Venus in Di

Wicked Sons Bc

By Emma V. L

Published by Emma V. Leech.

Copyright (c) Emma V. Leech 2024

Editing Services Magpie Literary Services

Cover Art: Victoria Cooper

ISBN No: 978-2-487015-26-5

About Me!

I started this incredible journey way back in 2010 with The Key to Erebus but didn't summon the courage to hit publish until October 2012. For anyone who's done it, you'll know publishing your first title is a terribly scary thing! I still get butterflies on the morning a new title releases, but the terror has subsided at least. Now I just live in dread of the day my daughters are old enough to read them.

The horror! (On both sides I suspect.)

2017 marked the year that I made my first foray into Historical Romance and the world of the Regency Romance, and my word what a year! I was delighted by the response to this series and can't wait to add more titles. Paranormal Romance readers need not despair, however, as there is much more to come there too. Writing has become an addiction and as soon as one book is over, I'm hugely excited to start the next so you can expect plenty more in the future.

As many of my works reflect, I am greatly influenced by the beautiful French countryside in which I live. I've been here in the Southwest since 1998, though I was born and raised in England. My three gorgeous girls are all bilingual and my husband Pat, myself, and our four cats consider ourselves very fortunate to have made such a lovely place our home.

KEEP READING TO DISCOVER MY OTHER BOOKS!

Other Works by Emma V. Leech

Wicked Sons

Wicked Sons Series

Daring Daughters

Daring Daughters Series

Girls Who Dare

Girls Who Dare Series

Rogues & Gentlemen

Rogues & Gentlemen Series

The Regency Romance Mysteries

The Regency Romance Mysteries Series

The French Vampire Legend

The French Vampire Legend Series

The French Fae Legend

The French Fae Legend Series

Stand Alone
The Book Lover (a paranormal novella)
The Girl is Not for Christmas (Regency Romance)

Audio Books

Don't have time to read but still need your romance fix? The wait is over…

By popular demand, get many of your favourite Emma V Leech Regency Romance books on audio as performed by the incomparable Philip Battley and Gerard Marzilli. Several titles available and more added each month!

Find them at your favourite audiobook retailer!

Acknowledgements

Thanks, of course, to my wonderful editor Kezia Cole with Magpie Literary Services

To Victoria Cooper for all your hard work, amazing artwork and above all your unending patience!!! Thank you so much. You are amazing!

To my BFF, PA, personal cheerleader and bringer of chocolate, Varsi Appel, for moral support, confidence boosting and for reading my work more times than I have. I love you loads!

A huge thank you to all of my beta readers and cheering section! You guys are the best! An extra special thanks this time to my lovely sensitivity reader, Rebecca Vijay. I truly appreciate your input.

I'm always so happy to hear from you so do email or message me :)

emmavleech@orange.fr

To my husband Pat and my family … For always being proud of me.

Table of Contents

Family Trees

HOUSE OF CAVENDISH

To Break the Rules

Silas Anson
Viscount Cavendish *m.* Aashini Anson
aka: Lucia de Feria

Twins

Ashton Anson
b.1816

Vivien Anson
b.1816

m.

m.

???

August Lane-Fox

HOUSE OF BEDWIN

To Dare a Duke

Robert Adolphus
Duke of Bedwin *m.* Prunella Adolphus
nee Chuffington-Smythe

Lady Elizabeth
b.1815

Jules
Marquess of Blackstone
b.1819

Lady Victoria
b.1825

Lord Harry
b.1833

Lady Charlotte
b.1817

Lady Rosamund
b.1823 *m.* Lord Frederick
b.1827

Lady Octavia
b.1828

m.

m.

m.

m.

Mr. Barnaby Godwin

Cassius Cadogan
Viscount Oakley
b.1815

Sebastian Fox
Viscount Hargreaves

m.

Nicolas Alexandre
Demarteau

Miss Selina Davenport

Agatha de Montboc

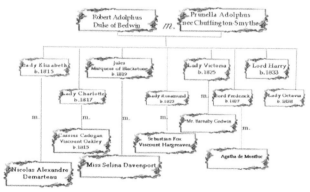

1

HOUSE OF HUNT
To Steal a Kiss

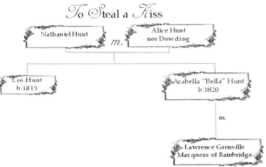

HOUSE OF TREVICK
To Follow her Heart

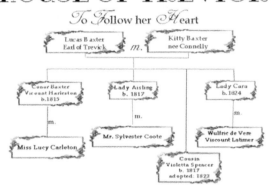

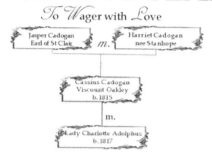

HOUSE OF ST CLAIR
To Wager with Love

Jasper Cadogan
Earl of St Clair
m.
Harriet Cadogan
nee Stanhope

Cassius Cadogan
Viscount Oakley
b. 1815

m.

Lady Charlotte Adolphus
b. 1817

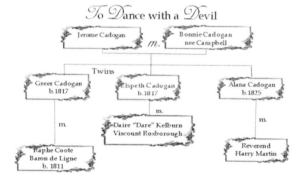

HOUSE OF CADOGAN
To Dance with a Devil

Jerome Cadogan
m.
Bonnie Cadogan
nee Campbell

Twins

Greer Cadogan
b. 1817

Elspeth Cadogan
b. 1817

Alana Cadogan
b. 1825

m.

Daire "Dare" Kelburn
Viscount Roxborough

m.

Reverend
Harry Martin

m.

Raphe Coote
Baron de Ligne
b. 1811

HOUSE OF MORVEN
To Winter at Wildsyde

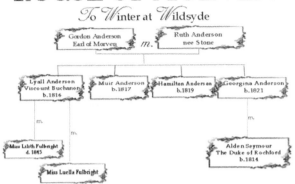

HOUSE OF DE BEAUVOIR
To Experiment with Desire

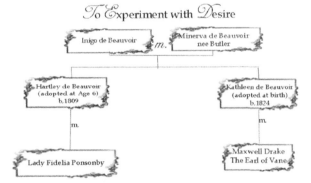

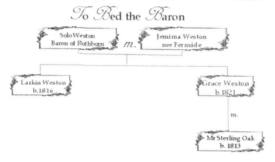

HOUSE OF ROTHBORN
To Bed the Baron

Solo Weston
Baron of Rothborn *m.* Jemima Weston
nee Fernside

Larkin Weston
b.1816

Grace Weston
b.1821

m.

Mr Sterling Oak
b. 1813

HOUSE OF KNIGHT
To Ride with the Knight

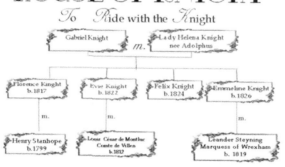

Gabriel Knight *m.* Lady Helena Knight
nee Adolphus

Florence Knight
b.1817

Evie Knight
b.1822

Felix Knight
b.1824

Emmeline Knight
b.1826

m.

m.

m.

Henry Stanhope
b.1799

Louis César de Montluc
Comte de Villen
b.1812

Leander Steyning
Marquess of Wrexham
b. 1819

Emma V Leech

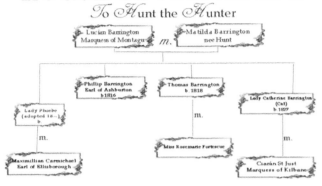

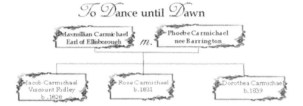

Prologue

Dearest Flo,

I hope you are well and bearing your confinement with fortitude, or ought I pray poor Henry is bearing your confinement with fortitude? The poor man must be at his wits' end, for I know how vexed you become with the world when you cannot get out and about. Still, only another two months and you'll have yet another wailing creature to clasp to your bosom. It's bound to be another girl, you realise. Poor Henry and Oscar will not stand a chance.

As for the gossip you pleaded for, there is little to relate for now. Hart is in alt, having gained a commission to create his first ever garden at Hardacre Hall. Personally, I'd stay as far from Beresford as it was possible to get. A meaner spirited, bigoted old muckworm it would be hard to find. I am biased naturally, but he despises me for my mixed blood and looks at me like I'm tainted. I danced with his eldest daughter once, Lady Fidelia. He told me to keep my filthy hands off her. I exchanged a few words of my own but thank God no one else heard. If Pa had discovered that, I reckon he'd have called the old bastard out.

I'm going to the Duchess of Bedwin's ball tonight. The male portion of the ton is all in a twitter, for Beresford is bringing his youngest daughter, Lady Narcissa. She came out last year and made quite a stir, not that I saw her. She was only allowed at a few select parties to dip her toe in the shark-infested waters of the ton. Though with a father like hers, I suspect it's the men who are the catch, and she's the one with the teeth.

We shall see.

Yrs etc,

Ash

—Excerpt of a letter to Mrs Florence Stanhope (daughter of Lady Helena and Gabriel Knight) from the Hon'ble Ashton Anson (son of Silas and Aashini Anson, Viscount and Viscountess Cavendish)

9th November 1849, Her Grace, The Duchess of Bedwin's Winter Ball.

"It's pitiful, really," Ash mused, shaking his head. "Have they no pride? Look at them, making great cakes of themselves over that little chit of a female."

His beautiful twin sister, Vivien, regarded her brother with amusement and took a sip of champagne. "So, you won't be going and introducing yourself, then?" she asked, her dark eyebrows quirking in enquiry.

"Certainly not," Ash said with a snort. "I never exert myself. She'll come to me soon enough, and I shall enjoy watching Beresford seethe with fury when she does so."

Vivien sighed. "Beresford is a loathsome toad. No one likes him, Ash. For heaven's sake, don't go out of your way to provoke him."

"I have no intention of doing so. I shan't give the girl the least bit of attention, so he can hardly complain of me sullying the sweet little innocent with my contaminating presence, can he?"

"No," Vivien replied coolly. "But you know as well as I do what will happen if you ignore the girl. You may as well bed her now and be done with it."

"Vivien, Vivien." Ash tsked and frowned at his twin. "I *never* touch innocent girls, you know that. They need marrying."

"Yes, you'd rather dally with ones who already enjoy that happy state," Viv drawled, shaking her head. "Really, Ash, you're worse than a tomcat."

Ash shrugged and grinned at her, which only made Viv's expression darken farther. "It wasn't a compliment," she said sternly.

With an unrepentant quirk of his lips, Ash replied with a sigh, "Ah well, what else is there to do but indulge in a little love affair? You know I never break up happy homes, but if the husband is a swine and bestows all his affection on tarts and opera dancers… sauce for the goose, my dear."

"You'll find your goose cooked one of these days," Vivien said crisply, gaining herself a bark of laughter. "It's not funny! It's high time you settled down. I have four children already, Ash, and you've not provided a single playmate for them. Not only will they be grown up before you even consider settling down, but you're wasting yourself and your talents."

"Indeed, I am not," he protested, smoothing a hand over a waistcoat that had received several admiring glances from the young bucks who strove to imitate such leaders of fashion as Ash had become. "I am exceptionally talented at looking beautiful, being adored, and punching great brutes in the nose. So here I am, glorious as ever, Mrs Crawford over there is quite desperate to adore me, and I have a fight at the club tonight. So, you see, sister dearest, I am putting all my talents to excellent use."

Vivien threw up her hands. "Oh, Ash, you are impossible. I wish you would stop pretending to be such a vain, selfish peacock. You take nothing seriously and you don't heed a word I say."

Ash put a hand to his heart and affected a wounded expression. "Oh, but I do, *I do*," he insisted, with such insincerity that his sister's eyes flashed with vexation.

"Go to the devil," Vivien replied succinctly, and stalked off.

Ash laughed and raised his glass to her as she stormed away. "Oh, I shall, Viv. I certainly shall."

Ash watched her go and then turned as laughter, sparkling and light as champagne, caught his attention. He turned to see the *ton's* newly crowned diamond surrounded by her admirers. The men vied with each other to get closer, each of them trying to capture her attention. Ash studied the girl with an expert eye, from her head to her toes, taking in the thick blonde hair swept back in a simple chignon. A single strand of pearls adorned her elegant neck, her fair skin flawless under the lamplight that touched her satiny flesh with gold. The gown was a delicate shell pink, almost white, and only emphasised her fragile beauty and innocence. It fit to her gloriously curved figure like a glove, splendidly highlighting a remarkably generous bosom for such a slight little thing. Whoever had the dressing of her had done a wonderful job, he had to admit. It was the perfect blend of provocation and artlessness.

His gaze travelled back up and he stilled as he found a pair of impossibly wide blue eyes staring back at him. He felt as much as saw the tremor run through her, the sharp intake of breath. *Ah, there she is*, he thought with amusement. Lady Narcissa gazed at him, her lush mouth slightly parted. Ash's lips curled a little, a vaguely mocking smile as he wondered what her father would say if he saw her staring at him with such open interest. He held her gaze for a moment longer, and then deliberately turned his back and walked away.

Chapter 1

Dear Diary,

I don't know how long I can keep this up. My father is so pleased with me, and it is such a relief to have him in this happy state after all the upset over whatever it was Fidelia did to infuriate him so. He returned to Hardacre last week, though, and my cousin, Mrs Chandler, has the unenviable task of chaperoning me about town. Now that his grace is no longer watching my every move, I am bound to go astray. It is much less of an effort to behave as I ought when I know he is watching every move I make. But now I have only Mrs Chandler and she is more interested in gossiping with her friends and flirting with her cicisbeos than keeping me out of trouble.

I am to go to yet another ball this evening, and I swear if that dreadful man ignores me again, ~~I shall…~~ Well, I have not yet decided quite what I shall do. I swear I am not so horribly vain as to expect every man I see to fall at my feet, but he makes such a point of ignoring me it is obviously done to provoke me, and I do not understand why. What can I have done to give him a disgust of me when we have never even been introduced? It is just so very peculiar when every other man is so very attentive. Too attentive to be honest. I am so weary of hearing my eyes compared to 'fathomless pools of blue' what nonsense, and if I must endure the reading of another mawkish sonnet to my beauty and innocence, I may just vomit.

I ought to hurry and choose a husband and get it done with. Then I need not endure this farce any longer. I long for a home of my own where I may find a little peace without my father's constant expectations of how I ought to behave and his never-ending cutting remarks. His standards are too impossibly high and surely a husband would be kinder to me if I choose well. Mr Winslow seems a sweet sort of fellow. No title but from an excellent family and vastly wealthy. I know his grace will not approve the match, but maybe if I push hard enough, I could wear him down. Winslow is the kind of man I might find something resembling contentment with, at least. He'd be an amiable husband who would not bother me overmuch. I know he's desperate to propose, but he's too spineless, the poor dear. I shall simply have to give him a nudge.

—Excerpt of a diary entry by Lady Narcissa Ponsonby.

15th January 1850, The Countess St Clair's New Year's Ball, St James's, London.

Ash watched as the carriage rumbled away, taking Baron Childe to the sanatorium, where he would likely spend the rest of his days. Thorn had finally freed his beloved Miss Fortesque of her vile brother, and the way she had gazed at Thorn had made an odd sensation stir in Ash's chest.

"Well, that went as it ought, then," Leo said cheerfully, clapping Ash on the back.

"Hmph," Ash replied glumly.

"Oh, cheer up. There's no point in sulking just because you didn't get to knock the fellow down. It was Thorn's turn to play the hero. He did it very nicely too," Leo said with a grin. "Come along, the ball is still in full swing, and I want a drink."

"Fine," Ash grumbled, following Leo back inside. He felt irritable and out of sorts for reasons he did not wish to examine too closely. He didn't think it was because he'd missed out on a fight, either. Well, not entirely.

Leo snagged a couple of glasses from a passing server and handed one to Ash. There was a lively polka in progress. Couples whirled about the floor, the ladies' gowns swishing. Despite his intention to continue ignoring her, Ash's gaze travelled unerringly across the twirling melee and found Lady Narcissa. The gown was blue this evening, no doubt ensuring she had received many compliments about her astonishing blue eyes. A pity her wit was not as bright as those glittering orbs. Ash had heard her chatter inanely as her acolytes feigned fascination, all the while staring at her cleavage. Why she continued to bother him, he did not know. He found no interest in pretty little ninnies. Ash liked intelligent women, lovers who challenged his intellect as much as his more intimate skills, and so his continued curiosity about her was out of character. Yet he could not tear his gaze away.

Finally, the dance ended, and Lady Narcissa turned from her partner and discovered Ash watching her. He raised his glass, his usual mocking smile firmly in place. The glare she shot his way could have etched glass. Ash grinned, knowing he had pricked her vanity by refusing to add to the ranks of her disciples. This was the first time he had even acknowledged her existence. She might have every other man here on his knees for the crook of her finger, but not him. He followed her progress as she left the dance floor, back to her admirers.

"Lovely, isn't she?" Leo mused.

Ash frowned, returning his attention to his friend to find Leo's gaze was following the same path.

"If you like that sort of thing." He turned to regard Leo. "You've no interest there, surely?"

"I've secured the next dance with her," Leo replied with a shrug.

"Why?"

Leo turned and gave Ash an odd look. *"Why?* Whyever not? She's gorgeous and rich and I shall enjoy holding her in my arms for the duration of the waltz. I'm not proposing to her."

Ash frowned. "I should think not," he muttered, annoyed for no good reason he could think of.

"Want me to put in a good word?" Leo offered, his eyes twinkling with mischief.

"Do, and I shall meet you in the ring tomorrow," Ash replied coolly.

Leo chuckled and pressed his glass into Ash's hand. "Hold this, then. I'm going to show the girl how it's done."

Ash's jaw tightened with irritation as Leo strode off. A moment later, his friend escorted the lady onto the dance floor and took her in his arms. They made the perfect couple. Leo, tall, broad shouldered and blond, holding his delicate female counterpart in his arms. They ought to be made of porcelain and set on a mantelpiece, Ash thought sourly, and then chided himself for his ill humour. But he could not help but presume the young woman would echo her father's opinion of his mixed blood and the idea made resentment burn in his chest.

He watched with growing antipathy as Lady Narcissa stared up at Leo with an adoring gaze that made Ash want to throw up. Insincere little baggage. Everyone knew she wanted a title and a fortune and Leo didn't fit. Oh, he was wealthy enough, but his father owned a nightclub, and Leo was a major shareholder in the Sons of Hades. *No, no, dear,* Ash thought with irritation. *You're barking up the wrong tree there.* She must know it too, which meant that treacly look of besotted fascination was nothing but a façade. He only hoped Leo wasn't fool enough to be taken in by it. Lesser men than him had been caught by such tricks.

"A pretty pair of turtle doves," murmured a sardonic voice beside him.

Ash turned to discover Felix Knight watching Leo and his companion, too.

"One of them is more of a vulture," Ash replied with a snort.

"And her a little wren, I suppose?" Felix mused, pondering this.

"No! *She's* the vulture," Ash replied in frustration. "Why can no one else see this?"

"Good Lord, Ash, she's just a girl husband-hunting, like all the rest, and she's the daughter of a duke with a vast dowry. She's hardly a fortune hunter. What's got you in such a lather, anyway?"

"Nothing," Ash muttered, folding his arms.

The dance ended with both Leo and Narcissa laughing, apparently well pleased with each other.

Felix grinned and nudged Ash with his elbow. "Ah, now we shall see for ourselves. Here they come."

Indeed, they did, and it was too late for Ash to escape without looking as though he was running away. Besides, he wanted to see the girl up close. Likely she was not as beautiful at close range as she was from a distance, or perhaps her voice grated upon the ear. She could not be as perfect as everyone seemed to think.

"Here we are," Leo said cheerfully, giving Ash a look of such innocence he was tempted to thump him right there in the ballroom. "My dear pals. Lady Narcissa, might I make known to you, Mr Ashton Anson and Mr Felix Knight?"

Felix beamed at the girl and executed an elegant bow over her hand. "Delighted to make your acquaintance, my lady."

Ash inclined his head slightly, merely acknowledging the introduction, his expression one of boredom.

Lady Narcissa ignored him and focused her attention on Felix.

"But you are Mr Gabriel Knight's son, I believe?" she asked, and Ash was disconcerted to discover her voice was surprisingly low and mellow. "You must be so very proud of him. I know little of such matters, but I understand he is vastly clever and innovative."

"Rich too," Ash murmured, *sotto voce.*

Felix ignored him and replied hastily, "Indeed, I have a great deal to live up to. As he never ceases to remind me."

"Oh, no. Indeed, I cannot believe it. I am sure you are following close in his footsteps, Mr Knight," she said, her expression so grave Ash was hard pressed not to laugh.

"I try my best. However, I feel I should need three lifetimes to equal his achievements," Felix said with a smile. "I understand a friend of ours is working at your father's estate at present. Mr De Beauvoir. He has designed a wonderful garden for you, I think."

"I believe so," Lady Narcissa replied with a wistful sigh. "And I wish I were there to see it come to life, but my father insisted I must stay in town."

"Of course you must, or half the male population of the *ton* would fall into a decline," Leo replied, grinning at her.

Lady Narcissa laughed, blushing a little, and gazed up at Leo with such patently false admiration Ash had to fight to hold his tongue.

"You flatter too outrageously, sir," she said, casting her eyes down.

"Oh, surely not," Ash drawled, losing the battle at last. "Every man here is your slave, is he not?"

Her eyes snapped to his, and he found it impossible to look away, caught in the passionate flicker of anger he saw there. Her voice was sweet and gently enquiring as she replied, however.

"If that were true, I would surely count you among my admirers, sir, yet you have avoided me so assiduously one wonders what it is you are afraid of?"

There was a taut silence as Ash's mouth curved into a slow smile. "I fear nothing, my sweet. But you ought to. Playing with fire is a bad idea for little debutantes. You don't want to singe your pretty gown, do you, now?" he drawled, before giving her an insolent bow and sauntering away.

Narcissa made a smothered sound of exclamation, blushing furiously, before remembering where she was and who was watching. Hastily, she rearranged her face and attempted to look as though his words had not cut her to the core. Embarrassment and hurt vied in her heart with the fervent desire to do murder. "I ought not to have provoked him," she said apologetically, trying to compose herself and unclenching her hands when she would have much preferred to put them about Mr Anson's neck and throttled the devil, or so she told herself. She ought to be furious with him for his rudeness, and it was foolish to feel so upset when she had goaded him into such a response after all.

"Nonsense," Mr Hunt replied, exchanging a significant glance with Mr Knight. "Mr Anson is an amiable chap usually, but he's a little out of sorts this evening. I'm certain he meant no offence."

Not much, he didn't, Narcissa thought ruefully. Of all the arrogant, impertinent, outrageous things to say. The urge to follow the wicked man and demand he apologise was hard to resist, but she made herself squash the impulse before she did something awful. She had discovered everything she could about him by eavesdropping shamelessly in the ladies' retiring room whenever she was there. It wasn't difficult, as Mr Anson was often the subject of conversation. It appeared he was having an affair with Mrs Crawford, an elegant and sophisticated woman whose far older husband preferred spending his nights at the gambling tables than with his wife. The latest *on dits,* however, suggested that affair was coming to an end and that Lady Sheridan was tipped to win Mr Anson's attentions next.

It was vile, the way men could behave with impunity in a manner that would have women labelled trollops. Yet *they* were given appellations such as 'rake' and 'libertine.' How strange those words seemed so enticingly wicked, when a lady was—if she were found alone with a man, no matter the circumstances—ruined, worthless, and of no further value. A widow or a wife had a little more leeway, assuming they were discreet, but Narcissa suspected it was a dangerous line to walk. No wonder Mr Anson had no interest in a woman who still had her virtue intact. He *might* have to marry her. The horror.

"You mustn't mind Mr Anson," Mr Knight said kindly, smiling at her. "Especially not when every fellow here would give his right arm to dance with you."

"Thank you," Narcissa said, grateful for his solicitude, even as a fire burned in her heart.

She did not understand why the vexing, presumptuous man was so determined to shun her, but she would make him regret being so awful to her if it was the last thing she did.

18th January 1850, The Haymarket Theatre, Suffolk Street, London.

Narcissa smothered a yawn and wondered how much longer the play would go on for. Though she was by no means the featherbrain she pretended to be for the sake of obtaining a suitable husband, she had to admit *Charles the Twelfth* demanded rather more concentration than she could give it tonight. Her eyes drooped, and she wondered if anyone would notice if she took a nap. The endless round of social events of the past weeks had left her feeling exhausted. Her feet hurt from dancing so much and her brain felt like porridge from the effort of having no opinions and agreeing with all the fatuous comments of the men she must consider as suitable husbands. She ought to just choose one and be done with it, then she could put an end to this ridiculous farce and settle down with a home of her own, free of her father's domineering influence on her life, having done just what he'd asked of her for once. The lure of a future where she would be free of his impossibly high standards was the one ray of light on the horizon of a life that had never felt her own. Yet she could not quite bring herself to do so. A quiet fury simmered inside her, the frustration of living a lie, of hiding her true nature and pretending to be meek and docile, an increasing strain upon her nerves. It was wearying beyond belief to act the pretty dimwit and disheartening too. Yet she dared not defy her father's instructions for fear of being sent straight back to Hardacre. Then he would arrange her husband with no say from her and she would lose all control over the choice. There was little enough as it was, but she must cling to what influence she had. Another yawn tugged at her lips, and Narcissa pressed them tightly together, doing her best to stifle it as she shifted in the chair. Though it was padded and upholstered in velvet, her derriere was numb from sitting still too long, and her corset had been laced so tightly it was hard to take a proper breath.

"Don't fidget," her cousin, Mrs Chandler, whispered, poking her in the side.

Narcissa winced and sat up straighter, fixing an expression of polite interest on her face. They could hardly expect more of her than that. The men here would consider the play far too complex for her to comprehend, she thought with frustration. She understood it perfectly well, but she was too tired to concentrate and her spirits too low to enjoy something so serious as well as she ought. If only it had been a romantic comedy, then she might have been able to set her own troubles aside for a few hours and that she might have stayed awake for.

Still, one went to the theatre to see and be seen, not necessarily to watch the actors on stage. There was a fair amount of chatter and movement from the audience and having lost the thread of the play, Narcissa's attention wandered. Gazing over the edge of the box, she surveyed all the elegant and fashionable patrons in attendance.

On the far side of the theatre was Lady Harriet St Clair and her husband, the Earl of St Clair, with their son, Viscount Oakley, and his beautiful wife. She saw too Mr and Mrs Nathaniel Hunt, the parents of Leo Hunt, the charming devil she'd danced with at Lady Harriet's ball. She saw now that he looked very much like his father, who was still a handsome man, though his hair was no longer the bright blond it must once have been. Travelling along the boxes with interest, she came next to one that was crowded with fashionable people, many of them young women. She saw then Mr Felix Knight, who raised a hand and acknowledged her. Narcissa was about to do the same when her gaze snagged on the man standing behind him.

Unwillingly, her gaze moved up over narrow hips to a broad chest and powerful shoulders lovingly encased in a beautifully tailored coat. The arrogant, sardonic curve of his lips was hardly a surprise, but she refused to look away, meeting those vibrant indigo eyes with defiance. Narcissa felt the snap of connection like an electrical charge, the irresistible pull towards him she found as incomprehensible as it was compelling. Her heart thudded hard in her chest as their gazes locked. Why did he hate her so, she wondered, for surely that was hatred blazing in his eyes? What had she done that had caused such enmity before she'd even said a word to him? She did not understand what it was about him that provoked her so, waking the devil that dwelled in her heart, the one who would tempt her into doing something rash if she did not force it back down. Perhaps it was simply that she wished to spar with him, for she was used to clashing with her father who was the most uncompromising and belligerent man on earth. Yet now and then she got her own way and he seemed to respect her for her courage in standing up to him. That Mr Ashton simply ignored her, refusing to give her the chance to cross swords with him was infuriating. Of course, she ought not to do so at all, being compelled to act the ninny, but she wanted to, quite desperately.

Narcissa looked away, breaking the connection and feeling shaken by it, unnerved by the intensity of his gaze.

"I need some air," she muttered, and sprang to her feet, thrusting the curtain aside and hurrying from the box.

"Not by yourself!" protested Mrs Chandler. "Maud, go with her!"

Narcissa fled. Maud Pinkerton was Mrs Chandler's companion: a tiny mouse-like woman with stringy grey curls and pervasive odour of peppermint. Narcissa found her to be a nervous, fluttery creature, at turns silent and docile or talking interminably about nothing of interest to anyone but herself. Narcissa pitied her and kept trying to befriend her with mixed results.

She had once mentioned the diary Maud kept, noticing how the woman often jotted in it and kept it close by her during the day. Narcissa had thought to find some common ground, only to be treated as though she was trying to steal the crown jewels rather than begin a conversation. She suspected this was because she herself was often a subject of discussion, and the observations Maud noted were probably unflattering.

Still, she had tried her best to be kind, for Maud's life was a precarious one. A dependent of Mrs Chandler's and a distant relation of the duke, who took no interest in her at all, she was a lady of a certain age with no means of her own and was reliant upon her cousin's generosity. Therefore, Maud was placed in the unenviable position of general dogsbody and went out of her way to ingratiate herself to her cousin and do her bidding.

Though in other circumstances Narcissa would have taken the opportunity to try to get the know the woman a little better, tonight she was too tired and out of sorts to make the effort. If she did not escape at once, Maud would stick to her like glue, and chatter inconsequentially about everything and everyone until Narcissa wanted to scream. Just for a moment, she needed a little fresh air, a bit of peace, and a moment for herself. Yet the corridors of the theatre were remarkably busy, with people laughing, flirting, and exchanging gossip.

Though she knew she ought not, Narcissa hurried on, too unsettled to behave as she should. Drat that odious man for making her feel so uneasy. Yet the idea that he despised her for reasons she did not understand gnawed at the edges of her mind and would give her no respite. The grand entrance doors beckoned and Narcissa glanced around, wondering if she was observed, but everyone was too interested in their own conversations and seemed to pay her no mind. She'd just step outside, just for a moment, just to get a little air before she screamed or, worse, swooned.

Narcissa pushed her way outside and the freezing air slapped her in the face as she sucked in a deep breath. A thin drizzle fell, slicking the street, but at least under the shelter of the grand portico she was dry, though her skin prickled with cold. Drunken singing and boisterous chatter reached her ears as she watched the passers-by, noticing now just how busy the road was. Mrs Chandler had hustled Narcissa inside the theatre so quickly there had been no opportunity to look about her, and now she saw why. The street was filled with young men, either coming from or on their way to the various night clubs that seemed to make up many of the surrounding buildings, and around them fluttered gaudily painted women. They were laughing brashly, making lewd suggestions to the fellows who stopped to talk to them. Plump breasts were unashamedly on view for the delectation of those fellows who had the task of choosing between them.

"Good heavens," Narcissa murmured, as fascinated as she was shocked by this other world, she had walked straight past and never seen.

"Hey, lads, that one is more to my taste, what a beauty!"

Narcissa gasped as a rowdy looking fellow caught sight of her and gestured to his friends.

"What the hell are you doing out here, you little fool?" The angry voice sounded close behind her and Narcissa turned, finding herself confronted with a superb silk jacquard waistcoat in such a violent shade of pink she could only gape for a moment in sheer astonishment. Then she looked up, and then up a bit more, and swallowed a squeak of alarm as she came face-to-face with Mr Anson's uncompromising scowl.

Grasping her by the wrist, he put his hand to the small of her back, turned her about, and pushed her back inside the foyer.

"Are you really that witless?" he demanded furiously. "Or were you hoping to start a riot?"

"N-No, of course not," she stammered, trying her best to gather herself. "I just wanted some air."

"The environs of the Haymarket Theatre are no place for a stroll," he exclaimed, shaking his head at her with incredulity shining in his blue eyes, and good heavens but they were blue, dark as indigo and fringed with black lashes so thick she almost wondered if he used something on them. No, she decided, her gaze moving to the lustrous dark hair that gleamed like ebony in the lamplight. No, he needed no help in that department, nor any other. The shoulders of his coat were not packed out with padding to give that huge breadth, either: he really was that large.

Narcissa swallowed, wishing she could dredge up anything resembling a coherent thought, but she could only stare at him, heart hammering. There was no other man in the *ton* like this one. Every inch of him exuded strength, a powerfully built image of masculine perfection, so gloriously beautiful that it almost hurt to look at him. His skin gleamed gold, his exquisite bone structure so impossibly flawless she wondered if he had artists clamouring daily for the chance to paint or sculpt him.

"Why not?" she asked, knowing the answer perfectly well but determined to keep him talking to her, for he looked as though he was ready to abandon her in the foyer. She might never get another chance to speak to him alone.

"Why—" he began, staring at her in astonishment, and then shook his head. "No."

"No?" Narcissa repeated, puzzled and quite unable to tear her gaze from his. She thought perhaps she might have forgotten how to breathe.

"You're not *that* dim," he said firmly.

"How do you know?" she countered, her determination to keep talking to him helping her to regain her wits.

He snorted, a slight curve tugging at the corners of his sensuous mouth. "No one is *that* dim," he said, studying her with such intensity that her skin felt hot all over.

Even though it was not a proper smile, Narcissa's heart quickened at the sight, and she pressed on. "Yes, they are. I know dozens of girls precisely that dim."

"Perhaps," he allowed. "But you're not one of them. Are you?"

For a moment she wondered what she could have done to give herself away, but the desire to test him was too hard to resist. So, she tilted her head to one side and fluttered her lashes at him, the very image of the pea-brained coquette. "I don't understand what you are asking me, Mr Anson."

"Fine, have it your own way," he said, turning away from her.

"Wait!" Panicked to think she had wasted her one chance to speak with him, Narcissa reached out and grabbed hold of his sleeve and was scorched by the glare he levelled upon her.

"You are wrinkling my coat," he said coolly.

Narcissa let him go like she'd been bitten. "I beg your pardon," she said at once, adding with a tentative smile so he knew she was only teasing, "I had no idea you were so very fragile."

"*I* am not," he replied. "My coat, however, is easily spoiled and I do not wish my valet to take a vendetta out upon you for having done so."

"I should take one out on him for that waistcoat," Narcissa said frankly, before she could think better of it. She swallowed hard, cursing her unruly tongue for speaking without thinking.

Mr Anson went very still and Narcissa held her breath. Oh, lud, now she'd done it. One thing everyone knew about Mr Ashton was his position as a leader of fashion, and most of all, his love of colourful waistcoats, and she'd just gone and insulted it *and* him.

"You find fault with it?" he asked, his voice perfectly pleasant, but a gleam in his eyes that told her she had best watch her step.

"I do," she said, recognising the challenging note in his voice. Hoping she was not reading him wrong, and he was not averse to crossing swords with her, she put up her chin, though her heart was hammering wildly now. The urge to turn and run was palpable, but she was no coward. There was no backing down now. "It's vile."

"It's pink, and it's silk," Mr Anson replied calmly. "Therefore, it cannot be vile."

"I disagree. I've never seen such a revolting shade," Narcissa declared, folding her arms. In for a penny… "What is it called? Blushing Megrim, perhaps?"

"It's called Rampant Fuchsia," he said, and with a straight face too.

Narcissa choked. *"No,"* she said, appalled and rather awed by this marvellous bit of insanity. "It's not really, is it?"

"Yes, as it happens," he replied, amusement lurking in his eyes as he folded his arms.

Unwillingly, Narcissa's gaze drifted to his biceps and the way his coat stretched tight over the bulge of hard muscle. She swallowed. "Well, I suppose you just knock down anyone who doesn't like it," she mused, unable to tear her eyes from his powerful arms. "Though I think even you are gentleman enough not to strike a lady."

"Even me?" His head reared back like she'd struck him. "What the devil does that mean?"

There was genuine anger behind the words now, and Narcissa paled. She had not expected him to take her words seriously. "I-I was only funning. I am sure you would n-never strike a lady."

"Then why did you say it?" he demanded. "Do you think me a savage?"

"No!" Narcissa replied in alarm, wondering what on earth had happened. For a moment there, she had believed he was enjoying their banter. "No, of course I don't think that, and I beg your pardon for speaking so unthinkingly. It's only you look at me with such hostility, like… like you despise me."

The simmering tension rolling off him in waves dissipated and Narcissa let out a breath of relief.

"I don't despise you," he replied curtly.

She snorted at that. "Oh, Mr Anson, how good of you to say so," she said, putting a hand to her heart. "I believe I may swoon."

His lips quirked, amusement lurking in his eyes. "Don't let it go to your head," he suggested dryly.

"I shall endeavour not to do so," she replied with equal gravity.

They stood, staring at each other, both bemused by the sudden lull in hostilities, yet Narcissa was still viscerally aware of the prickling sensation between them. She opened her mouth again, hoping to say something that would not set his hackles up, when a shrill voice called her name.

"Lady Narcissa! Oh, good heavens, my lady, I was worried to death. I thought I might never find you in this crush. You went off at such a pace, and my stamina is not great, you know, my dear. I had to pause for a moment to catch my breath, I quite thought I might swoon, but a gentleman was so very kind as to fetch me a glass of water, and then I was quite all right again. But of course, then you had disappeared and—"

"Please don't worry yourself, Maud," Narcissa replied kindly, though frustration at the interruption seethed in her veins. Maud was only doing as she'd been told after all. "I am perfectly well, as you see."

Maud sent Mr Anson a doubtful glance. "Oh. Umm… yes, well. Do come along, my dear. It doesn't do to linger in the foyer. You meet all sorts of… of odd people here if you dally, you know."

Narcissa winced and bit her lip as she dared a glance up at Mr Anson, dismayed to discover the mocking glint had returned to his eyes now.

"Yes, do run along, my lady. You never know what kind of fellow might importune you if you linger here unprotected," he replied before giving a curt bow and stalking away.

"Oh, Maud!" Narcissa said as the woman towed her back up the stairs. She was surprisingly strong for such an apparently scrawny creature. "That was too bad of you. How could you be so rude."

"Whatever do you mean?" Maud replied, her tone indignant. "You know very well you ought not to have run off alone, else Mrs Chandler would not have sent me after you."

"That's not the point. You were very impolite to Mr Anson, and he was good enough to look out for me when he'd no reason to do so."

"Mr Anson is not a respectable chaperone, as I'm sure I need not tell you," Maud replied doggedly. "And he's not a proper gentleman."

Narcissa scowled, wondering what on earth she could mean by that. She knew, of course, that some people thought less of him for his mixed blood, but she had not thought Maud could be so horribly judgemental. "His father is a viscount!"

"His father is *in trade,*" Maud hissed, her face the picture of disgust. "He owns warehouses all over the country."

"He does?" Narcissa asked, interested now. That *was* a dreadfully scandalous thing for a nobleman to do. Admitting to working for a living was even more shocking than discovering a woman with a brain in her head. More ridiculous rules she could not understand. "Well, I don't see why you should hold that against Mr Anson in any case."

"Don't be foolish, dear," was all Maud would say in reply.

Narcissa felt a surge of irritation. "So what if his father is in trade? He's dreadfully rich, isn't he?"

Maud returned a look of pained incredulity and shook her head. "Money cannot buy lineage, dear."

"But he's a viscount, he has lineage and money," she protested.

"He's tainted it by engaging in trade," Maud said firmly. "No gentleman would do such a thing."

"So, he would do better to let his family starve than earn an honest living?"

Maud looked at her in surprise. "Obviously."

Narcissa stared at her, baffled all over again, not only by the *ton* and its arbitrary rules, but by a woman like Maud agreeing with them. Maud had no money of her own, no means of supporting herself, and must therefore live on the charity of her family, yet she had the temerity to despise a man for having the courage and determination to make his own way and work for a living. The world was entirely mad. Narcissa had long ago concluded her father lived by a set of rules no sane person could consider normal, but he was a duke and, therefore—as far as Narcissa could tell—bred to live in a realm far removed from that of most other people. Maud, though? Surely, she could see this was madness.

"And that's hardly the biggest problem, is it?" Maud hissed, glaring at her. "His mother is *Indian*. The Earl of Ulceby's by-blow. His grandmother was an Indian servant! Can you imagine?"

It was hardly surprising to hear Mr Anson was Anglo-Indian. Narcissa had concluded as much from looking at him. Did he face this amount of prejudice from everyone, she wondered? Surely not, for he was popular and invited everywhere, but he must know there were some, like Maud, who looked down upon him. Was he too playing a part, acting unconcerned and at his ease in the face of people who secretly despised him? The thought made her reconsider the way he had acted toward her. Had he expected that treatment from her too? Her heart clenched at the idea.

"Can you imagine what your father would say if he'd seen you speaking to such a man?" Maud went on. "Good heavens. Do you want to be isolated at Hardacre for the rest of your days, like your sister?"

"What do you know of that?" Narcissa demanded sharply, for no one—not even Fidelia herself—would talk about what had befallen her.

Narcissa had only known that she had waved Fidelia off for a season in town, and then not seen her again for nigh on eighteen months. When she'd returned to Hardacre, her sister had been little more than a wraith, a frail shadow of the woman she had once been, shrouded in melancholy. Fidelia would never confide in her, only saying she had been unwell, a line repeated by their father. *Weak-minded*, he'd said of Fidelia, whilst fixing Narcissa with his steely glare and demanding to know if she was made of sterner stuff.

Of course, your grace, she had replied automatically. What else could she say? It felt like betraying Fidelia, who had never been weak-minded in Narcissa's opinion, only far too biddable. She had always done what his grace had asked of her without question, whereas Narcissa had always tried to find a loophole, or a way of doing precisely what she wanted to do. If the duke demanded she practise her needlework when she wanted to be outside, she would do just as he asked—whilst perched halfway up a tree. If he demanded she practise the piano, she would do that too, choosing the bawdiest song she could think of, learned from the grooms with whom she was not supposed to associate. Despite this, and despite the way he ranted and raged at her, Narcissa was aware she was the favourite child. She had come to believe that he despised any show of weakness and, whilst her behaviour might drive him wild, he respected her for not bending to his will.

"Well?" Narcissa pressed, when Maud failed to reply. "What happened to Fidelia? What do you know?"

Maud turned, glaring at her, her voice brittle with irritation. "I know nothing. Good Lord, child. Do you think the family confides in me? I only know that Fidelia must have done something wrong. Did she really become overwhelmed and suffer a nervous collapse? Perhaps, for she was so terribly shy, it's possible the season was simply too much for her. Or perhaps she went astray, perhaps she was ruined, perhaps, perhaps…" Maud threw up her hands, her thin cheeks flushed with colour. "What does it matter, other than to serve as a lesson to you? Your father will keep you a prisoner at Hardacre for the rest of your days if you do not marry well. I should consider that before you go tempting the likes of Mr Anson to take an interest in you. He's a libertine, a man with a reputation for violence, and as far from an eligible husband as you are likely to get."

Narcissa stared at the woman in astonishment. She had never heard Maud speak so passionately about anything, or even offer an opinion. Before this moment she had been a little grey mouse, terrified to irritate her charitable cousin, and in her terror, doing just that with her over polite anxiety and obsequiousness.

Maud stared back at her, chin up, eyes sparkling a little too brightly. "You think I would not have liked to marry, to have a home and family of my own? Do you think I chose this for myself?"

Narcissa shook her head, admitting silently and with a surge of shame that she had not thought about it at all.

"There are not so many chances in life for a woman, my lady. You have been blessed with beauty, position, and wealth, but even that won't save you if you make a misstep. Tread carefully, and don't go wanting something that does not fall within the boundaries of what your father will accept. It will lead to misery, that I promise you."

With that uncompromising statement ringing in her ears, Narcissa watched as Maud swept back the curtain to their private box. "Here she is," she said with a too-shrill exclamation of pleasure. "Just in time for the second act."

Obediently, Narcissa went back into the box, and watched the rest of the play without fidgeting even a little. Yet, try as she might, her mind returned to the foyer, to the man with the outrageous waistcoat and indigo eyes. She wanted to see him again, to apologise for Maud's behaviour and to make him see she did not think that way about him. Despite the dire warning she knew she ought to heed, her mind was focused on one goal—how to see him again.

Chapter 2

Dear Diary,

I attended yet another ball this evening and danced until my feet hurt so much, I cannot endure the idea of doing it all again tonight.

It's now been almost two weeks since I last saw Mr Anson. He seems to have absented himself from society completely much to my disappointment. I had so hoped to speak with him again and apologise for Maud's rudeness to him.

I wish I could stop thinking about him.

Dear Diary

I heard this evening that Mr Anson was involved in some ghastly fight at the club he frequents. He won apparently and the fellows have been reliving the fight blow by blow, not that they knew I was listening, or else they'd have not carried on so. The club is called Hades, or some such name. A gaming hell, I suppose. I cannot understand why men take such joy in knocking each other senseless. Admittedly, sometimes I should like to deliver a well-aimed blow myself, but not repeatedly, and only in the heat of the moment. Men do it for fun! Such odd creatures they are.

Oh, I wonder if he was hurt? Is that why he's been away so long? Oh, my. Whyever did I not consider that before?

—Excerpts of diary entries by Lady Narcissa Ponsonby.

29th January 1850, Hanover Square Rooms, London.

The concert was wonderful. Not least because she could watch it sitting down. It was the first concert, in fact, by a new performer by the name of Mr Aguilar. He played a lively Chopin Scherzo and beautiful trio for piano by Mendelssohn to a rapt audience before entertaining them with Capriccio. Still, Narcissa found herself glad when the interval arrived, and she could stretch her legs. Though the idea of another ball filled her with dread, sitting still for any length of time was a challenge for a girl who had more energy than most, even when the entertainment was sublime.

"Maud, run and fetch me a glass of champagne, there's a dear. I'm parched," Mrs Chandler said, waving her fan in a disconsolate fashion.

The lady was not in a particularly jolly mood this evening, as none of her beaus were here to entertain her. A pity, as she'd spent an age on her toilette and looked very fetching in a gown of dark green velvet matched with a splendid set of emerald and diamond jewellery. Still, it made her poor company, and Maud had been at her most irritating in her eagerness to avoid an inevitable set down.

"Oh, I'll go," Narcissa offered, giving Maud a quick smile. "Poor Maud has been on her feet all day, fetching and carrying."

Mrs Chandler gave Narcissa a sharp look, perhaps questioning if she had intended the words as a slight. She had, in fact, for as exasperating as the woman was, Narcissa found herself dismayed by the way Mrs Chandler treated her. As a guest in her cousin's home, she did not feel equal to openly criticising her, but she had attempted to illustrate how Maud was ill-used by more oblique means.

Rather to her surprise, Maud scowled at her in response, but Narcissa escaped before she could voice any complaint.

It took some time to work her way through the crowd, avoiding elbows and keeping her toes out of squashing range as she went.

"Lady Narcissa! Cooee! Cissy, darling, over here!"

Narcissa turned on the spot, wishing she were tall enough to see over the crowd and discover the owner of the insistent voice.

"Here, darling. *Here!*"

Finally, her gaze fell upon a lovely young woman, her hair a similar gold to Narcissa's own, but a darker shade. She gave a squeal of delight as Narcissa waved back and watched as Delia pushed her way through the crowd with quite ruthless indifference to those she elbowed en route.

"Cissy!" she cried, falling upon Narcissa's neck and hugging her tightly.

"Delia!" Narcissa replied, laughing and hugging her in return. "Oh, how wonderful to see you. I thought you were still on the Continent?"

"We got back last week," Delia replied, grinning. "Everyone is hoping my last little faux pas will have been forgotten by now," she added, in a whisper that could have been heard two streets away.

Narcissa smothered a laugh and took her friend's arm, towing her towards the refreshments room. "Oh, I am so glad to see you. The season has been so utterly grim I wondered how on Earth I could bear it, but now I think I may survive."

"Of course you shall survive. We shall divide and pillage and share the spoils, or something like that," Delia added with her usual joie de vivre.

"Isn't that divide and conquer?" Narcissa queried, so delighted by discovering Delia in town she could hardly keep the smile from her face.

Delia shrugged. "So, we'll divide and conquer and pillage, and then divide a bit more when we share the spoils."

"What exactly are the spoils?"

Delia paused, staring at her thoughtfully. "I've no idea."

Narcissa gave an unladylike snort of laughter and covered her mouth with her hands as a dowager lady turned and glared at her. "You are the most ridiculous creature," she said fondly.

"I know," Delia said sadly. "My poor brother is at his wits' end. He's so desperate to see me securely married, but all the fellows think I'm odd. Am I odd, Cissy?"

"No, of course not," Narcissa replied stoutly, if not entirely truthfully. Delia was somewhat… eccentric. "You are delightfully original, that's all, and the men of the *ton* are all such stick-in-the-muds they can't see it. Someone will, though, you'll see."

Delia sighed. "I hope so, Cissy, for I'm getting terribly tired of parading my wares and finding no one is interested. I'm practically on the shelf! I mean, they seem interested at first, but then I open my mouth and they look at me like I'm deranged. It doesn't put them off, exactly, but I don't want to marry a man who thinks I'm deranged."

"I should think not," Narcissa replied. "But take heart, love. I'm having no luck either, and I've been a perfect ninny the entire time. They adore me, and I want to run, far, far away from each and every one of them. I can't though, not with the duke breathing down my neck."

"Oh, isn't it ghastly," Delia said with a sigh.

"Ghastly," Narcissa agreed, so intent on her conversation with Delia that she didn't look where she was going.

"Oof!"

Delia steadied her as Narcissa stumbled back, having run into something that felt like a brick wall. Righting herself, she looked up, and felt her stomach turn a peculiar somersault.

"I might have known," drawled a resigned voice.

"Oops," Delia said softly, for she had noticed what Narcissa could now see, champagne dripping from Mr Anson's sleeve, his snowy white cuff sodden with the stuff.

"I b-beg your pardon," Narcissa offered with a hesitant smile. "I didn't see you there."

The fellow snorted, as well he might. Now she looked, he was rather hard to miss.

"Forgive me, my lady. I would have worn a brighter waistcoat to make myself more noticeable, but you took such offence last time we met, I did not dare."

Narcissa smiled. "I was horribly rude about it, wasn't I? I am sorry, but I'm so glad to see you are well and in one piece. I have been so dreadfully worried and—" She closed her mouth with a snap, a surge of heat burning her cheeks as she realised too late she had spoken without thinking, as evidenced by the surprise in Mr Anson's eyes. He had been dabbing at his drenched sleeve with an equally pristine handkerchief, but now he paused, regarding her with interest.

"You were worried?" he repeated sceptically. "About me?"

"The fight," Narcissa managed, wishing she had not given herself away so thoroughly. Oh, good Lord, now he would think she had been daydreaming about him and he'd be quite impossible. If only it weren't true. "I h-heard you were involved in a big fight."

"A boxing match," he corrected, regarding her with an inscrutable expression.

"Yes," she agreed, deciding to keep her words to a minimum for safety's sake. "That."

"I fight regularly, Lady Narcissa, and I won. Why would you trouble yourself to worry about me?"

Narcissa wished fervently he would just drop the subject, but his blue eyes were gleaming with curiosity now and she knew he wouldn't leave it. "Because you disappeared for two weeks, and I was afraid you were badly injured."

He took a step closer, too close, and lowered his head to hers, murmured wickedly, "Have you been counting the days, sweet?"

"Certainly not," she replied, glaring at him as defiantly as she could manage, though the heat warming her cheeks seemed to be spreading through her entire body. Drat the man for his egotism. Steeling herself, she wondered if perhaps she could tempt him back into exchanging the kind of teasing banter they had shared the last time they had spoken. "I only wondered if repeated blows to the head might be responsible for your rudeness, that's all. Besides which, I wonder that such a conceited fellow dares do anything that risks spoiling his pretty face," she added sweetly, praying he could tell she was only jesting with him.

"*Cissy,*" Delia whispered in awed tones.

Narcissa glanced at her friend to discover her eyes dancing with mirth at the exchange. Looking up at Mr Anson, she found to her dismay his expression was far harder to read. He might be contemplating wringing her neck, or he might be amused. It was impossible to tell.

"Well," he said at length. "As you see, I am entirely in once piece."

Oh, yes he is, Narcissa thought wistfully. One big, gorgeously impossible piece. To her relief, she recognised the glint in his eyes when he spoke again and knew he was not angry with her.

"However, I am pleased to note you think me pretty, and the next time I find myself bloodied and bruised, it is comforting to know I might call upon you to wipe my fevered brow."

Delia wrinkled her nose at that. "If you're bloodied and bruised, you wouldn't have a fevered brow. Unless you'd had the misfortune to contract some vile disease at the same time," she added thoughtfully.

Narcissa choked, her eyes flying to Mr Anson's countenance to see how this had gone down. To her delight, he grinned at them, showing strong white teeth.

"I stand corrected, Lady Cordelia. How good it is to see you again. And, in that case, perhaps Lady Narcissa would bandage my wounds?"

"I might, at that," Narcissa said coolly, enjoying herself now. "Around your neck."

His eyebrows flew up and her courage failed her. Smothering a choked laugh, she fled before he could see her cheeks were blazing, towing Delia along in her wake.

Delia was crying with laughter by the time they finally made it to the refreshments room.

"Oh, Cissy, I have missed you!" she exclaimed, shaking her head. "There's no one else in the world I like better."

Narcissa gave a huff of amusement. "Well, I'm glad to know it, for there are not many women who like me at all. That's the trouble with being named the season's *diamond*: most every other marriageable female wants to scratch your eyes out."

"Oh, poor Cissy. Has it been very awful?" Delia asked with sympathy. "I mean, it's always been awful for me, but I'm peculiar."

"Original," Narcissa corrected.

Delia sighed. "Yes, let's say that, even though we both know it's a big fat lie. Oh, lud, look out. Lord Malmsey is heading this way."

As one they turned and fled, hurrying to the withdrawing room where it was impossible for the vile man to follow them.

"He's not courting you?" Narcissa asked in concern once they were safely inside.

Delia pulled a face. "My brother would never allow such a brute anywhere near me, but he's such a horrid man. He won't take no for an answer. I shall be forced to give him the cut direct if he persists, but then I'm afraid people will talk and assume he's done something worse than make disgusting comments and try to grope me when the chance allows."

"Delia, you must stay far away from him," Narcissa insisted. "Tell your brother he's bothering you and get him to warn the fellow off. He's one of my brother Richmond's intimates, and that should tell you well enough what kind of man he is."

"I will," Delia replied, patting Narcissa's hand and smiling. "Don't fret, love. I may be an odd duck, but I'm not stupid. But never mind that. Shall I call on you tomorrow? We could go shopping. I'm desperate to buy the next instalment of Mr Dickens's latest work. Have you been reading it?"

Narcissa shook her head gloomily. "Mrs Chandler does not approve of ladies reading and the duke insisted I leave all my books at home."

"Oh, Narcissa!" Delia exclaimed in horror. This was apparently by far the worst fate she could imagine befalling her friend. "Don't worry. I shall bring all the chapters I have of David Copperfield. It's really quite wonderful. The opening line has stuck with me and gives me courage when I am at risk of falling into the dismals."

Narcissa watched with amusement as Delia cleared her throat and recited solemnly, *"Whether I shall turn out to be the hero of my own life, or whether that station will be held by anybody else, these pages must show."*

"Oh," she exclaimed, much impressed. "That is rather good."

"It is," Delia said, delighted. "And we shall be the heroes of our own lives too, Cissy darling. Just you wait and see."

Ash made his way back to his seat and handed a fresh glass of champagne to his sister.

"Did you go to France for it?" she enquired mildly, for it had taken him an age, considering he'd had to go back a second time after Lady Narcissa had thrown the first over him. Viven's gaze fell upon his wet shirt cuff. "Good heavens, did you swim?"

Ash grimaced. "I had a run in with Lady Narcissa. Quite literally."

Vivien made a sympathetic sound and shook her head. "Such a pretty child, but she really is a nitwit. Do you know I heard her talking the other day, and she mentioned the Grenadine guards, *and* she thought Leeds Castle was in Leeds! Honestly, the men all thought she was delightful, so sweet, so innocent and guileless. I could only pity the poor little fool."

"Hmm," Ash replied thoughtfully. The more he saw of Narcissa, the more he suspected she was a long way from stupid.

"Where on earth has August got to?" Vivien shifted in her seat to see if she could spy her husband. "I might have known. The poor dear has been caught by Mrs Cadogan. The wicked woman always makes him blush. I'd best rescue him."

Ash nodded automatically, not really listening to a word. Instead, he remembered the way Narcissa's satiny cheek had flushed pink as a new dawn when she'd let her tongue run away with her. He suspected she had not meant to admit she had worried about him, that she had been thinking about him. The knowledge that he had been on her mind pleased him far more than it ought. Especially knowing how badly it would vex her father.

Some sixth sense made him turn his head as the sensation of being observed prickled the back of his neck. Narcissa jolted as their eyes met and hurriedly looked away from him. Ash grinned to himself. He wondered how hard it would be to entice the girl to fall in love with him. She was certainly curious about him. That was hardly an unusual reaction. The pampered princesses of the *ton* viewed him like some species of exotic pet they wished to tame, to drag about on a leash to prove they could. Ash was more than happy to play along at first, until the moment they believed they had him where they wanted him, and then he disabused them of the notion. Any woman who thought she could rule him got a rude awakening. But a woman who was his equal, who challenged him and admired him, *loved* him… ah, well, that was the goal one of these days. Not for a long time yet, obviously, but he had to admit—to himself, at least—the growing evidence of how hard such a woman would be to find worried him far more than it had when he was younger.

Vivien returned with her husband just as the musicians struck up again. As if drawn by some invisible force, Ash turned his head once more. He concentrated his attention upon the fairest head of hair, willing her to turn around once more. When she did, he smiled, a confident, devilish smile that invited a reaction, that told her he knew she was thinking of him still. Narcissa's cheeks flushed crimson, but she held his gaze for far longer than he expected before finally looking away.

Ash let out a huff of laughter, admitting himself surprised by her boldness. He could not help but wonder just how bold she really was.

Chapter 3

Dear Diary,

What quirk of fate is it that the only man who piques my interest is one my father would disown me for even contemplating? It's all well and good to spend one's time pretending to be a halfwit for the purpose of securing a matrimonial prize my father approves of, but to be such a reckless fool as to purposely court disaster shows true idiocy. My father will not be satisfied unless I do justice to the family name and marry someone he believes is worthy of the connection. Yet the temptation to provoke the dreadful man into speaking to me again is undeniable. But then I never did things by halves.

I must have a care though. His grace wrote to tell me he is coming to town for two weeks to see how I go on while he deals with some business affairs. What those affairs might be fills me with dread. Perhaps it is just as well, though. With the duke at my elbow, I shall have no choice but to be the perfect little puppet, with him pulling the strings. I know I am a spoiled little madam, but Lord, there are days when I hate my life.

—Excerpt of a diary entry by Lady Narcissa Ponsonby.

30ᵗʰ January 1850, Claridge's, Bond Street, London.

Delia eyed the last cream cake wistfully and bit her lip.

"I want it but I'm afraid my corset will burst," she said frankly.

Narcissa sighed. "I've eaten far too much. Still, at least I shan't struggle to pretend to only eat enough to keep a sparrow alive at dinner tonight. It doesn't do for a lady to enjoy her dinner too much, you know. Smacks of greed and self-indulgence."

Delia grimaced. "Are you dining at Elsmere House tonight?"

Narcissa nodded. "The dowager is a bosom bow of Mrs Chandler. I'll probably spend half the evening evading Lord Elsmere, though. Her son is one of my dowry's most ardent admirers, though he's a fool if he thinks my father would give him the time of day. He tried for my sister too, you know. Quite shameless."

"He's a charming rogue, though," Delia said with a smile. "I rather like him."

"Will you be going, then?"

Delia nodded. "Yes, I'm going with Lady Rose Carmichael. Do you know her?"

"Narcissa shook her head. No, we've not been introduced. She's very pretty, though. Isn't she Montagu's granddaughter?"

"Yes, she is, and yes, she's perfectly lovely," Delia agreed. "And the nicest person, too. You'll like her."

Narcissa pulled a face. "Then do me a kindness and don't introduce me. It pains me to act like a brainless twit in front of people I wish to like me."

"Must you really act so?" Delia asked, darting another glance at the cream cake.

"If I want Mrs Chandler to tell his grace that I've been making every effort to secure a husband, yes, I do. He'll be here in three days," she added gloomily. "I have a horrid suspicion the business he is coming to deal with involves giving permission for men to offer for me."

"Lud! Not really?" Delia asked, wide-eyed. "Already? But you've only been out five minutes."

Narcissa shrugged, her spirits sinking. "The sooner the better, as far as his grace is concerned, I assure you. One of them is bound to be the Earl of Wishen," she added, shuddering at the idea.

Delia gasped, her hand going to her throat. "But he's old enough to be your father, not to mention being fat enough to crush you flat if he tried to embrace you, never mind anything else," she added, pulling a face.

"Delia!" Narcissa exclaimed in horror, for she needed no help in conjuring the most revolting images of what marriage to such a man might look like. "Please don't," she begged, as the cream cakes and sandwiches they'd devoured stirred uneasily in her belly.

"Sorry." Delia bit her lip. "He's a very kind fellow," she offered with a tentative smile.

Narcissa nodded grimly. "He is. The truth is, he'd be an excellent husband and I should want for nothing. If only I could bring myself to bear the idea of his hands on me."

She closed her eyes against the revulsion that rose inside her at the idea. *Don't think of it*, she told herself, and instead the image of Ashton Anson crushing her in his powerful arms illuminated mind's eye. Heat surged through her at the idea, as she wondered how it would feel to be held so tightly, to feel that sinful mouth come down upon hers, and—

"For heaven's sake, eat that cake, will you, Cissy? Before I do," Delia exclaimed, startling Narcissa out of her wicked imaginings so violently she blushed.

Good Lord, whatever was wrong with her? Daydreaming about the wicked man whilst out in public now. She was out of her mind.

"W-What?"

Delia paused, narrowing her eyes. "Whatever were you thinking about? You're bright pink."

"I wasn't thinking about—" Narcissa protested, but Delia gave a delighted bark of laughter.

"Oh, oh, I know," she crowed. "You were dreaming of Ashton Anson!"

"Delia, hush!" Narcissa hissed, for Delia had no concept of how to keep her voice down. "You dreadful girl."

Delia snorted, grinning unrepentantly. "I'm right, though, aren't I? Not that I blame you, he is quite splendid," she added with a sigh. "He's very charming, too. Oh, and he dances like a dream. It's quite something, you know, being held in his arms for the waltz. Just thinking of those big shoulders and muscular arms makes me feel quite silly. I should love to see him fight."

Narcissa frowned, not entirely comfortable with Delia's enthusiasm, nor the realisation she seemed so very well acquainted with the man. She liked the idea of seeing Mr Anson fight even less. The thought of him being hurt bothered her more than was good for her.

"Oh, stop looking so mutinous. I'm not about to steal him from you. As if I could," Delia added with a snort. "This cake, however…"

Delia snatched up her fork and broke off a large piece, putting it in her mouth and chewing with an expression of dreamy delight.

Sighing, Narcissa shook her head. "I suppose I'd best save you from yourself," she muttered sadly, taking her fork in hand once more. "I can't have you exploding all over Bond Street. We've a good deal of shopping to do yet."

With a laugh, Delia pretended to fight off Narcissa's fork with her own and by the time they had reduced the cake to a few meagre crumbs they were both in a far better humour.

They exited the elegant interior of Claridge's arm in arm, having deposited the morning's purchases with Narcissa's footman. Delia's maid trailed behind them at a discreet distance whilst the ladies window shopped and stopped now and then to pass the time of day with acquaintances. Pausing to admire a cleverly arranged window display of this season's spring bonnets, Narcissa was torn from her survey of a pretty chip bonnet lined with pale green satin by the sensation she was being observed. She looked up, turning to her right and left and seeing no one, before turning back to the window display and giving a gasp of surprise. Behind her own reflection in the glass stood another, much taller. Narcissa turned, glaring up at Mr Anson.

"Are you shopping for a new bonnet too?" she asked him gravely. "I should choose the one with the blue silk roses. It will go beautifully with your eyes."

Mr Anson considered this, folding his arms and regarding the window display with an expression of lazy interest. "The blue is insipid," he declared. "The pale green is the only one worth your time. I should snap it up before someone else does, you'll look quite charming in it."

Narcissa huffed, annoyed he'd singled out the one she liked. Now, if she bought it, he would think it was to please him. "I had already chosen that one," she replied rather crossly.

"Of course you had," Mr Anson replied with a patently false tone of reassurance.

"I did," she insisted. "Oh, you wretched man, now I can't buy it, and it would have gone perfectly with my new green redingote."

Mr Anson laughed, shaking his head. "What a ridiculous girl you are. Just buy the bonnet if it pleases you."

"No, because it pleases you," she said sulkily, which made her sound like a spoiled child, but she didn't care.

"Then I shall buy it for you," Mr Anson said, heading for the door.

Narcissa stifled a squeal of anxiety and caught at his sleeve. "Indeed, you will not, you madman! Do you want to set tongues wagging?"

"You're wrinkling me again," he said reproachfully, gazing down at her fingers.

"I beg your pardon," Narcissa said, letting him go.

"No, I beg yours," Mr Anson replied, his voice dripping insincerity. "I would not wish for anyone to believe you had an interest in me, or vice versa. How terribly shocking. Your papa would suffer an apoplexy."

"Not before he'd murdered Cissy," Delia said frankly. "She's got to marry someone ghastly, or he'll not be satisfied. Don't be vexed with us, though, Mr Anson. Please."

Narcissa elbowed Delia and shot Mr Anson a sharp glance, wondering if the knowledge her father disapproved of him hurt. She hoped not, for surely everyone knew her father was a hard and unsympathetic man who was not well liked. Mr Anson ought to care nothing for such a man's good opinion, for it was not worth having. She wondered, not for the first time, why on earth she tried so hard for it, but he was still her father, and her only living parent. The only time she got a modicum of respect from him was when she behaved like a spoiled child and demanded her own way. With a sudden burst of clarity, she wondered if this was why she behaved so ill around Mr Anson.

Mr Anson regarded Delia for a moment, his expression unreadable, before turning back to Narcissa. "Buy the bonnet," he said shortly. "It's perfect for you and it would be a shame not to, for the sake of pride."

"What would be perfect for me, Mr Anson?" Delia demanded, before Narcissa could speak. "You've such a good eye for fashion and I'm perfectly hopeless, as I'm sure you are aware," she added sadly.

Mr Anson regarded Delia with an expression of blunt amusement and Narcissa stiffened with anxiety in case the man was unkind to her friend. Delia was a beautiful girl, but she loved frills and bows and adornments. Somehow, she managed to look perfectly charming in them, when any other woman would look as though she'd narrowly escaped an explosion in a draper's shop. But Delia was rather out of the ordinary… and Narcissa did not wish Mr Anson to hurt her friend's feelings.

"Indeed, you have a style all of your own," Mr Anson said kindly, though he gave her over-furbished bonnet a slightly pained glance. "I think perhaps something in pink."

"Oh, I love pink," Delia said, clasping her hands together with delight. "That one with the roses?" she asked hopefully, pointing to a monstrosity of lace and petals that Mr Anson was regarding with undisguised horror.

"No," he said hastily. "The darker pink, with the cherries."

Frowning, Delia regarded a simple straw bonnet with a broad dusty pink ribbon and a small cluster of white blossoms embellished with two wax cherries. It was not, at first glance, terribly interesting, but then Narcissa considered how it would look on Delia and smiled.

"Oh, that is perfect," she agreed.

Delia looked between them sceptically, apparently unimpressed. "Come along," Narcissa said firmly, towing her inside the shop. Barely ten minutes later they emerged once more, both holding hat boxes and Narcissa admitted herself surprised to discover Mr Anson waiting for them outside.

"Well?" he asked, curiosity glinting in his eyes.

"It's splendid," Delia admitted, beaming at him. "I should never have chosen it in a million years, but I adore it. Though I wonder if perhaps I should add—"

"No." Mr Anson gave her a stern look. "No adding. It needs nothing more than your lovely face, I assure you," he continued in a milder and rather flirtatious tone.

Delia turned quite pink. "Thank you," she said faintly.

Mr Anson inclined his head. "If I can be of no further service then, I shall—"

"You can," Narcissa said in a rush, before he could escape them. "Be of further service," she added, boldly meeting his eyes even as her insides squirmed at her temerity.

"Indeed?" he asked, one dark eyebrow quirking. "I am alight with curiosity to discover how."

"I need a new gown, f-for a ball," she said, avoiding Delia's gaze. Her friend knew that was a lie as well as she did, having discussed the small fortune she'd recently spent on her wardrobe over tea and cakes.

"Which ball?" Mr Anson asked, narrowing his eyes.

"Er…" Narcissa's mind immediately became a blank canvas as panic turned her into the ninny she thought she only pretended to be.

"Lady Roxborough's," Delia said promptly, naming an event to be given in three weeks, bless her heart. "We're both going. I need one too. A dress, I mean."

"Hmmm." Mr Anson looked from Narcissa to Delia and back again. "Lady Roxborough is *very* fashionable."

"She is," Delia said with a sigh. "Which is why we need your help in case we make spectacles of ourselves."

Narcissa shot her a glare. Delia was over-egging the pudding somewhat, and Narcissa would not have the arrogant devil thinking she would look like a fright if he didn't help her. Mr Anson caught her eye, his lips twitching a little.

"Well, I cannot have you both going to such a splendid affair looking like dowds, can I? I suppose I had better give you the benefit of my expertise. It's the charitable thing to do."

"I don't need your ch—oof!" Narcissa rubbed her side where Delia's remarkably pointed elbow had just struck her.

"You're so very kind, Mr Anson," Delia said, giving him a look of besotted admiration. "A veritable good Samaritan."

"Oh, that's me," Mr Anson agreed, offering Delia his arm. Delia hurried to take it, darting a look at Narcissa that warned her she had best do the same or else.

"My lady?" Mr Anson said, a glint of challenge in his eyes.

"Too kind," Narcissa murmured with a saccharine smile. "If you are certain your coat can stand it. I should not wish to wrinkle you."

"I'll risk it," he replied.

"Very well, then." Narcissa regarded his proffered arm dubiously, for she knew this was a terrible idea. Yet for once she wanted to do something for no other reason than because she wished to, not to please her father, or to keep herself out of trouble with him. Quite the reverse in fact. She was playing with fire, and she knew it, but she would not change her mind now. Hesitantly, she placed her fingers on his sleeve, far too aware of the muscular strength of the arm beneath the well-tailored fabric.

They continued along Bond Street, with Delia chattering happily as Mr Anson offered the occasional answer to any direct question. Narcissa was silent, deeply uneasy at having got herself into this situation, though it was entirely her own doing. Many acquaintances had by now seen her on Mr Anson's arm. It was bound to get back to Mrs Chandler, and yet she could not regret it, even as her stomach churned with anxiety.

They paused before another shop window, this one with a colourful display of fine kid gloves, leather boots, and prettily embroidered silk shoes. Having no interest whatsoever in any of the lovely things on display, Narcissa dared a glance up.

Sighing inwardly, she admired the hard line of an uncompromising jaw, the sharp angle of a chiselled cheek bone and the sweep of thick black lashes. A subtle scent reached her nose, a faintly citrusy melange of sandalwood and amber that made her long to press her nose against his skin. Belatedly, she realised she was leaning closer, pressing against him in her desire to follow the tantalising scent to its source.

Naturally, Mr Anson looked down at that moment. Heat swept Narcissa from head to toe as his incinerating blue gaze met hers. Narcissa's breath caught as he stared down at her, uncertain what the intensity in his eyes meant, but assured that there was powerful emotion behind it. Whether he wanted to kiss her or snatch his arm from her grasp, however, she could not have said. He looked away a bare second later, leaving her all at sea, trembling inside and wondering if she had imagined that look, as he asked her—with perfect politeness—if she liked the cream silk dancing slippers.

Somehow, Narcissa managed a reply, though she couldn't have said what, and they carried on until they got to Madame Blanchet's. Both Delia and Narcissa slowed their steps, assuming this was where they were going, as Madame provided many of their gowns for them.

"No." Mr Anson shook his head and kept walking. "Madame Blanchet is well enough, but rather uninspiring. She is also indiscreet, and I assume you would rather no one knew of my involvement in the choosing of your gowns.

Delia and Narcissa exchanged glances. Though she had known she was behaving badly, Narcissa had not stopped to consider quite how shocking it would be if anyone discovered he had helped them do anything so intimate as choose their gowns.

"I suppose that is an excellent reason for going elsewhere, but she is the most sought after modiste in town," Delia ventured.

Mr Anson let out a huff of laughter. "That is because people have no imagination. I, however, do."

With that, they had to be satisfied as he led them onto Brook Street and to a small but elegantly appointed shop announcing the owner as Madame Amandine. In the window, a dressmaker's dummy was richly swathed in a gown of dark aubergine embellished with tiny jet beads.

"Oh," Narcissa said, avarice burning in her heart as she imagined wearing such a stunning creation.

"Indeed," Mr Anson replied, his tone smug. "Though not for the likes of you, I'm afraid, my lady. Not until you're wed could you dare something like that. Until then, you need spring colours that highlight your youth and innocence and bring all the gentleman buzzing around you like—"

"Flies?" Narcissa replied, her disappointment over the gown having restored her wits somewhat.

"I was not intending to conjure such an unpleasant image, but if you prefer," Mr Anson replied coolly.

He opened the door for them and, in short order, a feminine army of seamstresses appeared, all under the sway of the rather terrifying Madame Amandine.

Madame was a tall woman of ample proportions who showcased her own talents splendidly. Jet black hair was coiled in a complicated arrangement of plaits at the base of her neck, highlighting a face that was handsome rather than beautiful. At perhaps the high side of forty, she was elegance personified and

Narcissa and Delia immediately relaxed, aware they were in the presence of a woman with an innate sense of style.

"Monsieur Anson, 'ow charming to see you in my little shop," the woman replied, curtsying to him in grand style.

Delia shot Narcissa a wide-eyed look as she pressed her fingers to her lips to stifle a giggle, for if Madame Amandine was a French woman, Narcissa was a chimney sweep. The accent was ludicrous and Narcissa stammered through the introductions as she exerted a tremendous effort to keep a straight face. She did not dare look at Mr Anson, uncertain if he would be offended, as he obviously regarded the woman's skills with admiration.

"I apologise for the short notice, Madame," Mr Anson said smoothly. "But it is a desperate case. These two lovely creatures are to go to Lady Roxborough's ball and, like Cinderella, they have nothing to wear."

Madame clucked and tsked over this as her ladies fluttered about bringing this bolt of fabric and that sample of lace as the lady demanded.

"Voyons," Madame announced after much cogitating. "For the Lady Narcissa, it must be the acid green, bright and so vibrant, *n'est pas?* She will be like the springtime, all that promise yet to come. For the Lady Cordelia, it must be the blush pink, so sweet. A perfect confection of spun sugar with a sprinkle of star dust, *oui?"*

"Oui, Madame," Mr Anson said gravely. "And if I might be so bold as to make the smallest suggestion."

Madame tilted her head in acquiescence as Mr Anson gave detailed instructions for this trim and that cut, with a flounce here and a detail there whilst Delia and Narcissa listened with growing fascination.

"Isn't he marvellous?" Delia said, clearly delighted by him. "Just think, one moment he's discussing the merits of satin and taffeta, and the next he's drawing some fellow's cork."

Narcissa nodded mutely, vibratingly aware of the large masculine figure which was highlighted far too dramatically by the excesses of lacy femininity currently surrounding him. Though Madame could easily have become a figure of fun to a fellow with a cruel streak, Mr Anson treated her with the utmost courtesy, discussing the designs the two of them finally settled on with obvious enthusiasm.

Having arranged everything to his satisfaction, Mr Anson presented each of them with a rough sketch of the gowns he had arranged, asking if they approved or wished to make any changes. As both Narcissa and Delia were aware the gowns were things of exceptional beauty, they could do nothing more than nod their agreement.

Mr Anson returned to Madame and just as Narcissa had begun to despair about him ever being done, he bade the lady a good day, thanked her for her time and expertise, and escorted them from the shop.

"She will have them ready in plenty of time and will send word to you by the end of the week to come for a fitting," he said as he walked them back towards Bond Street.

"Thank you," Narcissa replied.

"I am so excited to see my new gown," Delia added, beaming up at him. "Thank you so much."

Mr Anson inclined his head. "It was my pleasure. Now, if you ladies would excuse me. I am afraid I must leave you here. Enjoy the rest of your shopping trip."

He executed an elegant bow and strode off, not looking back.

Narcissa stared after him, watching as he disappeared into the crowd.

"Well," Delia said, giving a heavy sigh. "That was unexpected."

"Unexpected. Yes," Narcissa replied faintly, whilst inside a little voice was repeating, *oh dear, oh dear, oh dear...* for she was horribly aware that her interest in Mr Anson had evolved, turning far too swiftly into fascination, into the need to know everything about him, and to be in his company again no matter what she had to do to make it happen. He was quite the most captivating and aggravating man she had ever met, and she was in deep, deep trouble.

Chapter 4

Dearest Emmeline,

Well, here I am, thrown headfirst into the season and doing my best to behave like the well-mannered young lady we both know I am not. Still, things are looking up, for Lady Narcissa is here. We met last season, though she could only go to a few of the smaller events, but the duke allowed me to visit her and for us to walk out together and to visit museums and the like. He's not a very nice man, I'm afraid, but dukes generally are not. Just look at my Papa.

Still, Narcissa is a lovely creature, named the diamond of the season, for obvious reasons, though some call her the pocket Venus on account of her being rather petite.

We did some shopping today and ran into Mr Anson, who I believe is a friend of yours. He was so very kind as to take us to a new modiste and help us choose gowns for Lady Roxborough's ball. Not that we did much choosing, the occasional nod was all he or madame seemed to require, but I believe the gown will be a thing of beauty. Narcissa will look quite stunning, of course, and throw the rest of us in the shade but I do not mind that.

Now, if I can only try not to say something that makes everyone stare, I shall be doing remarkably well.

Do write back at once, Em darling. I long for news from home. How does Suki go on, and my scrumptious little Jasper? Give them big kisses and lots of hugs from their Auntie Delia and tell them I miss them. I miss you all horribly, in truth. Even Wrexham. I can't wait until March when you all come to town.

Give everyone my best love.

Delia x

—Excerpt of a letter from The Lady Cordelia Steyning (youngest daughter of Philip Steyning, The Duke of Sefton) to her sister-in-law, to the Most Hon'ble Emmeline Steyning, The Marchioness of Wrexham.

30th January 1850, Claridge's, Bond Street, London.

Ash strode away from the two women, though he was certain he could feel Narcissa's gaze upon his back as he lost himself in the crowd.

"Idiot," he muttered furiously.

What the devil had he been thinking? Taking them shopping, of all things! He must be losing his wits. Lady Cordelia was a sweet creature, too kind-hearted and gentle to survive the *ton*, but she had no side to her, she was not anything but what she appeared to be. Lady Narcissa, however...

He ought to have sense enough to stay away from her. Whilst it might be fun to work her father into a lather of bigoted fury, or perhaps even to rile her vile older brother enough to force him into settling their differences in the ring, it was not worth the risk. Ash was many things, but he was not dishonest, and the truth was the Lady Narcissa tempted him like the sirens had tempted Odysseus. If he was not very careful, he would need someone to lash him to the mast.

He told himself that was ridiculous; he was overstating the attraction he felt. It was no more than any man would feel for a beautiful young woman. But… it was not like any other attraction he had ever experienced, not even close. Whenever their eyes met, he felt the connection like a snap of electrical current. Whenever he looked upon her, he could not help but wonder what was going on behind her eyes. Did she feel the surge of heat as fiercely as he did? He was certain she did. Even if, perhaps, she did not understand it, she felt the pull of attraction.

Forbidden fruit, he thought sourly, wondering if that was all it was for her. Perhaps for him too. For hadn't the duke forbidden him to lay his filthy hands on Fidelia? Now her even lovelier younger sister was here, flirting with him. Naturally, he was tempted to behave badly. He was a man, wasn't he?

Yes, that was all it was. Desire for a beautiful woman, and one, moreover, from whom he had been told to stay away. A recipe for obsession if ever there was one. The thought was comforting, but the real truth nagged at his consciousness, nipping at the edges of his mind like a vexatious little mongrel. Lady Narcissa intrigued him.

Ash groaned inwardly. There it was, staring him in the face. She might act the sweet little innocent who nodded demurely when a prospective husband blathered on about how women ought to confine their attentions to the home and child rearing and leave politics, finance, art, and literature—basically anything of interest—to men. He had seen her accept the most outrageous statements with apparent equanimity, but if you studied her closely you saw it, felt it even. If you paid enough attention, you saw the glittering flash of anger in her eyes before she quelled it, saw the barely perceptible stiffening of her shoulders, her fingers twitching with the desire to… to do what? Deliver a slap? Throw something? Ash was desperate to find out.

Then, too, one had to consider the characters of the men she cultivated the most. Not one of them could be considered over-endowed in the brains department. Financially endowed, certainly, with the requisite title, of course. Men she could probably manipulate without ever exerting herself. Was that it, then? Was that what she was after with this saccharine little façade? Why not? Inside that demure little half-wit could lurk a woman with a will of iron, a volcanic temper, and the intention to make a slave of whatever poor fool fell into her trap.

The idea of such a wicked, not to mention lovely, young woman ending up the property of some thick-headed oaf who wouldn't have the slightest idea of how to handle her, made resentment and something that felt uncomfortably like jealousy burn in his chest.

No, he told himself frankly. *No. No. No, Ashton, old man. No matter the temptation, no matter the provocation, you will stay far, far away from her.*

Ash groaned.

He was doomed.

2nd February 1850, Mrs Bishop's Rout Party. Mayfair. London.

Narcissa craned her neck, standing on tiptoes, hoping against hope to find Delia was attending the rout party. Certainly, every other member of the *ton* seemed to have been shoehorned into the house, for it was stifling despite the chilly night outside and there was barely room enough to turn around.

"Stop that," Mrs Chandler scolded. "You are not a giraffe."

Maud gave a titter of laughter at this observation. "Oh, no. No, not a giraffe, for she is a tiny thing. No neck for it. Oh, how very droll you are, my dear."

Mrs Chandler rolled her eyes and moved on through the crush of people, leaving Maud and Narcissa to follow in her wake. Narcissa sighed, having little choice, for she would be quickly left behind and lost if she did not keep up.

As she stepped forward, a glimpse of vivid purple caught her eye, however, and suddenly being left behind did not seem such a bad idea. It only took a moment's hesitation, her apparent interest in looking up at the staircase to see how many people were crowded on the upper floor, and Maud and Mrs Chandler were out of sight.

Biting her lip, Narcissa dithered uncertainly. She wondered if she hadn't best just continue on in the direction they had been heading in after all. Her father would be here tomorrow and the last thing she needed was Mrs Chandler—or worse, Maud, whom he despised—carrying tales to him. Then she caught another glimpse of that stunning waistcoat, and her feet were moving before her brain had the chance to catch up.

"I dinnae ken how ye can blether on about the cut of my coat when ye are wearing that monstrosity."

The voice, heavy with a thick Scottish accent, reached Narcissa's ears as she pushed through the crowd and found herself standing beside Mr Anson. She prepared herself to make an exclamation of surprise at seeing him, as if she'd no idea he was there.

"Oh!" she said, her hand pressing to her heart. "Excuse me, Mr Anson. I did not mean to burst in on your conversation."

"No?" he drawled, looking as though he did not believe a word of it, drat him.

"No," Narcissa replied with as much innocence as she could muster. "I was looking for Mrs Chandler."

"'Tis a wonder ye can see ye own hand in this crush, my lady. Though this fellow's waistcoat is nigh on blinding, which dis nae help," said the jovial Scotsman, whom she now recognised as Muir Anderson.

"Why, how good to see you again, sir," she said, meaning it, for the fellow was lively, good–natured, and fun to be around. "And how fares your brother, Mr Hamilton?"

Muir beamed. "Aye, Hamilton goes on well enough, I thank ye. He will be pleased you remembered him."

"You are both rather hard to forget, I assure you," Narcissa replied, meaning it.

"Ach, 'tis a pity there is no dancing tonight," Muir lamented. "I would have insisted on a dance after a fine compliment such as that one."

"Perhaps it wasn't a compliment," Mr Anson suggested dryly. "Lots of things are hard to forget and are not necessarily pleasant, are they, my lady?"

"True enough," Narcissa replied, more pleased than she cared to admit to discover him ready to fence with her again. "But unlike some people, I should never be so unkind."

"Is that so?" Mr Anson mused, regarding her steadily. "In my experience, the innocent young ladies of the *ton* are all teeth and claws beneath those charming exteriors. Terrifying to behold when out of spirits, and willing to tear a rival to bits for the smallest slight."

"Ash," Mr Muir said under his breath, giving his friend a bewildered look.

Narcissa stiffened, momentarily uncertain if he was in earnest, but she kept her nerve. "Perhaps you deserved the experience, if you spoke to any of those young ladies as you speak to me."

A slow, crooked grin spread over his sinful mouth, and the sight of that wicked smile sent a jolt of pure excitement and triumph lancing through Narcissa.

"Perhaps I did," he allowed, holding her gaze.

Encouraged by his reply, Narcissa carried on. "It is true, however, that society has claws, and I don't doubt you both know that as well as I. Being named the diamond of the season is certainly enough to have some pretty cats sharpening their claws."

"Aye, I've wondered about that myself," Muir offered, regarding them both uncertainly. "There's a fair amount of jealousy to deal with, I imagine."

"Indeed, though Lady Narcissa is well equipped to chase off any rivals. She is Venus, come to walk among us mere mortals. Such grace and beauty, such wit and poise," Mr Anson said gravely. "No one can compare."

Narcissa met his mocking gaze, wondering why she was standing here allowing him to insult her, albeit obliquely, except she had the feeling he was playing a game, and inviting her to join in. If she got the joke, if, perhaps, she wasn't fool enough to take his words at face value.

He knew, she realised with a jolt. He knew she was playing a part, and he wanted her to admit it. To him, at least.

Though her heart beat too fast as she wondered how she dared be so bold, Narcissa turned her face up to him, her eyes wide with innocent pleasure, her tone perfectly sweet. "Why, Mr Anson, you are too generous. To compare an innocent maid with such a *well-loved* deity, how very charming you are."

His eyes sparkled as he registered her riposte, for the reality of the Venus myth had that lovely goddess taking many, *many* lovers, and scattering illegitimate children hither and yon.

"I am delighted you recognise that fact," he said softly. "I should hate for my compliments to fall by the wayside, unnoticed."

"I find it hard to believe you are ever unnoticed," Narcissa replied, her gaze falling to his waistcoat. It was actually a glorious colour, a rich purple, delicately embroidered in black, and with black jet buttons. It suited him to perfection and Narcissa struggled against the desire to reach out and touch it, to feel the silk slide beneath her fingertips, the heat of his body saturating the luxurious fabric. "You would never allow it," she added serenely.

"I do hate to hide my light under a bushel," he agreed, watching her as he lifted the glass he held to his lips and drank. When he spoke again, his voice was low, too intimate, as though Muir Anderson and the rest of the world had gone far away. "I cannot understand why anyone would."

"Then you have not the imagination you claim to have," Narcissa replied, feeling heat sweeping up the back of her neck. It was suddenly stifling in here, her skin sticking to her corset unpleasantly, making her too conscious of her body, of how he made her feel.

"Ah, indeed, for there are devious motives for hiding the truth of oneself, even if the truth is far more splendid than the lie. If, for instance, one was hoping to catch some poor fool in a snare, then it would be as well to conceal that truth with a saccharine exterior, like a meringue hiding a sour secret inside. What a shock it would be, to discover tart, bitter lemon exploding on one's tongue instead of sweet strawberry."

The blush scalded her cheeks as she held his gaze. His intense regard stripped her bare, his words proved he had her measure, that he knew what she was about and thought her despicable, no doubt. Their exchange suddenly appeared in a far different light, his teasing banter no longer amusing, his opinion of her exactly what she had first believed it to be. To her dismay, tears pricked at her eyes.

"Excuse me," she said tightly, and fled, pushing her way blindly through the crowd.

"Damnation," Ash cursed, as Lady Narcissa ran from him.

"You rotten bastard," Muir said in a savage whisper. "What the hell has got into you?" he demanded.

"Shut up. You don't understand," Ash replied tersely, shoving his glass into Muir's hand. "I thought she did, but... bloody hell."

He hurried after Narcissa, no easy feat, as unlike her he could not elbow people out of the way, especially not ladies. At least his height gave him the advantage of seeing over the crowd, so he could track the direction in which that head of bright blonde hair moved. To his dismay, she went to the back of the house, leaving the main rooms. Ash cursed as he was waylaid by Mrs Travers, a friend of his last mistress, Mrs Crawford. She had been angling to get him to herself ever since he had ended that affair. It took all his diplomacy and a promise to call on her the following week before he could get away.

By the time he was free, there was no sign of Narcissa, though when he followed the corridor to its end, the door leading outside was not quite shut. Looking around to be certain no one was watching, Ash turned the handle and stepped outside into the frigid night. He blinked in the darkness, for the terrace was unlit, their hostess having assumed no one would be witless enough to dally outside on such a freezing night as this.

Nonetheless, it was easy to find her huddled against the corner of the terrace. She was crouching down, her skirts billowing around her, her back to the brick wall of the house, her arms wrapped around herself for warmth. Ash stepped cautiously closer, approaching her as he might something wild, likely to flee if he moved too quickly.

"My lady?" he said, but she did not look up, only stared ahead, into the dark.

She looked fragile and very alone. His heart felt squeezed with regret for having treated her so unkindly.

Ash crouched down in front of her, so they were almost level, and she was forced to meet his gaze.

"And here I was thinking you were clever enough to understand what I was saying," he said reproachfully.

She let out a little huff of laughter, though it was not a happy sound. "I understand perfectly," she said, her voice dull. "You despise me for pretending to be witless, for wanting to catch a husband my father will approve of. One I can bend to my will," she added bitterly. "Not that I blame you, I rather despise myself for it too."

"Then you were not paying proper attention," he said crisply. "So perhaps you are not as clever as I'd believed."

As he'd hoped, it was the right tack to take. If he'd been too kind, she would have been suspicious, disbelieved him, but now her eyes narrowed, glaring. Ash smiled.

"Well, personally, I can't stand over-sweet desserts," he told her frankly. "Too syrupy and dull. Offer me something sharp that makes my mouth water, however... something with a tart surprise to shock my senses, well, that's another matter."

His voice was low now, coaxing, as he stood and offered her his hand.

After a moment of hesitation, she took it, her small fingers curling about his and sending that unwelcome snap of electricity dancing over his skin. Unsettled by the connection, he pulled her a little too hard and she stumbled towards him. Ash steadied her with a hand on her waist, viscerally aware of how delicate she was. His gaze fell to her mouth, which was parted in a silent gasp of surprise. Plush and soft, her lips were the sweetest temptation, a perfect cupid's bow above, a lush, generous curve beneath. Unconsciously, Ash licked his lips, aware he ought to take his hands from her, ought to step back, but quite unable to do so.

"Do you mean that?" she asked, studying his face so intently he wondered what it was she sought, and if she'd found it.

He nodded, unwilling to speak, for he was afraid of what he might say. If it were another woman here, he would do all in his considerable power to seduce her, as he badly wanted to do. Her petite frame was a delectable landscape of curves, a temptation created by Lucifer himself to make men stupid. He was not stupid, he told himself, but his brain was being overridden by the unruly part of him that did precisely as it wished, no matter the consequences. Yet this was no neglected wife or lonely widow, but a maiden.

Unfortunately, Narcissa seemed blithely unaware of the strain she was placing upon his instincts as a gentleman. She must be, or else she would not have courted danger so readily, reaching out a hand and sliding her fingers down his chest, over the silken fabric of his waistcoat.

"Truly? You… You weren't mocking me?"

"Well," Ash replied, his voice too low, the seductive tones he reserved for his lovers too easy to give her, despite his best efforts. "Maybe I was mocking you a little, but only in the hope you would return the compliment. Sparring with a woman with a brain in her head is a most… invigorating exercise, you see."

Step back, he willed her silently. Behave as every governess and every book on propriety must surely tell you and *run*.

She didn't run. The foolish chit moved closer. Her skirts rustled provocatively about his legs, a froth of petticoats and skirts sliding against him. Both palms pressed against his chest now and he felt the heat of them through the layers of silk and linen as though she branded him, leaving a mark upon his skin that marked her property. *Be damned to that*, he thought irritably, but he did not remove her hands from his chest.

"I am not your quarry," he reminded her, in case she had forgotten. "I am not the kind of man to dance to your tune, and your father thinks me a half-breed. You ought not be here, with me, Lady Narcissa."

The words were coolly delivered, hard and matter of fact, though Ash was not feeling the least bit cool or matter of fact. Everything inside him was on fire, visions of exactly what he would do to her dancing behind his eyes. If she were not an innocent, he amended with a curse. Which she was.

Innocent. Untouched. Untouchable.

"I know that," she said, her voice low, her warm breath blowing a cloud on the chill night air. "But I want to be all the same."

"The devil take you," Ash muttered furiously.

What the hell did she expect if she said such things, looked at him in that agitating way? Giving into his instincts and ignoring the shrieks of his conscience, he pulled her against him. She went willingly—without so much as a murmur of protest, curse her— and his mouth crashed down upon hers with far more heat than it ought to have. Her first kiss, he reminded himself, and he forced his lips to soften when they would have plundered and demanded. She melted against him, pliant, turning to him like a sunflower following the sun. Her arms went around his neck, her soft body pressing against him, leading him farther along a road he could not afford to travel. Out of bounds, he told himself savagely, remembering her father's fury when he had merely danced with her older sister. *You're asking for trouble*, snarled an angry voice in his head. Frustration and resentment burned in his chest, giving him the will to reach up and grasp her wrists, pulling them from his neck.

"Enough," he told her, his voice colder than he'd meant it to be. "You've had a taste of what you wanted. Now run along and catch yourself a nice biddable husband, one your father will approve of."

She drew away from him as though he'd slapped her, and he hated himself for the uncertainty in her eyes.

"I want to see you again," she said, her candour so disarming he could only gape at her for a moment.

"Don't be a little fool," he snapped, too impatient with her to explain the myriad reasons why that was the most idiotic idea she'd ever had.

"Why not?" she demanded, an implacably stubborn glint in her eyes, the wilful little minx. "You want to see me too, I know you do."

He snorted at that, shaking his head in incredulity. She could *not* be that naive. "Any man here would want to see you again when you throw yourself into his arms so willingly."

She blushed scarlet at his words and Ash relented, not wanting to hurt her, only to make her see sense. "Wait, I'm… I'm sorry. That was—"

"That was true enough," she said, putting her chin up. "I suppose you must think me horribly brazen. I assure you I don't go about kissing men on terraces in the dark, as a rule."

He smiled at that despite himself. As if that hadn't been obvious.

"I don't think you brazen. I think…" *I think you are delicious, fascinating and I want to peel away the layers of that façade until I find the woman beneath*, he didn't say. "I think you are young and lovely and trying to find your place in the world, as we all do. But you really are a fool if you think there is anything but trouble waiting for you if you dally with me. My lovers are women of experience, women who know how to play the game. This game is not made for the likes of you, my lady. Run along back to Mrs Chandler now, before you realise too late you've chosen badly and got your wings singed."

"But—"

"Go," he said coldly. "Now."

Hurt flashed in her eyes but she went with a rustle of silken skirts, leaving him alone in the darkness. Ash clenched his fists, angry with her for stirring him up when he could do nothing about the feelings she provoked in him. What he needed was a fight.

Chapter 5

Dear Cissy,

I thought I ought to drop you a note about how we go on here. Things are much the same, except that we have all been holding our breath, waiting for his grace to leave. The house was in chaos this morning as he prepared for the journey. The relief of his absence is palpable, the atmosphere so much lighter the moment his carriage pulls away. I'm sorry that you'll have to deal with him now but cannot pretend I do not relish his absence.

I know I'm not much of a correspondent – neither are you, I might add, except for scribbling in that diary of yours, but I thought I ought to tell you, Fidelia fell in the lake last night. Don't ask me what she was doing walking about outside at all hours, alone, but you know how she is. Strangely, it seems to have done her good. When I spoke to her afterwards, she was far more like her old self. She even apologised for not being the sister I deserved, which is nonsense, of course, but a good sign, I think? Don't you?

Also, Mr De Beauvoir is here, the landscape architect who has designed gardens for the duke here at Hardacre. Thank God he was, for it was he who rescued Fidelia, pulling her out before she drowned. It makes me go cold to consider what might have happened if not for him. He's a jolly decent fellow too, though he doesn't say much.

He looked at some plans I had drawn up for glass houses yesterday, and he liked them! I have some work to do yet, but he said that if I create proper designs, and if he believes they will stand up and his clients would like them, that he'd buy them from me! Isn't that splendid?

I was so pleased I hardly knew what to say. I'm sure he thought I was a blithering idiot – he certainly thinks I'm a pampered puppy who can't lift a finger for himself – but all the same, Cissy. I felt so proud of myself I could have burst.

How are you, by the way? Do write back.

Alex x

—Excerpt of a letter from The Lord Rufus Alexander Ponsonby to his sister, The Lady Narcissa Ponsonby (children of The Duke of Beresford).

3rd February 1850, Kemble House, Mayfair, London.

Narcissa sat on the hard chair by the fire in Mrs Chandler's late husband's study, outwardly tranquil as she traced a finger over her lips, unable to keep the memory of Mr Anson's hot mouth crashing down upon hers from intruding into her thoughts. Harder still to forget was the way his kiss had softened, becoming tender, coaxing, as his powerful arms had crushed her against his chest. She'd felt her heart thrashing behind her ribs like a bird caught behind the bars of a cage, yet it had not been fear making her heart hammer so wildly, or not just fear, she amended. There had been anxiety enough thrumming beneath her skin, as in some far-off part of her mind the word *consequences* scrawled itself upon her brain in vast red letters that only an imbecile could have ignored. Yet, she hadn't cared. Not even a little. Not in that moment. All that she had cared about was how it felt to be close to him, the first tantalising taste of a drug far more addictive than opium, one that offered far more pleasure, yet danger in abundance. He was dangerous, which naturally only made him all the more alluring.

"Narcissa! Have you heard a word I've said?"

She started, her eyes flying to those of her father's: a cold, austere blue grey, about as warm as the North Sea and just as pitiless. This was the reason she should have had a care, the reason her behaviour seemed even more reckless in the light of day.

"Yes, your grace," she said automatically.

"What did I say then?" he demanded, his voice a growl of irritation.

Smoothing her skirts over her knees to give herself a moment, Narcissa gathered her wits. She had long ago perfected the talent of listening to the duke with half an ear whilst wandering off with her own thoughts. It was a survival tactic honed over many years and one, thankfully, at which she was adept.

"You said that you will receive several gentlemen in the following weeks. Those who have contacted you, asking to court me," she replied softly, eyes down, the picture of the demure daughter.

The duke grunted. "Don't give me that butter wouldn't melt look, you little wretch. We both know you're a wicked creature, but I prefer it when you don't dissemble to me. Wrap them about your finger as tight as you like, but don't try to play me, child. However, I'm pleased with you. I'll say that. You've done well. Some very flattering offers so far; you should be proud of yourself."

Despite knowing better, Narcissa's heart leapt as she looked up at her father. As a child, she had held him in awe, so desperate for any tiny shred of his attention, his regard, that she had been willing to behave dreadfully to get it, just so she might be sent to him to be reprimanded.

"Thank you," she said, hardly daring to believe the words.

By some miracle, he had not heard about her walking down Bond Street on Mr Ashton's arm. Not that it meant she was out of danger; someone might yet mention it. She wondered if what Fidelia had done to get herself banished to Hardacre was worse than what Narcissa herself had done last night, and her stomach twisted into a knot of terror. That his grace might discover it made her palms grow clammy. Yet though she knew the stakes were impossibly high, and her fears were well-founded, it was not enough to make her behave as she ought.

Mr Anson had warned her off too, telling her she was attempting to play a game that was forbidden to unmarried ladies, unless they courted ruination. Yet it was all she could think of, the temptation to see him again, to demand he take her in his arms and kiss her... *good heavens, Narcissa.* Heat prickled up her spine at her own audacity. She would *not* demand he kiss her again. She was not that bold. She wasn't, she told herself. Lord, now she was lying to herself as well as the rest of the world.

"—the Earl of Wishen."

"What?" Narcissa's attention snagged on the title of the man she feared his grace would choose to accept as her husband.

"I beg your pardon?" the duke said coldly, glaring at her as he stood leaning against the mantelpiece.

"Forgive me, your grace. I'm afraid I— Did you say you would accept the earl's offer for me?" she asked, struggling to keep her voice steady as revulsion rose in her guts.

The duke regarded her steadily. He was a large man, an imposing presence, and one used to dominating every encounter. He had stood during the whole interview, forcing her to look up at him from her lowly position on the chair.

"If you had been paying proper attention, which one might suppose you could trouble yourself to do, as it is your own future we discuss, then you would have heard me correctly. I said that so far, the earl's offer is the only one I have received in detail, and generous he has been too. He holds you in the highest regard, and the earldom is an ancient title, a respected one. However, I have not yet accepted his offer. I'm willing to give you time, providing you behave yourself. Perhaps you can bag yourself a greater prize, you're pretty enough to manage it, though I'd be more than content with the earl. Wishen is a fool, I'll grant you, but that ought to suit you well enough. You'll rule the roost and his vast wealth within a matter of days, which ought to please your mercenary little heart."

Narcissa swallowed, forcing a smile to her face, which felt stiff and unnatural. She had long ago allowed her father to believe she was motivated by money, often using an apparent desire for a new gown, horse, jewels or what have you to give her an excuse to seek him out, to annoy him and badger him into giving her a few moments of his time. He always gave her whatever she wished— after a clash of tempers. It seemed to please him when she wrangled whatever it was she wanted from his tight-fisted clutches, and he was far more generous with her than with her siblings… but then they never dared ask him for anything.

"Well, that's all for now. I'll be staying at my club, but I shall call on you again in a few days to update you on how your list of beaus is coming along," he said dryly. "Run along now, child. You may tell Mrs Chandler that I won't be staying for dinner."

Narcissa got to her feet, dropped a respectful curtsy, and left the room. Her stomach churned as she considered the earl. Not a monster, she reminded herself. He was a decent man, one who would not beat her or ill-treat her, and yet... He was sixty if he was a day, and she remembered how the spittle had gathered at the corners of his thick mouth as he'd spoken, how his sweaty hand had patted hers fondly as he'd called her a *sweet little dove*.

"Oh, God," she murmured, and sucked in a breath.

Was any amount of control, or freedom, worth the sacrifice of marrying a man who physically repelled her? Yet she knew that's what it would come down to. Of all the men she had cultivated, had encouraged the most, he was the one her father would approve. There were others she might catch, but she was far less certain of her ability to manage them, and she would not find herself in the keeping of a man who would bully and abuse her. Not that. Not ever.

So, short of Prince Charming falling from the heavens and madly in love with her in the next couple of months, her fate was sealed. Panic fluttered in her chest as she ran through the list of eligible bachelors still on the market in the vain hope she could think of an alternative. Leo Hunt was obviously out of the question; the duke would never consent to that match. Neither would he accept Lord Elsmere, who was handsome but feckless and not the kind of man she could manage in any case. He was far too enamoured of less than respectable ladies and spent most of his time among the *demi-monde*, spending money he didn't have.

Lord Harry Adolphus would be quite a catch, even if he was a second son, but he was only seventeen. The Duke of Bedwin would never allow his son to marry so young. Who else? The Anderson brothers were no good, though their older brother was a viscount. Their mother had been in trade, and they were Scottish, which the duke would never approve. Lord Marlowe was still on the market, though rumour was he'd set his sights on Lady Rose Carmicheal. He was also rather intimidating: a brusque, no-

nonsense fellow who had few social graces despite his title. Narcissa strongly doubted he would be a manageable husband. If the Earl of Ashburton ever deigned to come to town, he would be perfect. Not that she thought him manageable from what she'd heard of him, but having such a beautiful husband would be compensation enough. He was said to be a decent fellow too, not the kind to beat or mistreat a wife, but he'd become a recluse, for reasons which the *ton* delighted in speculating over. Some said he'd lost the woman he loved and mourned her still. Others said he'd lost his wits, or that his father had banished him for doing something terrible. Either way, he was no good if she could not get near him.

Mr Justin Ogilvy, she mused. He was young and handsome, from a good family, too. Though he had no title at present, he was next in line for an earldom through some tangled family connection. Narcissa doubted her father was patient enough to wait for that to come about, however. Nor did she know his financial situation, but there were no rumours about him having pockets to let or being an inveterate gambler, so… maybe if fate was kind?

Narcissa swallowed down a knot of misery that lodged in her throat. She had always known this was how it would be, and she had never allowed herself the fantasy that she might fall in love and live happily ever after. That was an impossibility, and something she would be a fool to imagine within her grasp. So, it was likely she would marry the Earl of Wishen. Well, it was hardly a surprise. It would not kill her. She would make a life for herself and, if all went well, she would have the consolation of children to love, though the getting of those children would require her to have a stronger stomach than she had at present. Perhaps when she had produced the requisite heir and spare, she could fall in love then, so long as she was discreet about her affair. It seemed a bleak future to look upon, but she would be financially secure. She would be a countess, and a title like that would bring her a deal of power and freedom.

It was certainly a far prettier fate than many young women faced, that much she knew. Yet tears pricked at her eyes all the same, regret for the kind of life she might have lived a weight in her chest. Mr Anson's handsome face filled her mind, and, despite herself, she smiled. If she had been free to choose, she would have pursued him. He was without a doubt the least manageable man she had ever met, and yet she did not care. Mr Anson offered her a challenge of such magnitude it made her heart leap with anticipation. The temptation to win him, to capture his heart for herself was so irresistible she knew she would do something rash if ever she saw him again, no matter the risk.

And, if her future was already written, as it seemed increasingly to be, then she ought to take the chances offered to her now, before it was too late, and her fate was sealed.

Chapter 6

Dear Alex,

His grace arrived in town this morning and I have endured my interview with him. By some miracle, it appears he is pleased with me for having caught one of Fidelia's <u>old</u> beaus. Lord Wishen. Aren't I a lucky girl?

I am so glad to hear Fidelia is well, better even, than she has been. Not that it would have been hard, she has been so distant of late. Please hug her for me and tell her I look forward to seeing her again when the season is over, assuming I do not go directly to a husband, I suppose.

Mr De Beauvoir sounds splendid, and I shall be forever in his debt for rescuing Lia. Send him my deepest thanks for what he did. We must think of a way to repay him for his kindness. I am so glad he liked your plans too, Alex. Not that I am surprised, you have a marvellous talent for drawing and such a good imagination too. Well done. It is certainly a splendid achievement, and I don't doubt, the first of many.

To answer your question, I am well enough. My feet hurt from dancing and my face aches from smiling but I am healthy as a horse as usual, if a little dispirited. Choosing a husband his grace approves of is not an especially fun prospect.

Much love to you, brother dear.

Cissy x

—Excerpt of a letter from The Lady Narcissa Ponsonby to her brother, The Lord Rufus Alexander Ponsonby (children of The Duke of Beresford).

5th February 1850, Kemble House, Mayfair, London.

"For heaven's sake, Maud, are you ready? We have been waiting for you this age," Mrs Chandler snapped impatiently.

"Oh, yes. Yes, I am, only… I have been looking for my shawl," Maud fretted, turning in a circle as if she expected the thing to appear at her feet in a puff of smoke. "You know, the pretty blue one I bought in Bath last year. Such a lovely colour, like a summer sky. It reminds me of lovely days at the seaside when I was a child. Such happy memories. We used to go to Brighton, you know. Of course, in those days, the old king—"

"Maud!" Mrs Chandler snapped, her eyes flashing. "The shawl."

"Oh, y-yes," Maud stammered.

"Here it is." Narcissa handed the shawl to Maud with a smile, having hurried off during Maud's soliloquy and found it on the back of the chair in the library where Maud had left it.

"Thank heaven for you, Narcissa. I swear I shall lose my wits over that vexing creature one of these days," Mrs Chandler muttered, stalking towards the front door and the waiting carriage.

Maud shot Narcissa a venomous look of dislike and hurried after Mrs Chandler. "I'm so sorry, my dear. Such a shatter-brain I am, I know. But I swear I looked in the library and it was not there. How very odd it is, I declare. Perhaps someone naughty is playing tricks on a poor old lady."

Narcissa opened her mouth to protest that she could not possibly have looked in the library and failed to discover the dratted shawl but closed it again. Maud was truly a pitiable creature and not worth causing a scene over. Yet every attempt she made to make the woman's life a little easier was met with increasing hostility. Narcissa decided she'd leave the woman to her own fate from now on, for her help was certainly unwanted.

"Now, Narcissa," Mrs Chandler said once they were comfortably installed and on their way. "His grace tells me that the earl will attend tonight's ball. He has informed his lordship that you have saved the first waltz of the evening for him, so be sure to write his name on your card. I trust you will remember to behave as you ought and not go disappearing like you did at Mrs Bishop's rout party, which was very bad of you."

"No, ma'am," Narcissa replied meekly, aware of the smug smile on Maud's lips. "Though that was purely accidental," she added, lying through her teeth.

"Whether it was or not, is neither here nor there. A woman in your position must be on her guard. The world throngs with fortune hunters, just waiting for the opportunity to get an innocent girl alone, but you know the duke better than I do. You must know he'd see you ruined before anyone blackmailed him into an alliance he felt beneath the family's dignity."

"Yes, ma'am," Narcissa replied, a sensation akin to iced water sliding down her spine.

Was that true? She had never really considered it before but there was a horrid ring of truth to Mrs Chandler's words. Her father was about as high in the instep as a duke could be, and the idea of their bloodline being sullied by a connection he felt inferior—No. He would not stand for it. But would he truly set her adrift, rather than lift a finger to save her? Though it pained her to admit it, she knew he would do so to Fidelia, for her father had never given her older sister the credit she was due and did not hide the fact he did not care a button for her. Was that what had happened, she wondered? If so, it must have been hushed up, for she had heard not even a breath of scandal attached to Fidelia, which would account for her still being allowed to live at Hardacre. Would he really do that to her, too? And if there was a scandal, would he have abandoned Fidelia? Would he abandon *her*, if it came to it? For she was his favourite and always had been, but...

Yes, she thought, the bleak realisation settling in her stomach like a lump of ice, cold and heavy with the knowledge that she had been a fool to think otherwise. Her father was utterly ruthless, and he would cut off any branch of the family tree that he believed was unworthy of the connection without hesitation.

"Narcissa!"

Narcissa jumped, bringing her attention back to Mrs Chandler. "Pay attention when I'm speaking, child. I am not of a mind to waste my breath, so heed my words. It has come to my attention that you were seen walking down Bond Street in the company of Lady Cordelia and a gentleman with whom you must know better than to associate. I know Maud warned you of the dangers of that connection," she went on, and Narcissa was unsurprised to see a malevolent glint of triumph in that lady's eyes. "But her warning seems to have fallen on deaf ears. So let me spell it out for you. I forbid you to speak to Mr Anson. You are not to dance with him, or to engage in any but the most formal of conversation with him. If he addresses you, you may reply cordially, but coolly. You will give him no reason to pursue you, or to believe that his advances are welcome. I do not think I need to explain to you what would happen if this information reached the duke's ear, do I?"

"No, ma'am," Narcissa said faintly, her stomach churning.

"I thought not. Then we shall say no more about it. Ah, here we are. Lord, what a bustle. We shall be sadly crushed, I fear."

The carriage stopped outside their destination, the grand façade of Linford House lit up for the night's festivities. Mrs Chandler took the footman's proffered hand and stepped down from the carriage, swiftly followed by Maud. Narcissa sat for a moment, the weight of truths she had been too blind to face until now, pressing down upon her until she thought she might buckle under the weight. Her corset seemed suddenly far tighter than it had, squeezing her lungs. It was hard to breathe, a suffocating sense of an inescapable future looming ever closer, crushing the breath from her. She wanted to flee, to run far, *far* away to a place where no one knew her, where her father and the Earl of Wishen could never find her, but that was a child's dream.

Narcissa was no child but a woman, the daughter of a duke, and one who knew what was expected of her. So, she put up her chin and stepped out of the carriage, showing the world the serene face of this year's most eligible heiress, and she smothered the scream building inside her, pushing it down as she smiled and made inane comments, and did all that anyone could expect of her.

"Now darling, you know you are very unkind to treat me so," Mrs Travers purred in Ash's ear as he swept her around the dance floor. "You promised to call on me this week, did you not?"

"I did, but the week is not yet at an end, I think," Ash replied mildly, wishing fervently he had thought of another way of keeping the woman at bay. Mrs Travers was a lush widow, well-endowed physically and financially. Recently back in society after being bereaved of a husband she had not liked above half, she was enjoying her newfound freedom to the utmost. Ash didn't blame her for that either. At thirty, she was still a young woman and, having borne her husband two strapping sons, she had done her duty by him. Now it was her turn to have some fun, but rather to his surprise, Ash was not interested in helping her do that.

He watched the swirl of dancers around them as they moved through the throng, scanning the crowd. Though he told himself he was just looking to see who was here, who might prove more amusing company than the woman in his arms, he knew it was a lie. He was looking for *her*, damn the girl. Though it pained him to admit it, he knew she was here, because he had made it his business to find out. She had arrived in the company of her cousin, as usual.

Mrs Chandler was a piece of work, he reflected bitterly. The kind of woman who wanted him in her bed whilst disparaging him as mongrel to her friends. The way she had spoken of his mother made his blood boil. Aashini was a lady to her bones, a woman who had endured situations that Mrs Chandler would swoon to even contemplate, and yet she was a loving mother, a devoted wife, and a woman he admired above all others. Mrs Chandler had cuckolded her late husband, and everyone knew her eldest son was likely Lord Bradford's bastard. Despite that, she had the temerity to look down on his bloodline whilst trying her best to seduce him. Not that he had been fool enough to bed her, thank the Lord. He'd had her measure from the outset, not that it had stopped the woman pursuing him. She had been less than happy when he had made it clear he was not interested. A woman scorned was a dangerous creature, and one he would do well to stay far away from.

A cry of pain came from Mrs Travers, and she stumbled against him, clutching at his lapels.

"Sorry! Beg pardon, entirely my fault," boomed a jovial voice as Ash found the Earl of Wishen, red-faced and perspiring, had crashed into his partner.

"Really, my lord," Mrs Travers protested. "I believe you may have broken my toe."

"Oh, no! Surely not," the earl protested earnestly. "It was only a glancing blow and—"

"You stepped on my toe, my lord!" the lady insisted.

Ash was about to intervene when he noticed the woman who had shrunk behind the earl's bulky form, trying her best to make herself invisible. Some hope she had of that, when the gown she wore moulded to every splendid inch of her. The soft turquoise made her wide blue eyes appear a truly startling shade, the kind of endless blue only seen on the most perfect summer days.

"Lady Narcissa, I hope you were unhurt in the scuffle," he said politely as Mrs Travers leaned heavily on the earl and made a deal more fuss than Ash thought strictly necessary. He wondered if she had a mind to make herself a countess with her next marriage. If so, he wished her luck.

"I was, thank you," Narcissa said, her cheeks blazing with mortification. He wondered at that, for the incident was hardly her fault. Everyone knew the earl had two left feet and rarely danced, for incidents of this nature were not uncommon.

"Come, my dear, I shall escort you to a quiet corner and make you comfortable. A nice glass of champagne and a little something sweet will set you to rights, you'll see," the earl said kindly, guiding the lady from the floor. "Anson, please continue the dance with Lady Narcissa and look after her, there's a good fellow. You don't mind, my dear?" he asked Narcissa belatedly, but did not wait for her answer, moving Mrs Travers out of the way of the dancers with far more skill than he'd showed whilst taking part.

"Fate has a sense of humour, it appears," Ash remarked, smiling at Narcissa.

She did not return the smile, her posture taut. "Fate," she whispered softly. "Fate is no laughing matter."

Ash frowned, moving closer. "Come, dance with me. Everyone is staring."

He took her in his arms, though her movements seemed mechanical, her gaze far away, as if she were not there at all.

"What is it?" he asked. "What has happened?"

"Nothing but what I always knew would happen," she said dully. "My father is choosing my husband. You probably just spoke to him. I shall find out, I suppose, in a few weeks."

"Wishen?" Ash said sharply, hardly able to believe his ears. "He's sixty if he's a day!"

"He's an earl, one with impeccable lineage, and he needs an heir now his fool son has got himself killed. He is also a kind man. I could do worse," she said, though her voice quavered, proving she was not half so sanguine as the words might seem.

"If the bridegroom were a corpse, perhaps," Ash said savagely. "How can your father— But what am I saying? Of course, the duke would choose you such a husband. What would he care for your feelings, for your happiness? You're only his daughter, after all."

She smiled at that, a wan expression that made his heart clench. "I have always known my father viewed us all as chess pieces, to be moved about and played as suited him best, but I had pride enough to believe I was a piece with some value. A knight, perhaps, or even a bishop. I was wrong," she said sadly. "We are all of us pawns, and he'll sacrifice us without a second thought if he thinks we are no longer of any use to him."

"My lady," he began, not knowing what he would say but wishing to take that bleak expression from her eyes.

"No. Don't be kind to me, please," she begged him, tears threatening as her voice trembled. "I shall make a spectacle of myself, and that I cannot do. I ought not be dancing with you. Mrs Chandler said I must not even speak with you, and now… she'll be so cross, only the earl told me to, and—"

"Hush now," Ash said sharply, for her eyes were glittering, her cheeks flushed, and he very much feared she would lose her composure. "Take a deep breath and steady yourself."

She did as he told her, as Ash surreptitiously guided her towards the far end of the ballroom, away from where he had first seen Mrs Chandler that evening. He was hardly surprised to hear the woman had warned her off and demanded she not speak to him. Ash glanced down at her, relieved to see she had gathered herself and seemed relatively calm, if pale. "The dance will end shortly, when it does, you go directly through that door on the right there. Turn left and keep going until you come to an atrium. Then open the second door on your right. I'll come and find you presently."

She stared up at him, wide-eyed.

"It will be all right, I promise. No one will know," he assured her, even as his pulse thrummed with a combination of fury and anticipation. He was out of his tiny mind, but she needed a moment to gather herself and he... he needed time to think. The idea of this beautiful young girl married to that doddery old fool made his skin creep. Surely, she had other options. Every unmarried man here would likely cut off his right arm for the chance of a bride like her, and one with such wealth and breeding. There must be someone?

The dance ended, and Narcissa obediently went off in the direction he had showed her as Ash moved back through the crowd to find his twin.

"Viv," he said, drawing her away from her husband. "I need your help. Watch my back, will you?"

Vivien gave him a sharp, suspicious glance. "Watch your—? Ashton, if you are having an assignation," she said crossly, as he recognised the signs of her working herself up with righteous indignation.

"It's not like that," he said, his tone sharp enough to silence her. "Not this time, but it will look that way if anyone finds out.

Please, Viv. I'll be in the library. Just make sure I'm not disturbed."

His twin let out a breath of annoyance, glaring at him. "Oh, drat you, Ash. What the devil are you up to now? Who is the damsel in distress?"

"That's none of your affair. Just do as I ask. I'll be in your debt," he added with a smile.

"That you will," Vivien replied caustically. "And I'll have payment from you this time too, mark my words."

Ash kissed her cheek, knowing Viv's bark was far worse than her bite, and she would take care of things for him.

Narcissa stood in the library of the grand old house, the comforting aroma of old books and leather doing nothing to ease her anxiety. She ought not to be here. Her situation was too tenuous, far more fragile than she had ever realised before. Yet, here she was, waiting alone for a man she had been forbidden to even speak to. Surely, she was out of her mind. Yet when the door opened and Mr Anson appeared, her fears fled, replaced by the urgent desire to be with him, to know this man who seemed to speak to her soul in a way no one else had ever done.

"It's all right, my sister is keeping guard," he told her, smiling reassuringly. "There's nothing to fear."

She gave a choked laugh, and his smile faltered.

"That was a stupid thing to say," he admitted wryly. "I meant only that we shall not be discovered, at least. Now, tell me about the earl and your father's plans for you."

He moved to the settee and patted the space beside him. Narcissa swallowed, and after a moment's hesitation, she sat down.

"There's nothing to tell," she said. "I am here to secure a husband the duke approves of. His grace wants a connection that is worthy of his title. The earldom is an old one, his lineage impeccable, and the earl is wealthy. He says he will give me time to see if I can do better, but he knows I can't as well as I do. In his eyes, it is the perfect match."

"If you disregard the fact Wishen is old enough to be your grandfather," Ash replied in disgust.

Narcissa shrugged, wrapping her arms about herself, for she was suddenly cold. She did not look at him, not wanting to see the revulsion in his eyes when he realised she was not going to fight her fate. "You know how these things work as well as I do. You know I'm hardly innocent in all of this. I have encouraged his advances because I know he's a man I can handle. I'll have a title and wealth and a husband I can wrap about my finger, just as I wanted, just as you predicted."

He reached out and put his fingers to her chin, turning her face towards his. Narcissa swallowed as he studied her, looking into her eyes as if searching for the truth of who she was. "That's not what you want, though, not really. It's simply all you think you can have."

She let out a soft huff of laughter. "They must be the same thing. I must make them the same thing, or I shall never find a moment's peace."

"You can't marry such a man," he said, dropping his hand and looking away from her. His tone was angry, but whether with her or the situation she wasn't certain.

"I can if my father insists upon it, for I have no means of fighting him," she said simply. "Girls marry men they neither know nor even like all the time. It's not such an unusual fate, and at least I feel reasonably confident he will never beat me."

"And that's the best you can hope for? A husband who will not beat you?" he repeated, a dark note in his voice.

Narcissa shrugged. "Most likely, yes. Unless some miracle brings the Earl of Ashburton to town and he falls head over ears for me," she said with a wry smile. "He's about the only man I can think of who my father would accept over Wishen, though he despises Montagu."

"Ashburton?" he said sharply. "You want him? Well, you'd make a pretty pair, I'll admit," he added with a sneer.

Narcissa regarded him cautiously, aware of the tension behind the words. "I've never met him," she replied, puzzled by the sudden outburst. "Though I believed he was a friend of yours. I only meant that he's one of the few men my father would choose over Lord Wishen. I hear he is young and handsome, and so it must be obvious I would prefer him as my husband. I'd be a fool not to."

"Yes," he muttered, and then shook his head. "I'm sorry, my lady. I'm not being of much help."

"There's nothing you can do, and besides, you have helped," she said, feeling suddenly a little shy as she glanced at him. "It is nice to have someone to talk to, someone who I can be frank with and who doesn't constantly remind me of the duty I have to my father's title and consequence, to my bloodline."

He was silent for a long moment before he replied. "My father ran away from home when he was fifteen because his sire was a brute who beat him savagely. He lived on the streets for a while and disappeared from society. Everyone thought him dead. Then, years later, he returned, having made his fortune in trade. People looked down upon him for that."

Narcissa stared at him with wide eyes, astonished by the revelation. He paused for a moment and then carried on. "My mother is everything a lady ought to be, kind and intelligent, and so strong. She is a loving mother who raised us to have empathy for others, and to take a pride in ourselves. I live in terror of disappointing her, of either of them, but all they really want is for their children to be happy. They are still as madly in love now as they were when they first met and to be in their presence is to bask in their happiness, to have it touch everything around you. These wonderful people are my parents, and I am so proud of them, of everything they have achieved, and yet there are still those who look down upon them and believe themselves superior when they are not fit to breathe the same air. It makes me crazy, and then to see a man like your father, who seems to view his children as a means to an end, who would sell you to a fat old man, and to know *he* is respected and revered." He shook his head and let out a breath. "I shall never understand the values of the *ton*. I don't want to understand."

She reached out, taking his hand. For she heard the hurt, the frustration at people's stupidity and bigotry, and she felt it too, on his behalf. "They sound like wonderful people. Brave and resilient people," she added with a smile.

He stared down at their clasped hands, and she followed his gaze, seeing her slender fingers entwined with his. Pale alabaster set against his golden skin.

"You don't despise my father for having worked for a living?" he asked sceptically.

"I know I ought to," she admitted, frowning over the admission. "But in all honesty, it seems strange to me to think that way. Your father succeeded despite the odds stacked against him. He fought back against fate and won. That's rare, I think, and rather wonderful."

"Yes. It is," he said, and his gaze met hers, a look in his eyes she could not read but that made her skin feel hot. Looking away quickly, she took a breath.

"I wish I could feel such pride in my father, and know that he loved me, that he cared for me at all. You are lucky, Mr Anson, and no amount of spiteful or judgemental comments can ever take that from you. I have been meaning to apologise to you for how Miss Pinkerton spoke to you that night at the theatre. I was never more vexed with her. I did not wish for you to believe I felt the same way and I wish… I wish…" Her voice trembled, and she took a moment to compose herself before she spoke again, her eyes fixed upon their hands. "I have never seen a relationship like you describe your parents having. I never really believed that existed outside of books. I have never dared even dream of it, but I… I would like to know what it feels like, to be loved and wanted and admired."

She started as warm fingers caressed her cheek and she turned to look at him, stunned by the compassion in his eyes, by the warmth and understanding.

"You ought to be loved," he said softly. "You deserve to be loved, to be the woman a man would sell his soul to win, the kind he would spend the rest of his days with, knowing he was the luckiest fellow on the planet."

"Oh," she said helplessly, her eyes prickling with tears as she fought for composure. Yet a tear spilled down her cheek all the same. "How strange it is. I've heard so many extravagant compliments these past weeks, and yet, I never cried before. You really are as dangerous as they all say, aren't you? I shall be a puddle at your feet if you keep on," she added with an unsteady laugh, confused by the powerful surge of emotion that his words had provoked in her heart.

His finger traced the line of her jaw, making her shiver. "That's because they were just words before, spoken by foolish men who don't know the true value of what they behold. They want to own you, to buy you and keep you for themselves, like setting a pretty piece of porcelain on a mantelpiece. They do not see the woman behind the façade. It makes their words meaningless, for such declarations need truth behind them before they can touch your heart." He leaned in and kissed her cheek, the place where the tear had fallen. "I cannot bear to see you cry," he whispered.

"Then you had best stop being so sweet to me," she said shakily, entirely undone by the tender way he spoke to her, the gentle touch of his hand, the brush of his lips against her cheek.

"I fear I cannot," he murmured, nuzzling her cheek. "You've caught my attention, something few women can do. Worse than that, you have made me think of you, and now I cannot stop."

She gasped as lips pressed against the sensitive spot beneath her ear. "Jasmine," he said, his breath warm against her neck. "Jasmine and something else, something delicious."

Narcissa closed her eyes, holding her breath as the pleasure of his touch sent little darts of electricity shivering over her skin. He was still holding her hand, but the other had settled on her waist. She felt the heat of it through the layers of her gown and her corset and chemise and could not help but wonder how it would feel if there were no layers beneath his palm and her skin. The thought was so very shocking heat surged through her, but still, she did not pull away.

His lips moved over her skin, trailing a path to the curve of her shoulder.

"Ah, vanilla," he said, and she felt the words as they shaped themselves against her skin. "Good enough to eat," he murmured as his lips moved over her cheek to her mouth.

She sighed as he kissed her, as though she had been waiting her whole life for the touch of his mouth against hers and only now could she breathe easy. Though she hardly knew how she dared, she raised a tentative hand and stroked his hair. He captured the hand and turned into it, pressing a kiss to her palm before returning to her mouth and kissing her again, her hand still trapped in his, pressed against his chest.

Narcissa was lost, her senses swimming in a sea of which she had no experience. Though she knew it was dangerous, she trusted him to guide her, to see her to safety, though there was a part of her that knew it was foolish to do so. This man was adept at seduction, everyone said so, and surely that was what this was. He was seducing her with sweet words and soft touches so that she would give herself over to him. But she wanted to give herself over to him, could think of no pleasure sweeter, no greater happiness than spending however much time he would grant her in his arms. For if she was to marry an old man, could she not have this moment for herself, was that too much to ask?

His hand moved up her side and cupped her breast and she sucked in a breath, shocked both by the fact he had done it, and by the jolt of pleasure that had darted through her, tugging at a place even more intimate than the one he caressed. "M-Mr Anson," she said hesitantly, wondering if they were truly as safe here as he supposed.

"Ash," he murmured, capturing her mouth again.

Narcissa sighed, forgetting what it was she had been worried about as his tongue traced her lower lip and then slid into her mouth. Startled at first, she did not know what to do, but he teased her, touching her tongue and inviting her to do likewise. It seemed to be a delicate form of fencing, advance and counter-parry and riposte, but the deeper the kiss, the more lost she became in the intimate encounter.

He pulled her closer, raising their still entwined hands and settling her arms about his neck, pressing her gently but inexorably down against the sofa cushions. The weight and breadth of him so close to her made her dizzy with an unsettling combination of longing and fear. Was this just a game to him, the game he had warned her that she dares not play?

A sound outside made her stiffen, and he reacted too. Ash raised his head, alert and listening. Whatever it was, it seemed to be nothing to worry about, however, and she lifted her face to his, expecting him to kiss her again, but he stared down at her as though he had woken from a dream.

"Devil take you!" he exclaimed, surging to his feet and putting distance between them. "Were you ever going to stop me?"

Narcissa blushed, staring at him indignantly. "Stop you? Why should I? Why is it my job to stop you?"

"B-Because," he stammered, and then shook his head. "No. No, you are quite right, this is on me. I ought never... Good God, woman, what you do to me. I think I may have lost my mind."

Hurt and humiliated by his sharp words, Narcissa stumbled to her feet, her legs not entirely steady. "I beg your pardon," she said, trying her utmost to keep her composure. She would not cry in front of him again. "I did not mean to—to cause you such trouble."

Aware she was about to break down despite her best efforts, and determined to spare herself that much humiliation, she fled towards the door.

"Narcissa!" He moved as she did, catching her before she could grasp the door handle. "No, you little fool, I didn't mean—"

She struggled in his arms, pushing him away and he let her go, but held a handout, standing between her and the door.

"Don't go, not like this, not when you don't understand. I meant no insult, I swear it. That... Damnation, Narcissa, that was the sweetest kiss I ever tasted in my life and I... I lost my head. I ought never to have allowed things to go so far, but you are so delicious I forgot myself. I forgot my manners and the fact I was a gentleman... or something resembling one, at any rate," he added wryly.

Narcissa looked at him doubtfully, uncertain of whether to believe him.

"I was chastising myself, not you," he told her, his voice gentler now. "You did nothing wrong, though you will end up losing your innocence if you don't learn to tell me *no*. The truth is, you make me stupid, recklessly stupid, and so I need you to keep your wits about you or we shall both end in the basket."

Narcissa stared at him, mollified by the frank explanation. Slowly, her lips quirked, as she discovered she was not entirely displeased by the idea this sophisticated, experienced man had lost his head over her, albeit it momentarily.

"I'm sorry, Narcissa, I behaved badly. Do you forgive me?" he asked, a wary look in his eyes now.

She smiled at that. "I didn't want to tell you no," she admitted.

He groaned and ran a hand through his hair. "Don't say that," he pleaded. "We're in enough trouble as it is."

"We are?" she asked him softly, for she had been aware of the danger she was courting, not only the possibility he might ruin her for fun, or that they might be discovered, but the growing awareness of the way her heart was cleaving to him, wanting him above all others. The idea he might feel the same way made hope blaze to life in her heart.

"I think so," he admitted, holding out his hand to her. She stepped closer, taking it as he looked down at her. "I'm not sure this is one of my brighter ideas, and I've had a few really bad ones in my time."

"That's not very complimentary," she chided, though she knew what he was saying.

"Narcissa," he said, and his voice was grave now. "It would be best for you, for both of us if we did not see each other again."

"I know," she said in a small voice, desperately disappointed but determined to be brave, knowing she had no right to ask more of him. She'd had more than she ever expected, a few moments of his time that were hers alone, and that no one could take from her.

"Is that what you want?" he asked, a flat note to his voice that struck her as odd, that made her gaze fly to his as her heart lifted.

"No," she admitted, holding his gaze. "No, it isn't."

He searched her face, his expression unreadable. "Well," he said, the words a little softer now. "You'd best go now, before you're missed, and be careful my sister doesn't see you. She can be trusted, but I'd rather not have her scolding me all night if you can manage it. Your father is not one of my greatest admirers, which I am certain you have figured out."

She nodded gravely, knowing all too well what her father would say if he knew where she was. The idea was too terrifying to contemplate, so she pushed it away, turning her attention back to Ash.

He stroked her cheek, his expression serious. "When you find Mrs Chandler, an excuse about a torn hem is probably your best bet if you're questioned. Hardly surprising after a dance with Wishen," he added with a smile. "Now, you'd best run along."

Narcissa nodded and waited while he cracked open the door and looked outside.

"It's safe," he told her.

"When will I see you again?" she asked, not wanting to leave him without having something to hope for.

"I'll think of something," he promised.

Narcissa smiled back at him, uncertain now, and went to let go of his hand but he tightened his grasp, lifting her hand to his mouth. He closed his eyes as he kissed her fingers.

"Goodnight."

"Goodnight," she whispered as he let her hand go, and slipped quietly out of the door.

Chapter 7

Dear Diary,

Tonight was dreadful and wonderful, and I am terrified and yet so ridiculously happy. Oh, what I tangle I am making of everything, and yet I cannot be sensible, not now, not when I have been given a glimpse of a life I never dared dream of before.

—Excerpt of a diary entry by The Lady Narcissa Ponsonby.

5th February 1850, Linford House, Hyde Park, London.

"Bloody hell," Ash muttered, once Narcissa had gone. "You are out of your tiny mind."

He paced the room, his nerves all on end, heart thudding.

"Beresford's daughter," he said faintly, his voice disbelieving. He took another turn about the room, trying to make sense of what the devil had happened, at precisely what point he had realised he had fallen into a trap entirely of his own making. "Well, you don't do things by half, I'll say that much for you."

"Talking to yourself is the first sign of madness," said a dry voice.

Ash started and then let out a breath as he saw Vivien in the doorway.

"I take it your intriguing rendezvous is over," she asked mildly. "And were you considering letting me know at any point this evening?"

"Sorry," he replied, shaking his head. "I was a little distracted."

"So I see." Viv narrowed her eyes at him. "Who was it?"

Ash relaxed a fraction, relieved that Narcissa had returned to the ballroom without Viv seeing her. "None of your business, Viv," he replied mildly.

Vivien stared at him, and Ash prayed she wouldn't take it into her head to get the truth from him. It was impossible to keep a secret from Viv if she had decided she wished to know about it. "You're not getting yourself into trouble, are you, Ash?" she asked, and then threw up her hands. "What am I saying? Of course you are."

"Of course I am," he repeated amiably, walking over and giving her a kiss on the cheek. "Thank you for helping."

Viv snorted and followed him to the door. "I hope you know what you're doing," she muttered, shaking her head. They went out and Ash paused as movement down the corridor caught his eye. He thought he saw a glimpse of blue, but it was gone too quickly to be certain. Forgetting it, he escorted his sister back to the dance.

The rest of the evening passed in a blur, as far as Narcissa was concerned. She danced, and she smiled, and she did everything Mrs Chandler could expect of her. To her relief, Lord Fotherington was here tonight and, as he was Mrs Chandler's favourite beau at present, the lady was too happy flirting and laughing with him to worry overmuch about Narcissa.

The excuse about her hem worked like a charm, and Narissa managed to quiet her over-excited heart enough to behave properly instead of like a besotted lunatic who had become ridiculously infatuated in such a short space of time.

Ashton. *Ash*. She repeated the name he had given her leave to use over and over again in her mind, hugging it to herself alongside the beautiful words he had spoken.

You deserve to be loved, to be the woman a man would sell his soul to win, the kind he would spend the rest of his days with, knowing he was the luckiest fellow on the planet.

She repeated them to herself, wanting to remember so she could write his exact words in her diary. The memory of his tenderness, his soft voice, made emotion expand in her heart, filling it until she thought her ribs could not contain the happiness rising inside her.

Even when Lord Wishen sought her out again, looking at her as though he were famished and she the last cream cake, her spirits were too buoyed to be diminished. All the way back to Mrs Chandler's home, as her cousin and Maud chatted animatedly about the ball and all the juiciest *on dits* they had gathered over the past hours, Narcissa just stared out of the carriage window. She wanted to be alone with her thoughts so she could relive those moments in Ash's arms, the feel of his mouth upon hers. She smiled to herself, still stunned how wonderful a kiss it had been, and oh, how she wanted another, and another, and all his kisses all to herself.

Finally, the carriage arrived back at Kemble House and the three women made their weary way up the stairs to bed.

"Goodnight, Cousin. Goodnight, Maud," Narcissa said, turning down the corridor to her own room.

Mrs Chandler waved her fan dismissively before entering her own room and closing the door, but Maud lingered.

"Oh, my lady, a moment of your time, if you would be so good," Maud said, her expression too sweet to be trusted.

"Certainly," Narcissa replied, uncertain of what she could want, even as a prickle of unease ran down her spine.

"In private, I think," Maud added, gesturing for Narcissa to carry on walking.

Narcissa glanced at her, her unease growing as she went to her bedroom and Maud followed. Her maid, Nancy, was waiting for her.

"Nancy, would you mind giving us a moment, please?" she asked politely as the girl bobbed a curtsey and hurried out.

"Don't worry," Maud said brightly, once the girl had closed the door. "I won't keep you above a moment."

"Very well," Narcissa replied, her heart thudding as a terrible sense of foreboding swept over her.

"I know what you did tonight," Maud said, with no preamble. "I know you met that man, your *lover,*" she said in disgust, her lip curling.

Narcissa caught her breath, one hand flying to her heart. Instantly a denial rose to her lips, but she closed her mouth, holding it back. She would not deny it, not deny Ash. It would be pointless for one thing, for Maud must have followed her, but more than that, she did not wish to deny he meant something to her, even to a spiteful creature like Maud.

"What do you want?" she said instead, her voice cold.

"Five hundred pounds," Maud replied, her eyes flashing defiantly.

Narcissa gaped at her. "You're mad," she whispered, stunned both by the realisation Maud really meant to blackmail her as much as the vast amount. "I have a little pin money, but nothing anywhere close to that sum. You know this. The duke pays all my bills directly. He does not trust me with anything more than the smallest amount of money and I have no jewellery to sell other than my pearls. He disapproves of unmarried ladies wearing anything else."

"Then you had best ask your lover for the money. He's a wealthy man by all accounts. His father certainly is."

"I c-can't do that," Narcissa exclaimed in horror. "It's impossible."

"Then I shall tell Mrs Chandler and she will tell the duke," Maud said with a shrug, turning and walking to the door.

"No! Wait," Narcissa cried, running after her. Fear, cold and sickening, made her skin clammy as she considered what her father would do when he discovered what she had done. Would she be made a prisoner at Hardacre too? Would he disown her? She stared at Maud in disbelief, not understanding how she could be so cruel. "Why, Maud? Why are you doing this to me? I have tried to be kind to you, to make things easier for you."

"Kind?" Maud spat in disgust, her expression venomous. "By making Mrs Chandler aware that she treats me like dirt? As if we don't both know it already. You think that kindness, do you? And what do you think will happen when she becomes uncomfortable, knowing you are aware of what a petty, vindictive woman she is? Do you think she'll change her ways? Or do you think she'll get rid of the reason for her discomfort altogether? The only reason she keeps me around is because it makes her feel superior and she can tell her friends about her charity and kindness in keeping such a poor dab of a woman as I am in her household."

"I'm sorry," Narcissa said, bewildered by this point of view, but seeing at once the possibility Maud had the right of it. "I had no intention of putting you at risk, Maud, you must see that. My intentions were good. I only wished for you to be treated with respect."

Maud snorted. "The road to hell is paved with good intentions, that much I've learned at my cost. Well, no more. This time I shall look out for myself. You are a stupid, spoiled brat, Narcissa.

You've beauty, position, wealth. Everything a girl could possibly want, you have. You could be a countess for the snap of your fingers, but no… that's not good enough for you. No, you must ruin yourself, throwing everything away on a man who does not belong in our world, nor his own."

"That's not true," Narcissa said, her temper rising.

"Do you know what his Indian brethren call them, those that are half-Indian, half-English? *Kutcha butcha,*" she said with relish, apparently savouring the strange-sounding foreign words. "It means half-baked bread," she said, laughing now.

"Stop that!" Narcissa cried angrily, tears springing to her eyes. "You spiteful creature."

"Spiteful? Me? Oh, that's nothing. Can you imagine if you married him, assuming he has even considered the idea—which I strongly doubt—but all your children would be like him. They wouldn't fit, Narcissa, just as he doesn't. They'll always be on the outside looking in."

Anger of the kind Narcissa had never felt before burned through her veins, chasing away fear. "If the world they are looking in at contains people like you, I shall be glad to remain on the outside of it with them," she said savagely, the rage in her voice making Maud take a step back.

The woman glared at her but looked a little less certain of herself. "I give you one week to come up with the money, Narcissa. Pay me, and I'll keep my mouth shut. Otherwise, you'll find yourself on the outside a deal quicker than you may have bargained for."

With that, Maud went out, closing the door.

Narcissa stood staring at it for a long moment after she had gone as the simmering rage dissipated, leaving her weary and terribly frightened. It was one thing to be brave and face down a creature like Maud. The Duke of Beresford had the power to imprison her for the rest of her days or cast her into the streets without a farthing to her name and that was quite another matter. She stumbled back and sat heavily down on the bed, a sob of despair rising to her throat.

Oh, lord, whatever was she to do now?

It was three interminable days before Ash saw Narcissa again, despite his best efforts. Having paid his valet to befriend Mrs Chandler's staff and find out where they would be each night, his luck had been poor. The first night they had attended a musical, but the affair had been oversubscribed and not only had Mrs Chandler and her companion been stuck close to Narcissa like glue, but they had left immediately after the concert. The second night, they had attended a dinner party to which he had not been invited. Ash had almost written today off as a bad job too, when his valet had rushed home to tell him they were attending a photographic exhibition that very afternoon and only Mrs Chandler and Narcissa were attending for her companion had fallen ill.

It was not an ideal opportunity, but he was willing to chance it when the alternative was slowly climbing the walls. Try as he might, he could not keep his mind from Lady Narcissa Ponsonby. He was a damned fool to have allowed his compassion for her to have tempted him into arranging that meeting last night. Before that, he had desired her, but he had kept his feelings in proportion, knowing she was out of reach. Now, however, he knew she had values that were akin to his own, he knew too how she felt in his arms, the taste of her mouth against his, and he was crawling out of his own skin with the need to put his hands on her again.

With belated clarity, he realised his initial animosity towards her had been because of her father. As she was Beresford's daughter and on the face of it, a complete henwit, he had assumed she would despise him as the duke did. As he began to suspect her intelligence matched her beauty, his interest in her had intensified alongside his frustration. Though he knew it was ridiculous, he'd had the feeling the duke had dangled the one woman in the world Ash might lose his head over in front of him, with the sole purpose of tormenting him.

That night at the ball, the things she had said, her admission she admired his father for his climb out of the gutter, her assertion of how lucky he was to be loved by such people, had surprised and touched him. She was not what he had expected her to be, and the desire to know more was tantalising.

He knew it was a pointless affair. There was no future for them, for he knew well enough the duke would see him dead in a ditch before he contemplated a marriage between them, not that he was thinking of such a thing. But she would be, and rightly so, for she courted ruin with this madness. If he had an ounce of sense, he ought to tell her not to seek him out again, he ought not be here now. It would cause them both nothing but trouble. It had been his intention to tell her that night. He *ought* to have said it and almost had, but he could be a stubborn devil and the idea of doing something to avoid the duke's wrath had smacked of cowardice. Yet it would be Narcissa who would suffer if they were caught. But then she had told him she wanted to see him again, and he had wanted her to want that so much he'd not done what he should and denied her. He must, however, for her own sake. She was an innocent and had not the slightest idea how an affair could escalate into something unwieldy and out of control when passions ignited, and his desire for her was already driving him distracted. He would end things today, he promised himself, but he could not do so if he couldn't speak to her.

Now Ash stood outside Mr Mayall's photographic gallery on the Strand, determined to speak to the woman he could not keep his mind from, no matter how briefly. It was not an especially large establishment and in normal circumstances, he would have not attempted to see her here, for he doubted there was a quiet corner to be found. But the added information that Lord Fotherington had escorted the ladies made Ash hope he might manage a few moments of conversation with Narcissa without Mrs Chandler noticing. An article about the gallery and Mr Mayall's wonderful photographs had been printed in the past week, so the crush of people swarming to view images of the famous and the fashionable was greater than Ash had dared to hope for.

Joining the throng pushing inside the gallery, Ash wasted no time on the photographs but scanned the crowd, his view impeded by a vast array of bonnets which hid the wearer's hair and face. To his astonishment, Ash discovered his heart racing with anticipation. Never in his life had he got himself in an emotional state over a woman. He'd experienced lust, certainly, and the excited anticipation of a new love affair without doubt. Though he admitted to himself now that the feelings of excitement a new lover usually engendered in him had been lacking of late, the sensation of going through the motions and treading the same old path, one that had been increasingly depressing.

Ash threaded his way through the crowd, trying his best to be discreet as he peered around bonnets, hoping to find the beautiful face he sought. A brittle laugh caught his ear, and he turned, following the sound and unsurprised to discover Mrs Chandler on Lord Fortherington's arm. Ash lingered behind them, out of their eyeline until he was certain Narcissa was not with them. Though it suited him perfectly, he felt a swell of anger towards Mrs Chandler for neglecting her charge at such a public gathering where any lout could importune an innocent girl. Still, a bird in the hand was not to be sniffed at and he pushed on, determined to track her down.

He found her in the next room, regarding a photo of Charles Dickens, her lovely face pensive. She wore a grey-lilac satin robe with a darker lilac velvet three quarter length pardessus over the top. Her bonnet was lined with the same grey-lilac satin as her gown, her pale blonde curls shining brightly against the soft colour. A large bow was tied jauntily under her chin and plumes of pale grey feathers draped becomingly about her face from the bonnet.

Ash stopped for a moment, unable to take his eyes from the picture she made, from the kind of beauty that made your heart hurt to look upon. He moved closer, perceiving close up that she looked a little pale, before bending to whisper in her ear.

"I would have a thousand photos of you if I could."

She gasped, her gaze flying to his, and the pleasure in her eyes upon seeing him, the wide curve of her lovely mouth, made all his good intentions fly out the window. How could he tell her he would not see her again, and dim the happiness he saw in her face, never mind the sensation of loss that stung his own heart whenever he thought of it?

"Mr Anson!" she exclaimed, and to his regret, the happiness in her eyes dimmed and she darted an anxious look around.

Still, he could not keep the smile from his lips at her startled surprise, and her evident pleasure in seeing him.

"What are you doing here?" she asked nervously, staring at the people around them.

"What do you think?" he replied, his tone dry. "Come with me. Don't look so anxious, Mrs Chandler is still in the first gallery, flirting with his lordship."

"Yes," she said, sounding breathless. "Indeed, I shall, for I must speak with you," she said urgently.

He nodded, a little alarmed by the tenor of her voice, the fear in her eyes, but they could not speak here, so he offered her his arm. "Come, then."

Obediently, she took it, following him down into the next room, though she became visibly agitated as he guided her down a corridor and through a door that led them outside to a small courtyard.

"That's better," Ash said as he closed the door on the noise and bustle inside. He turned to her with a smile that died on his lips as he realised just how anxious and unhappy she was. "Whatever is the matter?"

She took a deep breath, attempting to calm herself. "Maud—that is, Miss Pinkerton—saw us last night."

Ash went still as the import of those words sank in.

"Impossible," he said, shaking his head. "Viv would have seen, I'm sure."

"Well, Maud knew we were together," Narcissa asserted. "She must have followed me when I left the ballroom, before your sister came to stand guard."

Ash had not considered that, and a feeling of dread swept over him.

"Tell me what happened, what she said."

Concisely, Narcissa repeated what Miss Pinkerton had said to her, and her reasons for what she did to someone who had tried only to be kind.

Ash's expression darkened as he realised just how bad this was. "What does she want? I presume her intention is blackmail, else we'd not be having this conversation."

Narcissa nodded, her expression bleak, her beautiful face drained of colour and Ash cursed himself for getting her into this situation. This was his fault. It had been his idea to meet her in private, and he had assured her he would keep her safe.

"How much?"

Narcissa's lip trembled. "F-Five hundred pounds," she stammered, as well she might. "I don't have it, Ash," she admitted, wringing her hands together.

"Curse her," he muttered angrily, and curse him for a reckless fool. That he, who was so discreet in his affairs, should have made such a fateful error. The one time when it mattered more than ever before, and he had messed up. Damn him to hell.

"What shall I do? The duke gives me very little pin money, all my bills are sent directly to him," she said, and the fear in her voice was audible. Ash's expression softened as he saw how she trembled, and he could not help but reach for her, holding her in his arms. The swell of tenderness rising in his chest, the overwhelming desire to protect her from harm, was startling, his fury with himself and with Maud bloody Pinkerton such that he had to work to keep his voice calm.

"Firstly, you won't worry," he told her, holding her gaze, asking her to trust in him, though why she should when he had created this unholy mess he had no idea. "I shall deal with this; I give you my word."

"But how?" she asked fretfully.

"Leave it to me. I will deal with her," he repeated, his voice firm.

She stared at him, searching his gaze, and he was hardly surprised when she shook her head, unconvinced. "No, that's not good enough. Tell me how. Maud insists on having the money by the week's end or she will tell Mrs Chandler."

Ash raked a hand through his hair, wishing she might have given him time to think of a reassuring answer. "Well, I don't exactly know at this precise moment!" he admitted grudgingly. "But I shall think of something, mark my words. I won't let that woman upset you, Narcissa. I shall make it right, I promise. In the short term, tell her I will give her the money but that she will have to meet me, alone. That is non-negotiable."

Narcissa stared at him, alarm in her eyes. "B-But you don't m-mean to—"

"She will be quite safe, you may assure her of that. I'm not in the habit of murdering women," he muttered. "Nor terrorising them, no matter how richly they deserve it," he added reproachfully.

"I beg your pardon. No, of course you wouldn't," Narcissa said, sounding rather mortified. "Only I am so terribly frightened I hardly know what I am saying, what to think. If my father finds out—"

"I know," he assured her grimly, well aware of just what was at stake. "Believe me, I shan't rest until I have a solution that will keep you safe. Just tell her to go to the Calverley art gallery on Pall Mall and ask for Mr Weston. It's a respectable establishment but I know the owner. There will be no risk to her reputation."

She nodded, tilting her face up to stare at him. "You must regret ever speaking to me," she said sadly.

Ash smiled at that despite the situation, knowing it was far more his doing than hers. "Yes, I must. What a lot of trouble you have caused me for the sake of a private conversation and a kiss."

Her expression fell, her eyes swimming with tears, and he lifted his hands to her face, cradling it gently. "And yet I don't. I could never regret that night, that kiss, it is imprinted upon my soul."

"Then do it again," she pleaded, and stood on tiptoe, raising her mouth to his.

Gentleman he may be, in his finer moments, but he was not fool enough to refuse such an offer. With a swift tug, he released the ribbon of her pretty but bothersome bonnet and deftly removed it before he lowered his mouth to hers.

His breath caught as their lips met, fire exploding inside him alongside the burning desire to shelter this woman from harm, from anything that could cause her distress. Yet it was his fault she was in this mess in the first place, and he was only making things worse by dallying with her. Though the knowledge tore at his heart, he knew he must keep her safe. Though it was the hardest thing to tear his mouth from hers instead of deepening the kiss, prolonging it in any way he could, he knew it was for the best.

Pulling away, he rested his forehead against hers.

"Narcissa," he began, his voice low.

"No."

The implacable word made him look up at her.

"No?" he repeated in confusion. "I have said nothing yet."

"But you will. You're about to say we cannot see each other again," she said, the words choked, the sorrow in her eyes making his chest ache.

He had never thought to see such a look from this woman, to believe that she cared for him, even a little. Ash sighed, touched that she felt so strongly, or thought she did, but she was little more than a child who had never experienced feelings of this nature. She did not know what danger she courted, not really. At the first sign of trouble, she would likely blame him for it, and it would be as well he avoided such an eventuality for both their sakes.

"And what will you do when your father finds out?" he asked her gently. "For unless we say goodbye, he *will* find out. Do you prefer to wait until we are both tangled up in an affair that will hurt us both deeply, or to do it now, when we will be wretched for a time, but shall recover?"

Even as he said the words, the unsettling suspicion that it might take longer than 'a time; to forget her nagged at his conscience.

"Then you don't want to see me again?" she asked, her voice trembling.

He snorted at that, replacing her bonnet and tying the ribbons with swift, deft hands that longed only to untie them again and cast it aside.

"Don't be a little fool," he scolded her, annoyed by her disingenuous words. "I told you from the start, this was a game you could not afford to play. Neither of us can."

"Then that's it. I shall marry Lord Wishen," she said, resignation behind the words.

"Don't do that," he snapped. "Don't make out like it's a choice between the two of us when you would never have chosen me. Not when it came down to it."

Narcissa gaped at him, eyes wide with hurt. Ash cursed himself but perhaps it was better this way, better they part with anger and hurt on both sides. She would recover quicker under those circumstances. Besides, it was true. Ash was no romantic boy. He knew well enough how it would be. She would profess to love him until the stakes became too high, and then she would return to the safety of her life and her unimpeachable status.

Not that he blamed her entirely. It would be hard for her to be his wife, should he even offer her the chance. He and Viv, privileged and protected as they were by his father's fierce reputation, had still endured their share of snubs and slights. How would a young woman used to being treated with the greatest deference adapt to such a fall, to being seen as something no longer quite perfect, in some way sullied by her association with him? Badly, he suspected, and he knew that would hurt him more deeply than anything else ever could. The woman who became his wife must love him not only unashamedly but with pride, caring nothing for what anyone else thought, or he would not marry at all.

"I w-would choose you," she stammered, but there was enough doubt behind the words, enough fear to tell him he was right.

He stared at her, keeping his voice even. "Go back inside, my lady. Find yourself an alternative to Wishen. God knows you could bring the devil himself up to scratch if you put your mind to it."

"But not you," she said, tears brimming in her eyes.

"No," he replied, resolute, even as something bright and hopeful died inside him. "No. Not me."

She stared at him for a long moment and then nodded. Turning, she opened the door and slipped back inside the gallery. Ash stood frozen for a moment until he felt something like rage burning inside him, the need to hit something so fierce he looked around for a suitable target but found himself surrounded by brick walls.

It will pass, he assured himself, before striding down the courtyard to a back gate. He walked out, down the yard, back into the street while the simmering rage boiled inside him.

It will pass. It will pass.

Chapter 8

Dear Diary,

This week has been the most miserable of my life.

Maud is to meet with Mr Anson this afternoon. I no longer feel I have the right to think of him as Ash. That offer was rescinded when he parted with me. I feel utterly at sea, for I can settle to nothing, concentrate on nothing. Life seems to have lost all its colour. How I wish to go with Maud and see him again, except I have sworn to her we have parted company, for I can give her no opportunity to blackmail me again, not when it is Mr Anson who must bear the cost of my recklessness.

I have been a fool, and yet those moments with him linger in my mind, taunting me with a glimpse of what happiness looks like. I don't know what to do.

I wish I had asked him to run away with me, there and then, but I discover to my shame that I am not half so brave as I thought I was. I do not wish to end my days like Maud, unmarried and at the mercy of others who would use me for their own ends. Though it makes me sick to admit it, I fear even marriage to Lord Wishen would be better than that.

—Excerpt of a diary entry by The Lady Narcissa Ponsonby.

12th February 1850, the Calverley Art Gallery, Pall Mall, London.

Ash waited in the private receiving room at the Calverley Art Gallery. The sooner this interview was over, the happier he would be. Not that happiness seemed to be anywhere in sight. He stood by a window that overlooked the street below, watching the passersby as they went about their business. Turning away, he flexed his hands—which were still swollen after the punishment he'd put them through recently—swore and went to peer in the mirror over the mantel.

Christ, he thought, regarding his face with a grimace. He'd fought too many bouts in the past days, winning them all. At first, he'd been untouchable, fuelled by rage and frustration, but the anger was leaving him now, replaced with something less aggressive and far more insidious that made him want to reach for a bottle and not stop until it was empty. He'd deserved the black eye he'd received yesterday. He was lucky he hadn't got his pretty nose broken. His own damned fault for not paying close enough attention, but it was difficult to concentrate on anything now. Cursing, he swung away from the mirror and stalked back to the window. Where was the bloody woman?

Once he'd dealt with her, the entire sorry business would be over and done and he could move on. He'd agreed to meet Mrs Travers tonight, not that the prospect was especially appealing, but it was either that, another boxing match or drinking himself into oblivion. Mrs Travers did little to get his blood moving, but she was a distraction less likely to kill him, he supposed grimly.

Finally, there was a knock at the door, and Mr Calverley appeared. "Your guest has arrived," he said, expressionless.

Ash nodded. "Show her up."

Mr Calverley nodded and hurried away. As Ash was one of the gallery's best customers, he knew he could rely on the man's discretion.

Miss Pinkerton arrived a few minutes later, white-faced but resolute as she stood just inside the door, glaring at him. Her expression faltered with shock as she took in the black eye.

"I box," he said crisply. "Please don't alarm yourself."

Miss Pinkerton made a face which expressed disgust at such a pastime but said nothing.

"Do take a seat," Ash said, polite if cool as he gestured to a seat by the fire.

"No, thank you. I shan't be staying. Do you have the money?" she asked crisply. "For if you think you can browbeat or frighten me into giving up on—"

"Oh, I know I could," Ash replied quietly.

She let out an involuntary gasp, her hand going to her throat.

"Settle your feathers," he said in disgust. "You are quite safe. Here." Reaching into his coat pocket, he extracted an envelope, holding it out to her.

For a moment, she gazed at it longingly, as she vibrated with indecision.

"I don't bite," he said in exasperation.

Like a scurrying little mouse, she darted towards him, snatched the envelope from his hands, and retreated once more, tearing eagerly at the seal. She pulled out the contents and unfolded the papers, staring at them in bewilderment.

"I don't understand," she said, raising her eyes to his. "W-What is this?"

"The first is the deed to a property in Kent. It's only small, but it is yours, so you may live in it, sell it, or rent it out as you see fit. There are two bedrooms, so perhaps you might choose to take a lodger. The other is a draft on my bank for one thousand pounds."

Colour rose to her cheeks, indignation glinting in her eyes.

"What do you mean by this?" she demanded, holding out the papers to him, her hands trembling. "Is it some manner of cruel joke to punish me for my audacity?"

Ash let out a weary huff of laughter. "No. It is precisely what it appears to be. No one should be forced to live a life of servitude, grateful despite every insult and thinly veiled abuse. This gives you freedom, and I hope it gives you an incentive to let Lady Narcissa alone. She has enough to contend with, without you making her life a misery."

Miss Pinkerton stared at the papers in her hands, tears filling her eyes as a sob rose to her throat.

"Why? Why do this after… after everything I said about you?"

"Just because you say such things, it does not make them true," he said coldly, regarding her with indifference. "I know my own worth. I need no pretty words or approbation from you to validate myself, but I see your fear, your insecurity and jealousy, all the petty spitefulness that fuels you because of a life that has treated you unkindly. Well, this time you are to be treated kindly by a man you despise for the colour of his skin, and I do not want your gratitude, or your thanks, but you will live knowing you owe me this much, despite your vile treatment of Lady Narcissa."

She stared at him, white-faced, her expression pinched with shame and mortification. Ash took no pleasure in her discomfort. He only wanted it over and done with now. He went to the table where he had placed his hat and gloves and picked them up. Moving to walk past her, he paused, regarding her coolly.

"You could have been a friend to her, you could have helped her, and she would have loved you for it. She has a kind heart and is someone who would never see those she cares for suffer. Instead, you rebuffed her attempts to help you and used her for your own ends. At the very least, I believe you owe her an apology, but if it *ever* comes to my ear that you have done anything, said anything—"

"I won't," she said in a rush, shaking her head. Ash waited, and she tilted her head, looking up at him. "I know you do not want my thanks, and I don't blame you for that, but you do have my gratitude, Mr Anson. This... This is..."

She stared incredulously at the papers in her hand again.

Ash snorted. "Yes, now you are grateful, and in six months, a year, when you are speaking to your friends and my name comes up, you will disparage me just the same, because prejudice of that kind runs deep. Just know that I know this, and I was the one who set aside notions of revenge and did the honourable thing. Good day to you, madam."

He stalked out, leaving Miss Pinkerton to digest his words and praying he had done enough to keep Narcissa safe from her spiteful gossip. Either way, it was over now. His part in her life was nothing more than a footnote, a memory she might take out from time to time as she recalled her recklessness, and a man she had once cared something for.

14th February 1850, Goshen Court, Monmouthshire.

Pip set the accounts he was working on aside with a sigh. Finally, the estate was showing faint signs of coming back to life, the promise of profitability one that he could no longer deny, even in his most pessimistic mood. He rubbed the bridge of his nose and smiled as he reached for the little Valentine's card on his desk. It was handmade, with a slightly wobbly heart made of pink satin and trimmed with lace, stuck onto a folded piece of card. The heart had been applied with the liberal use of paste, and the card was still a bit sticky, but the sight of it made Pip's heart lift as nothing else could.

His daughter, the hand behind the card, was the brightest spot in his life, a source of wonder and joy, and often a source of alarm and the reason he did not always sleep soundly. She made him laugh and made him want to tear his hair out, and he would not be without her for the world.

"Bless you, Jenny," he murmured, remembering her beautiful mother.

He had uncertain notions about what heaven might look like, if such a place truly existed, but he hoped Jenny was happy and at peace wherever she might be. The sound of laughter caught his ear, and he got to his feet, moving to one of the immense windows that filled his study with light, and also made it about as cosy as a windswept moor. A chill draught blew through the ill-fitting frame and Pip made a note to get his workmen in here next. He had left many of the rooms he occupied most last on the list of those needing repair. Some masochistic idea of making amends for his past, perhaps, but enough was enough. He had dwelled in guilt for too many years. His parents loved and accepted his daughter, and they had forgiven him. Perhaps it was time to forgive himself, too.

He smiled ruefully as he looked down at the scene below. It had snowed the past days and Ottilie and her governess, Mrs Harris, were intent on making a snowman. There was a woman who would never forgive him for his well-earned reputation, or for having an illegitimate daughter. Thankfully, all her ire was reserved for him. She found no trace of shame in his daughter, else he would not have kept her on. He wondered if she would ever warm to him. She had been in his employ for five years, and yet he knew no more about her now than he had when she'd first arrived. Not that he hadn't been grateful, she had been a godsend, and she was the only one who kept Tilly in line. As her mother was dead and the circumstances of her birth such that made Pip's heart contract with shame, he spoiled her dreadfully. Naturally, this made her quite unmanageable at times and he knew he had only himself to blame. He knew this because Mrs Harris told him at regular intervals.

She was a strange creature, he reflected, bothered by his inability to charm the enigmatic governess. As haughty as a duchess at times, she seemed to look down upon him from a great height, despite the disparity in their situations. She was not the least bit afraid to vent her opinions about him to his face—none of them complimentary—if she thought it necessary.

It was often necessary.

Pip wondered why he bore it. Obviously, he kept her on because Tilly loved "Harry" and would have been devastated to lose her. He would not have his daughter lose another person whom she loved, and there was no doubt in his mind the feeling was reciprocated. There had been plenty of times when the two were alone and unaware of his presence, when that affection and care had been obvious. Indeed, when he was not around, Mrs Harris was entirely different, according to Tilly. It was only him who made her stiffen up and become all rigid and po-faced.

Curiosity gnawed at him. Though he was not an especially vain man, he knew what he looked like. Made in the same mould as his father, he had the kind of looks that made women do the most ridiculous things to get close to him. But not this woman.

Why?

Why could no amount of charm, no amount of kindness or consideration break through that barrier of ice?

Watching the snowman take shape, he caught his breath as he saw Tilly scoop up a handful of snow and throw it at her governess when her back was turned. It hit the woman on the back of the neck and Pip tensed as he imagined the icy shock of it, the cold water sliding down under the collar of her pelisse and gown. He held his breath as Mrs Harris spun around, for as close as she was to her charge, she was also a strict governess and a stickler for rules and propriety.

"Oh, you little fiend. You will pay for that," the woman cried.

Pip's eyebrows rose as a violent and somewhat hysterical snowball fight erupted beneath his window. Tilly knocked Mrs Harris' bonnet off and it lay abandoned as they ran back and forth. Screams and shrieks echoed around the frozen landscape, and he watched in growing bemusement as Tilly tackled the woman to the ground and sat on her, trying her best to stuff snow down her neck as Mrs Harris wriggled and exclaimed, laughing uproariously as she tried to fend his daughter off.

"Pax!" she cried breathlessly, when it became clear Tilly would not give way. "Pax! You win. I surrender."

"Huzzah!" Tilly shrieked, jumping up and running around in a circle waving her arms in the air.

Mrs Harris staggered to her feet, brushing snow from her skirts as her hair, usually pinned ruthlessly into a tight bun, unravelled and spilled down her back. Pip watched, fascinated to discover it reached way past her waist. In fact, he had never particularly noticed what a tiny waist the woman had, or the way it flared out, making him suspect the curves beneath her skirts matched those above. She reached up, re-pinning her hair in deft motions that spoke of many years practise. Turned sideways as she was, highlighted against the snow, her startlingly lush silhouette imprinted itself on Pip's mind. Lazily, he wondered what she might be like in bed, if she would scream and laugh with the same kind of abandon if one could only get past that impenetrable barrier of ice and—

"Christ!" he muttered, turning away from the window in alarm.

What the hell was wrong with him? Fantasising about his daughter's governess? *Mrs Harris?*

"Pip, old man, you are losing your mind," he told himself sternly. What the devil had got into him? Admittedly, he was not living the life he once had, but he wasn't a monk. With a little discretion, it was quite possible to arrange things with a lady to their mutual satisfaction. He had done so plenty of times. He was currently visiting a rather splendid little widow a few miles away. Not that he took any chances these days. He was rigidly strict with himself, never allowing the chance of creating another child out of wedlock.

Still, it was a rather depressing business, a tad too clinical. Yet his only other choice was to marry, and that idea was worse. He could not bring himself to marry for duty, knowing what his parents had, what kind of life might be possible with the right woman. Yet he could not bear to go back to town, to spend the time required to meet a woman he might have the chance of falling in love with, not when that meant leaving Tilly for months on end. Taking her to town was an obvious answer, and he knew he must, yet he shied away from the idea.

"Papa, Papa!"

Pip turned as the door burst open and Tilly barrelled in like a small but deadly cannonball, throwing herself at him and making him stagger. She brought the scent of cold, fresh air and snow into the room with her, and her face was flushed with pleasure and triumph as she stared up at him.

"I won, Papa! I slayed Harris!"

"You *slew Mrs* Harris," corrected her rather breathless governess, who hurried in after her.

Pip regarded her with interest and noted that her hair was still dishevelled and there was a rather becoming glow in her cheeks.

"And what have I told you about bursting into a room like a wild animal? You are a young lady, Ottilie, or so I am told. It is not done to throw yourself into a room as though you are running from

123

an army of savages. You must knock and wait for permission to enter."

Tilly made a moue of displeasure. "But Papa didn't mind. Did you, Papa?" she wheedled, gazing up at him with soulful eyes.

"Er." Pip hesitated, eyeing Mrs Harris warily, aware he was on a hiding to nothing. "I didn't mind, sweetheart, but Mrs Harris is quite right. You ought to heed her, for she is teaching you how to behave as you ought."

Tilly made a sound of impatience, burying her face against his coat. "Behaving is soooo dull," Tilly complained, her voice muffled.

"So it is, but misbehaving leads to a life of full of wickedness and shame," Mrs Harris replied crisply. "Does it not, my lord?" she asked him, her voice pleasant enough, though Pip was well aware she was making a point.

"Indeed, it does, Mrs Harris. So much wickedness." Though he did not know quite what had got into him, he lingered a little over the last word, holding her gaze, just for the hell of it.

Rather to his delight, her colour rose.

"Quite," she said sharply. "Come, Tilly. You must wash and change if you want to have any supper."

Groaning, Tilly went to her, hearing the voice of command as clearly as Pip did. A moment later, they were gone.

Well, he thought, amused. Mrs Harris really was a conundrum, but perhaps that icy exterior was not quite as impenetrable as he had thought.

Chapter 9

Dear Diary,

I have taken to my bed and pleaded illness, though I am not ill, only so very shaken, and shocked and beside myself at my good fortune.

I know what I did was wicked. Blackmailing Lady Narcissa to keep quiet about her private meeting with Mr Anson was a terrible, terrible thing to do and I know I must atone for such abhorrent behaviour. Yet I find it hard to regret the outcome.

Mr Anson was not at all what I expected, and his treatment of me was beyond anything I might have believed possible. I knew he would be well within his rights to give me a dressing down – and he did, but not in the way I expected. He was unexpectedly kind despite his harsh words, and I find myself at a loss to account for such behaviour. Though I still believe Narcissa would be a fool to throw everything away because of her feelings for a man who will bring her nothing but trouble, I find I have some sympathy with her, and can understand what tempted her to do such a reckless thing.

—Excerpt of a diary entry by Miss Maud Pinkerton.

19th February 1850, Kemble House, Mayfair, London.

Narcissa looked up from the cup of chocolate she was nursing, surprised to see Maud walking into the breakfast parlour. She had kept to her room ever since her meeting with Mr Anson, and Narcissa had seen nothing of her. Mrs Chandler had told her Maud was suffering one of her megrims, with a little curl of her lip that showed what she thought of that.

For once, Narcissa felt some accord with Mrs Chandler's impatience. She did not believe for a moment that Maud was unwell, only that the horrid creature was too ashamed to face her. This suspicion was born out as she glared furiously at Maud across the table, but the lady continually avoided her eye.

"I hope you are feeling better?" Narcissa enquired, keeping her voice sweet, determined that the wretched woman acknowledge her. "I was so sorry to hear you were unwell. Megrims are such a debilitating illness. I'm sure you do not deserve to be in such dreadful pain, but sadly, life is seldom fair. *Is* it, Maud?"

"Indeed, no," Maud replied, still avoiding her eye and buttering a slice of toast with quick, nervous swipes of her knife. "It rarely is, but I am much better now. Thank you, Narcissa, you… you have always been so very kind, and I do not think I have ever told you how… how grateful I am for that."

Narcissa's eyebrows shot up. Her words had sounded entirely sincere, so much so that she almost demanded to know what the devil Maud meant by them. Settling into anxious silence, Narcissa watched the woman curiously. Had she come up with another way to make Narcissa's life a misery?

Not that it was a round of laughter and giddy happiness at present, or anything close. Though she had hoped Mr Anson might change his mind in time, Narcissa had known it was a foolish wish. She had not seen or heard anything of him since that day at the gallery. According to Delia, whatever event Narcissa was attending, he had either just left as she arrived, or he was attending another soiree elsewhere. Though Narcissa had not confided in her, Delia knew she had a partiality for Mr Anson, and so did not find it amazing that she seemed despondent if he was not around.

Finally, breakfast was done. Narcissa had just got to her feet when Maud surprised her once more.

"Lud, but the rain has finally ceased. I thought we must build an ark if it carried on any longer. Would you care to take a turn about the garden with me, my lady? If we keep to the paths, we shall be quite dry, and you are looking for a little pale. Some fresh air will put the bloom back into your cheeks."

Narcissa struggled to keep the scowl from her face, aware Mrs Chandler was watching the exchange with interest. Her cousin was self-absorbed for the most part, but she was not a fool. If she sensed there was a dispute between them, something interesting that she could stick her nose into, she would not rest until she knew what it was about.

"That does sound like a good idea," Narcissa replied carefully. "Though we had best make haste, for I do not think it will be long before the next shower."

Having got her way, Maud nodded and hurried off. Less than ten minutes later, the two women found themselves in the high walled back garden of Kemble House. The few daffodils and spring bulbs that had dared make an appearance in the dreadful weather hung their heads, looking as dispirited as Narcissa felt.

"Thank you for coming," Maud said, her expression uneasy.

"What do you want, Maud?" Narcissa replied curtly. "If it's more money, then—"

"No! No, not that," Maud replied, colour rising to her cheeks. "I wanted to apologise and… and to explain."

"Apologise?" Narcissa said in disgust. "You think that is all it takes to be forgiven for what you did? You ruined *everything!*"

She sucked in a sharp breath, aware that her voice had trembled but too proud to allow Maud to see how very wretched she was. Though Narcissa hardly believed her eyes, a fat tear rolled down Maud's cheek.

"Oh, my dear. I… I'm so sorry. I beg you will believe that. I know it is no excuse, but you do not know what it is to be growing old, alone and with no one to protect me. You do not know what it is to wonder if I shall end my days in the poorhouse when Mrs Chandler finally grows tired of me, and my own pitiful savings run out. I know what I did was very, very wrong, and your Mr Anson, he—"

Narcissa stilled, aware of a fresh note of respect in Maud's voice. She waited as Maud fished out a handkerchief and dried her eyes.

"I do not deserve the kindness he showed me," she admitted. "The generosity, but he has saved me, Narcissa. He has given me a home of my own, a place that no one can ever take from me, and you cannot know, cannot imagine what that feels like after a lifetime of uncertainty."

Narcissa gaped at her as Maud came closer and took her hands, squeezing them hard.

"My dear, listen to me," she said, her voice serious and full of concern. "You have nothing to fear from me. I shall never betray you ever again. Indeed, if you can bear to forgive me, I should be the friend to you I ought to have been from the start, but I beg you will heed me this once."

"Go on," Narcissa replied hoarsely, still reeling from the revelation that Mr Anson had done such a thing for Maud.

"Mr Anson *is* a gentleman," Maud acknowledged gravely. "In the truest sense of the word. He is a good man, an honourable one, but he can still bring you nothing but trouble, my dear. I cannot advise you strongly enough to stay away from him. Your father is not a kind man, nor, if you will forgive an old woman's opinion, a good one. Disaster beckons if you allow Mr Anson to court you."

Narcissa let out a huff of bitter laughter at those words. "Have no fear, Maud. Mr Anson has no thoughts of courting me. Indeed, you have only echoed his last words to me. I shall not see him again, for he has no desire to see me."

Maud's expression pinched with compassion as she heard the undisguised pain behind the words.

"I *am* sorry, my lady," Maud said, and as Narcissa looked into her eyes, she saw the truth of those words and nodded.

"Then that makes two of us," Narcissa said, sounding defeated as they trudged listlessly about the sodden garden and dark clouds rolled in on the horizon.

♡♧◇♤

25th February 1850, Lady Kerseymere's ball, Mayfair, London.

Ash did not regret the end of the month of February. It had been grim on all fronts, the weather vile and his mood even worse. A short-lived and disastrous affair with Mrs Travers had ended acrimoniously, not that he entirely blamed her. He had been neither kind nor attentive, and all his much-vaunted charm had been absent. Everything had gone wrong during the weeks in which he had said goodbye to Narcissa, and even Vivien had told him to go to the devil after trying her best to discover what was wrong with him.

He told himself he didn't know what was wrong, what was making him act like a petulant child whose favourite toy had been taken from him, but that was a lie.

Narcissa had invaded his soul, his every thought. He even thought he could smell the scent of her lingering in rooms he entered, as if she were haunting him. It was a kind of madness, and yet he could not break free. He couldn't sleep, for heated dreams plagued him, the feel of her skin against his so real that he woke sweating and hard with an unfulfilled desire for a woman he could not have. He was losing his mind at a rate that was as startling as it was terrifying, and he did not know what to do about it.

Yet here he was again, and this time at an event he knew Narcissa was attending. He had tried his utmost to get out of it, but his brother-in-law was away mending some minor disaster his mother had instigated, and Vivien had told him he had better escort her himself to make up for his horrid temper. He had agreed, reluctantly, but only on the condition she find someone else to escort her home again, for he was not staying long.

For now, he lounged indolently in a dark corner of the ballroom, trying his best to remain unobtrusive, for he was in no mood for polite chitchat. People stood around the edges of the ballroom, chatting or watching the dancing. Numbers were a little depleted this evening as the weather had been so vile of late it had kept some guests away. Through the gaps in the milling crowd, he saw glimpses of the dancers as they whirled past, and his heart gave an unaccustomed leap in his chest as a familiar head of shining fair hair caught his eye. She wore a gown of delicate silver-grey tonight, so pale it was almost white.

Ash told himself not to torture himself, not to look, but his feet moved of their own volition, taking him closer to the dancers. She was dancing with Lord Elsmere, who was gazing down at her cleavage with ill-concealed desire in his eyes, though Ash suspected it was her dowry as much as her person that excited the bastard.

You've no chance, you poor fool, Ash thought sourly, even as a fierce surge of jealousy rose inside him. Elsmere might be feckless and irresponsible, and a terrible prospect as a husband, yet if he'd had money the duke would have looked upon him with far more favour than he did Ash. It didn't matter. It was hardly the first time he'd come up against such bigotry. Yet it was the first time it had kept him from a woman he suspected might have been one he could have loved, might have been the one for whom he would have reformed himself.

With something very much like sorrow filling his chest, Ash watched Narcissa circle the floor in another man's arms. *Turn away and leave*, he told himself, but he could not, his gaze fixed on her as though compelled by some magnetic force. Finally, the dance ended, and he watched as Elsmere led her from the floor. Despite knowing better, he followed at a discreet distance, watching as Justin Ogilvy appeared at her elbow and bowed, offering her his arm.

Enough, he thought savagely. There was nothing to be gained by torturing himself and gazing after her like some lovesick boy. He was no boy, but a man grown, and there were plenty more fish in the sea. If Narcissa had truly wanted him, she would have fought for him, would have refused to let him go that day, as Viven had fought for the man she loved, pursuing him unashamedly.

Despite the things Narcissa had told him, her feelings could not run deep. He'd done the right thing in ending the affair before it truly began, and he'd do well to remember that.

25th February 1850, Lady Kerseymere's ball, Mayfair, London.

Following her dance with Mr Ogilvy, Narcissa followed the duke from the ballroom, her heart thudding so hard she thought she might be sick. She had not expected him to attend the ball tonight and his sudden arrival seemed strange. She had been told only that he needed to speak to her at once.

Terrified at what it was her father had to say to her, she did as he had instructed as best she could, walking with her chin up, giving no outward sign that there was anything amiss. It might be nothing terrible, she reminded herself. Her father was always terse and irritable, even when he wasn't furious with her, so there was no reason to suppose she was in trouble… except that some sixth sense had her stomach churning. Mrs Chandler had been in an odd mood this evening, more brittle than usual with both Maud and Narcissa.

Too late, Narcissa realised Mrs Chandler knew something and, whatever it was, she had told the duke.

The duke led her to a small, brightly lit parlour where she was dismayed to discover Mrs Chandler and Maud waiting for her. Her gaze immediately flew to Maud, who gave a small but decisive shake of her head. The hard knot of anxiety balled in Narcissa's stomach released a little, yet the smug, rather catlike satisfaction in Mrs Chandler's eyes boded ill. Narcissa had always held the rather uneasy suspicion that her cousin was jealous of her and would be more than pleased to see her marry Lord Wishen. For, whilst it might make her a countess, it would also make her his wife. As Mrs Chandler's late husband had also been far older than her, and it had not been a happy marriage, her cousin must know what kind of life that would let Narcissa in for.

The duke closed the door. "Mrs Chandler, I received your letter but an hour ago and came at once. I shall not make the error of failing to act as I did with Fidelia." He turned to Narcissa, regarding her with disfavour. "I had hoped that you would not let me down as disgracefully as your sister did, but I see I was mistaken."

"Y-Your grace?" Narcissa said, her voice trembling as her worst fears were realised.

Whatever it was he had discovered, it was bad.

"I trusted you to behave as a lady, to conduct yourself in a manner befitting your station and the dignity of the name to which you belong, but I see now that I was mistaken. There is a flaw in the bloodline that shows itself in the female members of this family. You are all driven to wickedness and licentiousness, no matter what is expected of you, what you owe to me in deference to every opportunity I have granted you. I have given you everything you could ever have desired, and this is how I am repaid, with lies and deceit and behaviour of the kind that only makes me feel shame to have sired such an unnatural child."

"Your grace," Narcissa said again, her temper rising as the unfairness of his words made her blood boil.

"You will hold your tongue," he raged, and this time she saw the revulsion in his eyes, a depth of fury of the kind she had never before encountered. He knew. In that moment, she realised he had discovered her meeting with Ash. Though she ought to have known better, she turned to stare at Maud, who paled and shook her head.

"I n-never—" she began helplessly, wringing her hands together.

"No, but you ought to have done, and this is the thanks I get for all the kindness I have shown you," Mrs Chandler said, turning on Maud in disgust. "To think, all these years I have tended a viper in my own home. When I think of everything I have done for you and, at the first moment you could, you betrayed me. Instead of coming to me about this wicked child's behaviour, you turned it to your own advantage, and then to say you understand why she did it! La! I was never more shocked," she went on, pressing a hand to her breast, her lip trembling unconvincingly.

"You... You read my diary," Maud said, her voice quavering. "You unspeakable bitch!"

Mrs Chandler gasped at the violent words, her cheeks turning scarlet as Maud stood rigid as a bowstring, her skinny frame vibrating with rage. "And after *everything* you have done for me? You have the nerve to say that out loud after the years of insults, after having me fetch and carry, treating me like a servant? You have never given me anything I did not earn, and it has taken a man like Mr Anson to make me see that I have got so much wrong. I have spent too long revering a man who is nothing more than a spiteful bully, and doing as he told me I must. If not for you, I might be married," she said, glaring at the duke with such murderous fury that Narcissa wondered if she might actually strike him. "If not for you, I might have a family, people who loved and cared for me, instead of being at the mercy of a hard-hearted, callous slut. And as for you, Mrs Chandler, how dare you chastise Narcissa for being wicked? You should look to your own bed and the parade of lovers who traipse in and out of it before you berate that innocent girl."

Mrs Chandler let out a shriek of wrath and turned on the duke, flushed with indignation and mortification. "Are you going to let that evil shrew speak to me like that?"

"That will be enough," the duke growled, his tone low but menacing enough to silence Mrs Chandler. "Miss Pinkerton, I will thank you to return to Kemble House and gather your things. You are no longer a part of this family."

"Your grace, no!" Narcissa said, for as much as she could not help but blame Maud for her part in this, she could not see her turned out of doors. "She has no one else, no—"

"Then she ought to have thought of that before she betrayed my trust," the duke said implacably. "And I warn you, Narcissa, if you think I would not cut you off too, that would be a foolish mistake to make."

"I don't think it," Narcissa said, struggling to keep her voice even but determined to speak her mind. "I know well enough that you don't give a damn for any of us, past what it is you think we can do to further the family name."

The duke looked at her and shook his head. "What the devil else is there for you to do? Females marry and bear children, that is your purpose in life. When Miss Pinkerton failed to fulfil that purpose adequately, she failed the family and became a burden. I should think carefully before you follow in her footsteps."

"And what of happiness?" Narcissa asked dully, too miserable to cry, numb with shock and sorrow. "Do you have no room in your heart, no compassion at all for what our lives will be like if you choose a husband who will make us wretched?"

"Good God, this is what comes of reading novels," the duke said in disgust. "I suppose you hoped to fall in love, did you? What a fool you are, Narcissa. I granted you with a modicum more intelligence than that dullard of a sister of yours, but I was wrong. To think, a daughter of mine would dare to dally with a man who was not even English, whose blood is tainted by that of an Indian slave, of all things! It beggars belief."

"He is a better man than you, than you could ever hope to be!" Narcissa shouted, the words exploding from her in a show of rage she could not hold back.

The slap was so sudden and so violent that it knocked her sideways, and she staggered, crashing into a chair and falling heavily to the floor.

"Oh, you brute!" Maud shrieked, running to her. "Narcissa, my dear, are you all right?"

Narcissa blinked through hot tears that stung her eyes. She was shaking with shock and pain and the terrible realisation that she had underestimated her father. He truly was a monster, and one she ought to have feared far more than she had until this moment.

She nodded, dazed and unable to speak for fear she would break down, and she would not give him the satisfaction.

"We are leaving," the duke said, his tone merciless. "Get up, Narcissa. It is about time you learned what it means to obey, and that the price of defying me is one you will not enjoy paying."

Chapter 10

Sir,

I will thank you to meet with me this day at 4pm.

Beresford.

—Excerpt of a letter from His Grace, The Duke of Beresford, to Mr Ashton Anson.

26ᵗʰ February 1850, Kemble House, Mayfair, London.

Ash stared at the house in front of him, wondering what the bloody hell he was doing here. When the summons had arrived, his first instinct had been to throw it into the fire, for if the bastard thought he could make Ash jump when he said jump, he was very much mistaken. Yet there was only one reason he could think of for the man to ask him to come to the house, and that was because Maud had betrayed them after all.

Guilt lodged in his chest as he wondered if he ought to have done more to silence the woman. Perhaps he ought to have been less curt with her, but his damned pride would never have allowed it. He had believed she had been grateful, too, fool that he was.

Concern for Narcissa was a chill beneath his skin. Everyone said Beresford was a cold bastard, and he hoped the man had not been unkind to her. The impossible desire to rescue her from the brute left a hollow sensation in his chest. If he'd thought they might have a future together, that she could be happy living her life with him, he would have moved heaven and earth to get her out of her father's house. But there was little point in taking her from one unpleasant situation to another that would make her just as miserable, albeit for different reasons. That he might be mistaken in her was an idea he would have loved to believe in, but he was too cynical about the world. The sooner the girl married and got out from under the duke's control, the better it would be for her.

Resolute and keen to get the ordeal over and done with, Ash rapped on the front door and was promptly shown in.

"His grace is expecting you," the butler intoned, and led Ash through the hall and up the stairs to an elegant receiving room before discreetly leaving.

The duke was standing before the fireplace, arms folded. His expression as he regarded Ash was that of a man looking at something unpleasant that must be dealt with swiftly. It was a moment before Ash registered Narcissa was there, too. She sat rigidly still, her face pale and set, and she did not look at him.

"Mr Anson, thank you for arriving promptly," the duke said. "I will not beat about the bush, for I'm certain you wish this to be over as quickly as I do."

"That rather depends on what *this* is," Ash replied dryly, watching Narcissa, who was staring straight ahead as if neither he nor the duke were there at all.

"This, sir, is a warning. I have been plagued before by social climbers and fortune hunters, who have learned to their cost that I will not be manipulated or blackmailed. So, let me make this plain. There are no circumstances under which I would allow you to marry my daughter. Narcissa has confessed all to me and explained that you wheedled your way into her affections. How you could dare to meet in private with an innocent girl who knew no better, and what's more, a daughter of mine, is frankly beyond my comprehension, but then perhaps your kind knows no better."

"*My* kind?" Ash repeated with a sneer. "You mean, a man who actually cares for the fate of a woman, who considers her happiness of greater import than whatever monetary or social gain you can get out of her?"

Fury flashed in the duke's eyes. "No, sir, that is not what I mean, and you damned well know it, you impudent cur! By God, I ought to thrash you for having the temerity to lay a hand on what is mine."

"Try it," Ash said darkly, the rage in his chest burning with such heat he wished the bastard were not twice his age, for he would have given him a thrashing he'd not forget in a hurry.

"I would not lower myself," the duke replied, his lip curling. "But you will stay away from my family in the future, or you will discover to your cost I am not to be trifled with. The Lady Narcissa deeply regrets the shame she has brought to me, and to herself by her association with a man so far beneath her notice. Is that not so, my dear?"

"Yes, your grace," Narcissa replied, her voice apparently calm, her gaze fixed on some distant point as she looked neither at Ash nor at her father.

The duke nodded, satisfied.

"Is that all?" Ash replied, his heart beating very hard. The desire to go to Narcissa and shake her, to demand if that was really what she thought was hard to resist, but he would not demean himself in such a way before her father.

"That is all," the duke agreed. "I trust I have made our position clear."

Ash tore his gaze from Narcissa to look at the duke, hoping the man could see the depth of loathing in his eyes. "Abundantly."

He turned and walked away, not looking back. He did not take one last look at Narcissa, nor did he slam the door or hurry for the room. He thanked the butler for his hat and gloves, and walked away from Kemble House, and kept walking until he got to the club.

Then he went in, picked up two bottles of cognac and found a private room.

"You may go," the duke said dismissively, once Mr Anson had gone. "We will catch the five o'clock train. I suggest you do not keep me waiting."

Narcissa steeled herself, bracing her arms on the chair before she tried to stand, pain lancing through her. His grace had been entirely correct when he had told her she would not enjoy paying the price for her disobedience. She was still numb with shock, as for all her father's vile ways, he had never actually laid a hand on her before. The beating he had delivered had been coldly brutal, swift and humiliating and the backs of her thighs were red raw with the marks of his retribution. Sitting down was an exercise in pain management as she concentrated on her breathing and in not breaking down. She would *not* cry in front of him. Never again would he see any sign of emotion from her, any sign that he had hurt her. She would not give him the satisfaction.

She walked stiffly but resolutely out of the room, head up, not looking at her father. With every step the tight, abraded skin on her thighs shrieked and burned, but she neither winced nor made a sound. After all, such physical pain was nothing to the agony in her heart.

That Mr Anson had been subjected to such a scene, that he must believe she agreed with all the vile things her father had said, made her want to curl up and die. Her soul had been crying out to him silently the entire time he had stood before her father, pleading with him not to heed the ugly words, not to believe that she could ever regret the brief moments they had shared together. Not enough, she told herself wretchedly. It was not enough to feel it; she had to tell him, somehow, that she was not the two-faced creature her father had painted her as. She wished she'd had the courage not to say the words the duke had put in her mouth, but the beating had been too fresh in her mind, and her fear of facing another was so paralysing that she could not find the courage to defy him.

Coward, she thought in disgust. Mr Anson had been right not to believe in her, not to put his trust in her, for she was too weak to speak her mind when it mattered the most. If she had been a woman worthy of him, she would never have denied him, never have agreed that she had shamed herself by associating with him.

Self-loathing uncoiled inside her and she wondered if it were possible to feel any worse than she did. Though she had always known her sister's melancholy must have been because of something their father had done to her, she had never before had such understanding of how Fidelia must feel. The sense of utter helplessness, of having no autonomy over her own life, even her own body, had never been so cruelly brought home to her as it had over the past hours.

Her maid, Nancy, was waiting for her when she entered her room.

"Oh, my lady," she said, her voice heavy with sympathy. "Shall I fetch you some willow-bark tea? Maybe it would help a mite?"

"No, thank you, Nancy," Narcissa replied, her mind made up. Coward she may be, but she would get a message to Mr Anson, no matter the risk, no matter how pitiful a recompense that must be for everything she had put him through. Though the pain of sitting at the chair in front of her small travelling desk was enough to bring tears springing to her eyes, Narcissa reached for a sheet of paper. The words she wrote were a pale shadow of everything she truly felt, but she dared not write anything too incriminating in case she was discovered. Nancy was a kind-hearted girl, but she was terrified of his grace, and with good reason. If she panicked and betrayed Narcissa, things could get very bad indeed. She hoped that Mr Anson could read between the lines, that he could see the truth behind the things she wrote, and understand that she missed him, that she regretted every missed opportunity when she might have been braver, might have made him believe in her.

But perhaps it was just as well that he had not, as she had proven to them both she was not the dashing heroine she had once believed herself to be at heart.

"Well, everything is packed, and I've set a feather pillow aside," Nancy said, taking the coat Narcissa would wear for the journey from the now empty wardrobe. "I thought perhaps if you sat on that for the train journey—"

Narcissa sent her a wan smile. "You're very thoughtful, but if you really want to help me, there's something else I would ask of you."

"What, my lady?" the maid asked anxiously, regarding the sealed letter Narcissa held out like it was a venomous snake.

"Please," she begged. "Please see this sent to Mr Anson. I will give you every shilling of my pin money, Nancy. I have a little over two pounds remaining, and it's yours, if you can get this to him."

"My lady," Nancy said, shaking her head. "Oh, I don't dare. Truly, I—"

"Please," Narcissa repeated shakily. "Please. If you cannot get it to him, take it to Miss Pinkerton and ask her to do so on my behalf. I'm sure she must have left a forwarding address with someone. Please, Nancy."

Nancy let out a long-suffering sigh but nodded. "I'll see what I can do," she said reluctantly, and took the letter from Narcissa's hand.

Sir,

I pray you will forgive me for the ugly scene and my father's vile words. I write this in haste and hope that my maid will find a way to get it to you without discovery for I am to be banished from town, back to Hardacre Hall and I do not know when or if I shall ever speak to you again.

Please know that I do not share my father's views despite what you must think of me. I am foolish and frivolous and terribly spoiled, but not so shallow as all that. Please believe me. I could not bear it if you thought so ill of me as that. I had no intention of causing you distress or embarrassment, though I am horribly aware I am guilty on both counts.

I wish I could ask you to write to me, but I will be allowed no correspondence now, and you must see anything from your hand would be confiscated at once.

Now it is too late I wish I had acted differently, I wish I had not been such a little fool and given you a disgust of me, for you are the only man who I shall think of during my banishment. I hope this revelation is of some pleasure to you, if not a fitting revenge for my idiocy.

Forgive me.

—Excerpt of a letter from The Lady Narcissa Ponsonby to The Hon'ble Ashton Anson.

2nd March 1850, Goshen Court, Monmouthshire.

Ash waited at the front door of Goshen Court, still uncertain of what had prompted him to come here. But he had tried drinking himself into oblivion, which had produced the inevitable after-effects, and he had tried throwing himself back into a world filled with women more than willing to take his mind off of his troubles. Neither attempt to give himself some peace had worked. He had tried damned hard to make his mind stop replaying that scene at Kemble House repeatedly, but it seemed his brain was set on tormenting him.

Narcissa's white face and set expression nagged at him. The listless way she had agreed with her father's words made him want to believe she had not truly meant them, yet he had expected her to reject him, so it had hardly been a surprise. She would never have chosen him. Not when it meant that she would cut herself off from everything she had been taught to believe was important.

Perhaps if they had lived in a world where they'd had time to get to know each other, to trust in each other, perhaps then it might have worked. But when every meeting was brief and fraught with the danger of discovery, there was little chance for that. It made the meetings more exciting, heightened feelings so that they grew out of all proportion to reality. It was an unfulfilled fantasy, that was all. This sense of regret, of loss, was simply disappointment that he'd not had more time, that he'd not been able to seduce her. Not that he would have seduced an unmarried girl. Perhaps once she had a husband, they could meet again and… The idea made his stomach roil with unexpected revulsion and he sucked in a deep breath.

Mercifully, the door opened, and Ash hurried inside. The butler accepted his overcoat, hat, and gloves and a footman took the portmanteau from him just as Pip came down the stairs.

"Ash!" he said, beaming at him with such warmth that Ash realised this was why he'd come. He and Pip had been close once, but in recent years they'd seen little of each other. Of course, Ash knew why that was now, and the man's little daughter, Tilly, was a favourite of his. "Well, this is an unexpected pleasure."

"Sorry to appear out of the blue," Ash said with a crooked grin. "I came on the spur of the moment. Didn't have time to warn you."

"There's no need for any warning. You're always welcome, you know that," Pip said, before narrowing his eyes, his gaze shrewd as he looked Ash over. "You look like the very devil. What's amiss?"

"Nothing," Ash replied automatically, before adding, "Everything."

"Ah," Pip said, sympathy in his eyes. "Then you've come to the right place. Come through to my study, we'll have a drink."

Ash followed him, gravitating immediately to the fire in the hearth as the rest of the room seemed arctic in temperature. Pip went to the sideboard and began pouring drinks. "I'm dashed pleased to see you old man. It's been an age. Though I ought to warn you—"

Before he could finish the sentence, a door opened and Leo appeared with the huge cat, Mau, draped around his shoulders like a fur stole.

"Ash!" he exclaimed, grinning broadly. "Well, well, this is a turn up. I didn't expect to see you here. What brings you to these parts?"

Ash repressed a sigh. He was not in the mood to deal with Leo's brand of good-humoured nonsense. Still, he accepted Leo's hand, shaking it. "Needed a change of air," he said noncommittally, smothering a yawn. He'd not slept much the past days and was dead on his feet. "Lord, it was a devilish long journey, though. Couldn't you get a place in Surrey, Pip? Be a sight easier to get to."

"Then you'd not have your change of air," Pip observed dryly, holding out a drink for Ash.

"Don't mind if I do, thanks," Leo said, swiping it before Ash could get his hands on it. Pip sighed and went and poured Ash another drink. Ash took it gratefully, downed it in one go, grimaced, and asked for another.

"Blimey," Leo observed. "Like that, is it? Well, it's a bit early, but I'm game if you are."

Ash shook his head. The last thing he wanted to do was get drunk in company with his friends. Heaven only knew what he'd say in his cups. "I'm having this and going to bed."

Leo exclaimed, outraged that he would retire at such an hour. Ash ignored him, wanting only another drink before he went to bed. Hopefully, the combination of excellent brandy and sheer exhaustion would allow him to sleep without being plagued by thoughts of Narcissa.

"Are you sick?"

Ash looked around, only then realising Leo was still muttering.

"Yes," he replied, taking the second glass of brandy from Pip and treating it much like the first. "Sick to death."

Pip and Leo exchanged glances. "Who is she?" they asked in unison.

"Bugger off," Ash replied, irritated that they knew him well enough to understand what the trouble must be. "I'm going to bed."

"Top of the stairs and turn right, third on the left," Pip called after him as Ash disappeared.

Narcissa flung open her bedroom window, heedless of the frigid air that blew into her room. Leaning out, she looked down, searching for any escape route, even though she knew it was hopeless. There would be no daring descent via the window, not unless she wanted to break her stupid neck. She might be depressed, but she was too stubborn to give up.

The journey back to Hardacre had been an exercise in self-control as she fought not to cry whilst the train jolted and shuddered and the seat beneath her rubbed her petticoats against the raw skin on her thighs, despite the feather pillow Nancy had provided for her. The duke had seemed amused by her pain and anything resembling affection for him that Narcissa might have held onto had died, alongside any lingering desire to please him… which she now knew it to be impossible.

Now, she did not give a damn what he wanted. She must take back control of her own future, no matter how difficult it was going to be, and she did not underestimate that. The risk she was contemplating was so terrible it made her break out in a cold sweat just to contemplate it, but she had made up her mind.

At least her maid had got the letter to Maud, tracking the woman down just before she had left to go to her new home in Kent. Narcissa could only hope that any sense of regret the woman felt for her part in Narcissa's misery had prompted her to do what she could to ensure the note found its way to Ash. Perhaps then he would not be displeased to see her again. For she *was* going to see him again.

She did not know how she would escape Hardacre and go to him, but she was determined to do so. At least then she could explain herself in person, for she owed him that much. After that she did not know what she would do, but perhaps Delia's brother, Wrexham, would give her shelter until she could arrange something more permanent. Perhaps Fidelia would want to go with her, she mused. Not that she had heard from her, or Alex, since their father had locked her in her room.

The duke had given her no indication of how long she was to be kept there, or of what his plans for her were, but she could guess. If she knew her father, he had told Lord Wishen to arrange a marriage with all haste. It was likely a matter of days before her chances of finding a different way of life disappeared entirely.

Still, she must make plans and so Narcissa began searching through her belongings, hoping to discover something of value. The only thing she could lay her hands on easily were her gowns, but they were hardly portable when one was trying to slip away unnoticed. All her remaining pin money had gone to Nancy, for having taken the letter to Maud. Their mother's jewellery had all gone to Fidelia, and all Narcissa had worth pawning was a set of pearls. They were very fine, but she did not know how much they would fetch. Still, they were a start.

Dragging a chair over from her dressing table, Narcissa climbed onto to it and reached for a box on the upper shelf. It was heavier than she expected, and she swayed on the chair, jumping down before she fell as the box slipped from her grasp and landed with a thud.

"Devil take you!" she exclaimed crossly.

She stared in dismay as the box of beads and miscellaneous treasures she'd collected as a child exploded over her bedroom floor. With a sigh, she got to her knees to search through the mess, when there was a soft knock at the door.

"Love? It's Fidelia. Are you all right?"

"Lia?" Narcissa exclaimed at the sound of her sister's voice. Jumping up, she ran to the door. "Oh, I thought you weren't speaking to me, either."

Her sister made an impatient sound that warmed Narcissa's heart. "Don't be a silly goose. He's forbidden us from talking to you. Do you really think we wouldn't have come to see you otherwise?"

"No, I-I suppose not," Narcissa admitted. She had seen so little of Fidelia of late, and her sister had been so distant, but she had never been uncaring. "Only I'm so miserable, Lia. I've… I've made a dreadful mess of things," she admitted.

Fidelia's voice was soft, her concern audible even through the door. "What happened, pet?"

"A man happened. Obviously," Narcissa wailed in despair. "And I don't care what his grace does to me, I only care that *he* thinks I'm awful… and I'm not, Lia, not really. *Am* I?" she added, suddenly less certain of that. She had discovered she was far more afraid of the duke, and of the future, than she had ever realised.

"Of course not, but what exactly—? Hush, someone's coming. I'll come back when I can."

"Lia?" Narcissa called softly, desperately wishing she would not leave her alone.

It would have been so nice to confide her troubles to a sympathetic listener, but she knew Fidelia was even more afraid of their father than she was. Rightly so, as it turned out. For if the duke had treated her as he had treated Narcissa, she could well understand her sister's behaviour.

Chapter 11

Dear Diary,

I am going to escape. I don't know how, but I will not fail. Somehow, I must see Mr Anson and tell him how much I admire him. Perhaps, if he can find it in his heart to forgive me – but I dare not think of that.

—Excerpt of a diary entry by Lady Narcissa Ponsonby

10th March 1850, Hardacre Hall, Hardacre, Derbyshire.

Narcissa paced her room, trying to calm her growing sense of unease. She could not see her maid, who had been relegated to working below stairs once more. Not because the duke had discovered the letter—his retribution for that would have been far more severe—but simply because he wished to isolate Narcissa and make her life as miserable as possible.

As she had suspected, he had informed her she would marry Lord Wishen at the end of the week. Her own fears had been superseded, however, by the information that he meant to marry Fidelia to Lord Malmsey. The duke had concluded that the female line was fatally flawed, and the sooner they were safely married off, the better.

Terror for Fidelia, who was a quiet, gentle soul, made Narcissa's stomach churn, for Malmsey was a vile brute. Worse even than the duke, were such a thing possible. Yet no amount of pleading on her part had moved the duke, who had only commented that he would be relieved to be rid of them both.

Now Malmsey was on the premises, and Narcissa was desperate to warn Fidelia that she must get away however she could. Perhaps they could escape together? Hope stirred in her chest at the thought. Surely, they would fare better together than alone?

The sound of raised voices reached her through her bedroom door and Narcissa ran to it, pressing her ear to the door. There was some sort of altercation, but she could not quite make it out. Was that Fidelia's voice?

"Run!"

Narcissa gasped, for surely that was Alex. The anxiety in that one word was palpable. A muffled thud sounded, followed by a scuffle, before footsteps pounded past her door.

"I'll tear you to pieces, you little shit!"

That had been Lord Malmsey, Narcissa realised with a stab of fear.

What on earth was happening?

Narcissa beat her fist against the door. "Is anyone there? Please open the door. Fidelia? Alex? What's happening? Help! Help, please someone! Fidelia, are you all right?"

She rattled the handle, continuing to pound upon it for what seemed like hours before she slumped to the floor and put her head in her hands. She had almost given up hope when she heard soft footsteps passing her door.

"Help!" Narcissa shouted, resuming her hammering on the door. "Help! Please, who is that?"

"My lady?"

"Yes!" Narcissa exclaimed, rattling the handle again. "Who is that? Whatever is happening?"

"It's Sally," whispered the voice on the other side of the door. "Your sister's maid, my lady."

"Sally! Thank heavens! What on earth is going on?"

There was a pause before Sally answered. "Tell the truth, I'm not exactly sure, my lady, but… but think perhaps Lady Fidelia has run away with Mr De Beauvoir."

Narcissa stared at the closed door, her mouth agape. "Whatever do you mean? She's eloped with the gentleman designing the new gardens for the duke?"

"That's right. I reckoned my lady had taken a shine to the fellow, and he to her. Didn't bargain for this, though. Only that Lord Malmsey is a nasty piece of work, so I reckon she did right, beg your pardon for saying so, my lady."

"Oh, she did!" Narcissa exclaimed, so delighted by this piece of information she felt a jolt of happiness for the first time in days. "Oh, well done, Fidelia!"

"Yes, I reckon so," Sally said. "'Cept now I need to go and… well, I've things to see to, my lady, so if you'll excuse me—"

"No, Sally, wait, please," Narcissa begged. "Does… Does she love him, do you think?"

"Yes, my lady. Reckon she does, at that."

Narcissa smiled wistfully and sent up a silent prayer that her sister got the happy ever after she so richly deserved.

"If you'll excuse me, my lady—"

"No, wait!" Narcissa said urgently. "Please, Sally. *Please…* let me out."

There was a taut silence, and Narcissa held her breath.

"I don't dare, my lady," came the regretful reply. "I'm in enough trouble with what I've got planned."

"Will you go after her?"

"Reckon so," Sally replied. "This ain't a happy place to work and, with my lady gone, there won't be a place for me anyhow."

"Then what difference can it make if you let me out?" Narcissa asked in growing desperation, as she feared this might be her one chance to get free. Emotion made the words tremble as she pleaded again. "Sally, please don't leave me here."

There was silence on the other side of the door, then a scratching sound before something skidded over the polished wood floor by Narcissa's feet. Looking down, she stared at the key to the door.

"Thank you!" she whispered, but Sally had already gone.

Too aware that time was of the essence, Narcissa packed up everything she could carry in a portmanteau and stood before the locked door, the key clutched in her hand. If she did this, she would likely ruin herself and end up in even worse straits than she was now. At least if she married Lord Wishen, she would have a home and status. She would never have to worry, and she would be out of her father's control. But was that enough? After everything she had learned about herself these past weeks, could she bear to give up on the possibility there was something more, if only she were brave enough to reach for it? She was tired of allowing fate to sweep her along, tired of doing everything her father wished of her, only to be reviled and abused anyway. No one was coming to save her, but perhaps if she was daring, she could save herself. She knew the chance of Ash wanting her in the way she hoped was slim after everything she had put him through, but perhaps if she did this, he would see she was prepared to risk everything to be with him, that she could be brave for him. She would not despise herself for being a coward again. This time, she would take her courage in her hands, and make her own choice, for better or for worse.

Taking a deep breath, Narcissa stepped forward and unlocked the door.

12th March 1850, Goshen Court, Monmouthshire.

Ash stared down at the fire in the hearth. He didn't know what to do. Despite Pip's best efforts, and Leo's worst ones, he was still as restless and unhappy as he'd been when he arrived ten days ago. He did not know whether to go back to town. The temptation to do everything in his power to snatch a moment alone with Narcissa, to demand if those words had been true, burned in his chest. Yet what was the point? If it were true, he'd have gained nothing, and if they were not… what then?

Currently, Leo was staring at him like he was sandwich short of a picnic, an expression of pitying concern in his eyes that was damned irritating. Not that Ash blamed him. He had just confessed to Leo that he had *feelings* for Lady Narcissa Ponsonby. That certainly entitled Leo to have him locked up for insanity, in Ash's opinion. The chink of glasses told Ash that Leo had decided he needed a drink to cope with such a ridiculous confession and was more than relieved when Leo handed one to him.

A knock sounded, heralding the butler. "The post has arrived, Mr Hunt, Mr Anson."

Rather to Ash's surprise, Leo leapt for it, colour rising to his cheeks when Ash gave him a curious glance as whatever it was he'd been hoping for appeared not to have arrived. Too blue devilled to enquire, Ash let it go, about to turn away when Leo handed a letter to him.

"For you."

Ash stared at it, an odd sensation climbing down his spine as he stared at the unfamiliar handwriting. It couldn't be. Could it? He tore it open, discovering a sheet of paper and another note sealed within it.

Dear Mr Anson,

I was asked to see this letter delivered to you, but the gentleman I spoke to at your club informed me you were staying at Goshen Park. I pray it reaches you safely, for I did not know where else to send it.

I do not know if I am being kind or cruel in sending it on, for I fear I have already meddled unduly in an affair I had no business in criticising. Please understand that jealous and spiteful as I was, I truly sought to protect Narcissa from the fate that befell me.

When I had almost given up hope of ever marrying, I fell in love. I believe my gentleman loved me in return. He was a good man, though of humble origins, and the duke refused to countenance our marriage, though I am hardly an important figure in the family history. But Beresford wishes to control everyone and everything within his power, and he does so with cruelty and malice. I wish I'd had the courage to run away to my gentleman and to escape his tyranny, but life is full of wrong turns and regrets.

I cannot advise either of you what to do next, but I know Lady Narcissa admires and esteems you. So much so that she told the duke to his face that you were a better man than he, than he could ever hope to be. He struck her for that, so severely she fell to the floor with the force of the blow. She has realised too late just what a man her father is, and I do not see how she can ever escape his clutches now. I pray you will find a way to help her, if your feelings for her are strong enough to withstand the difficulties you will surely encounter.

Yours sincerely,

Miss Maud Pinkerton.

Ash stared at the letter, his heart beating very hard. The sealed note lay in his hand, unread but he did not trust himself to read it in front of Leo. That the duke had hit Narcissa made a sensation far past any anger he had ever experienced before burn like acid in his chest. He wanted to kill the man for laying a finger on her. And she had told her father that Ash was a better man than he—to his *face!* Regret at having not done more, at not realising she was speaking under duress when he had visited the house, made him feel sick to his stomach. Somehow, he had to get her away from the duke.

"Oh, the devil," Leo said in disgust, tearing Ash's attention from the letter in his hand. "It's from her, isn't it?"

Ash didn't answer, not wishing to discuss it with Leo, for there wasn't time. Instead, he tucked the letter and the note away in his pocket and said nothing, just downed his drink in one large swallow and headed to the door.

"Ash, where are you going?" Leo demanded, hurrying after him.

"I'm leaving," Ash said, not turning as he strode to the stairs.

"Why? What for? Oh, you great lunatic, you're going to do something ridiculous, aren't you?"

Ash paused on the stairs, regarding Leo with an enigmatic smile.

"Quite possibly," he said, and carried on his way.

14th March 1850, Albany Street, Regent's Park, London.

Two wearying days later, Ash stepped down from the carriage, his heart heavy as he wondered what the devil he was to do now. When he had reached Hardacre Hall, the place had been in a state of uproar. Not that he'd gained entry to the Hall itself, but the rumour mill in the village of Hardacre was working overtime. Not only had Lady Fidelia Ponsonby eloped, but she'd done it with Hart! Ash's mind boggled over this information, which he would normally have found intriguing in the extreme. Just at the moment, however, he didn't give a damn about that strange turn of events, his entire being focused on the second part of the scandal: Lady Narcissa had also disappeared.

After examining everyone he could get his hands on, it had become clear that Lady Fidelia, her brother, and Hart had all gone off together in the same carriage, bound for London. As for Narcissa, no one seemed to know. They hadn't noticed her disappearance until the afternoon of the following day, but no one could tell him more than that. He'd gone to the railway station, had visited every inn for miles, checked every source of transportation he could think of, and no one had seen a glimpse of her. How it was possible that such a dazzlingly beautiful female travelling alone could pass unnoticed, he simply could not imagine.

A steady drizzle fell, settling on his face as he turned towards his front door. The idea that Narcissa was out in this weather, alone and unprotected, made his insides twist into a savage knot. His fault, he told himself. If he had given her a chance, she might be with him now. Though he still did not know if the tentative relationship that had sprung up between them had any real substance, his instincts told him to trust his gut. Currently, his gut was damning him for losing the one woman who might have made him happy, if only he'd allowed her to try.

Utterly wretched and sick with guilt, Ash walked to his front door. He needed a change of clothes and a bite to eat before he headed back out again. Somehow, he had to figure out where she might go. Delia had been a close friend, so he would start there.

Perhaps she had heard from Narcissa, or perhaps Narcissa was already there, safe and well. God, he hoped so.

Ash was about to enter his house when a voice called his name.

"M-Mr Ans-son," it stammered through chattering teeth.

Ash turned, looking in surprise at a boy astride a bedraggled horse. Rain dripped sullenly off the lad's hat. His clothes, which were of excellent quality, were too big for him and soaked through. Though the horse looked a superb creature, it appeared as if it had endured an ordeal, its head hanging with exhaustion. Indeed, the two of them looked utterly dreadful, covered in mud from head to hoof. The young fellow held a sodden portmanteau before him on the horse, which slipped from his grasp and fell to the floor with a wet thud. As Ash watched, the boy's eyes rolled up in his face and he swayed.

Ash hurried forward, catching the lad just as he slithered from the horse's back.

"Take the horse round to the stables and see it's cared for," he shouted to the footman who had hurried out from inside his house.

"Come along, my lad," he said, hefting the boy, who weighed nothing at all.

Suddenly, Ash registered the softness beneath his hands. He glanced at the boy's white, mud-spattered face as he carried him through the door and his breath caught. Just as he told himself he'd run mad, for it could not possibly be… the lad's cap fell off, revealing a tumble of pale gold curls.

"Christ!" he exclaimed, slamming the door before anyone could see the figure he carried was female, and not that of the young boy she'd appeared to be.

"My lord?" exclaimed his housekeeper, Mrs Fenchurch, gazing at the figure in his arms with alarm. "God have mercy. Is he dead? Or… *is* that a he?" she demanded suspiciously.

"Fetch a doctor," he said, giving her a stern look. "And hold your tongue. No one can know she's here."

"Yes, my lord," the woman said with a sharp nod. "At once."

Ash didn't reply, knowing he could trust his housekeeper implicitly, too intent on carrying Narcissa up the stairs. She was soaked to the bone, filthy and shivering. He kicked open the door to his bedroom, carried her through, and slammed the door shut again after them before he laid her carefully down on his bed.

"Narcissa?" he said, patting her cold cheek.

She didn't stir, which made his heart leap with fear. Ash reached for her hands and rubbed them between his, terrified by how cold she was. She let out a soft sound of protest and he breathed a sigh of relief.

With fingers that trembled with fear at just how ill she might have made herself, for she had clearly been out in this dreadful weather for days, Ash reached for her boots. The laces were so wet they would not untie, so he found a penknife and cut them through, tugging the leather boots aside and stripping off the sodden stockings beneath.

He hesitated as he stared at the helpless figure before him, wondering if he ought to send for his housekeeper. A possessive desire to care for her himself, to keep her close, startled him but he did not question it. Like it or not, Narcissa was ruined now, and she had come to him. She had put her trust in him, and he would not let her down. As soon as she was well, they'd be married. Ash did not bother examining the surge of possessive satisfaction that thrummed through him at the idea, pushing it aside as irrelevant.

"For better or worse," he muttered under his breath as his trembling hands fumbled with her buttons. "I hope you didn't change your mind on the way, love, or we shall both be in the basket."

Narcissa mumbled and stirred as he stripped the wet coat and waistcoat from her. Lord, how had he ever thought she was a boy, even for a moment? Beneath the waistcoat she wore no corset, and the fine wet linen plastered itself to the decadent curves of her breasts.

"M-Mr Anson?"

"Narcissa?" Ash said in relief, as her eyes blinked open and she gazed at him, looking somewhat bewildered. "Oh, thank heavens. Come, love. We must get you out of these wet clothes. You're soaked to the bone, and you'll catch your death of cold if we don't get you warm and dry."

"Y-You're n-not cross with me?" she asked through chattering teeth.

"Cross?" Ash repeated. "What for? Never mind that. Can you stand so we can get these trousers off? Wherever did you get them?"

"My brother's," she said, allowing him to help her to her feet. "I stole them, and then stole one of the duke's horses," she added.

Ash looked at her. "My, you have had an adventure," he murmured.

She nodded, a shadow passing over her face. "N-Not a very pleasant one, but I... I had to see you. I had to tell you. I didn't mean—"

Ash pressed a finger to her mouth, a lump rising to his throat as regret filled him. "Hush, love, I know already. I ought to have realised, but.... I'm sorry, Narcissa. I underestimated you."

She shook her head, her face crumpling into one of abject misery. "N-No, you didn't. I was a coward. I ought n-never to have denied you like that. Only he... he..."

Ash pulled her into his arms and held on tight. "I know. Mrs Pinkerton told me a little, and you shall tell me everything. Once you are warm and dry, we will talk it all through, I promise. For now, though... Hush, love."

Ash reached for a handkerchief and wiped her eyes carefully.

"All right?"

Narcissa nodded and stood passively as he reached for the hem of the wet shirt.

Ash hesitated. "I don't have many female staff here, but I could send for my housekeeper if—"

Narcissa held his gaze boldly, though her cheeks blazed red. "I c-came to you for a reason," she said, her chest rising and falling quicker with each word she spoke. "I don't know if you want me or if—"

Ash pressed his mouth to hers, feeling her cold lips touch his warmth with a shock that ran through them both. He pulled away, the strange and powerful surge of protectiveness sweeping over him again.

"I want you," he said shortly, and stripped off her shirt before reaching for the counterpane and wrapping it swiftly around her.

Narcissa held it close, her cheeks burning with embarrassment as he knelt and tugged the trousers down her legs.

"Get into bed," he instructed, determined to keep this as businesslike as he could manage.

A knock at the door caught his attention, and he bundled up the wet clothes scattered about his room and went to the door.

"I've sent George for the doctor, and I brought this," she added, holding out a steaming mug. "A hot toddy ought to warm the poor mite. Shall I run a bath for her?"

Ash nodded. "If you would, yes. And, Mrs Fenchurch," he added as the lady took the wet garments from him, "as you are dying to know, the young woman is Lady Narcissa Ponsonby, and she is to be my wife."

"Oh, congratulations, sir," Mrs Fenchurch said, smiling at him now she knew things were going to be set right.

As loyal as she was, she would not have countenanced working in a house with an unmarried female under the same roof as him and he did not wish to lose an excellent housekeeper, nor to endure one of her morality scoldings. He'd suffered through a good many over the years. It was the cost of having an employee who had known him since he was a snot-nosed boy and had once smacked his arse for naughtiness.

"No one, and I mean *no one*, must know she is here," Ash said gravely. "Not until after we are married. Her father is a brute and I fear what he will do to her if he discovers her under my roof. Until she has my name, I have no legal right to keep her from him."

Mrs Fenchurch's expression was one of startled surprise, but her voice was calm and reassuring. "Yes, sir. I understand. No one here will breathe a word, I promise you that."

Ash nodded and closed the door, carrying the steaming drink to Narcissa, who was huddled in the bed. Her eyes were very wide as he approached and sat beside her.

"Married?" she repeated faintly, staring at him with anxiety in her eyes.

"Of course," Ash replied shortly, avoiding the scrutiny of her blue gaze. "You've been missing for days, and you came to me. You're in my bed. What else did you expect? Drink this."

"I'm n-not sure I know," she admitted, not taking her eyes from his as she accepted the mug. "I suppose I hoped you might wish to marry me, but I did not mean to force you into a situation you did not want, though, and if no one knows I am here—"

Ash looked away from her, uncertain of what it was he felt, of what he ought to say, only that he was damned if she was wriggling out of the situation she'd created now.

"We'll talk about it all later," he said, knowing that was evasive at best, but he needed time to get his thoughts in order. "Drink up, now. Mrs Fenchurch is running a hot bath for you. Are you hungry?"

As if in answer to his question, her stomach gave a furious growl. Narcissa looked mortified but nodded. "Very," she admitted.

"I'll have something sent up," he said with a smile, getting to his feet.

"Don't go," Narcissa said as he walked to the door.

Ash turned, regarding her tucked up in his bed. The desire to stay was almost overpowering, but he needed to get away, to clear his thoughts, which were running in ten directions at once.

"I won't be long," he said, and left the room.

Chapter 12

Dear Mau,

It is rainy and dreary here today, and I am feeling a little blue. I usually find a good deal of satisfaction in my embroidery and in books and painting, and the morning calls I make and receive. Trevick is such a beautiful place, and one I have always considered a sanctuary, but I am increasingly restless and out of sorts and I don't know why.

I received a note from a friend this morning. I believe you know the Lady Fidelia Ponsonby. Perhaps you have not yet heard, but she eloped with Mr De Beauvoir. They are married now, and I wish them truly happy.

Why have you not written to me?

Yours, ever,

—Excerpt of a letter from the Hon'ble Miss Violetta Spencer (cousin and adopted daughter to The Right Hon'ble Kitty and Luke Baxter, Countess and Earl of Trevick) to The Hon'ble Cat, Mau.

14th March 1850, Albany Street, Regent's Park, London.

Narcissa watched as Mr Anson left the room, her heart thudding too hard. Married? It was what she had wanted, of course, only... she had not wished to force him into it. Though it had been foolish, she had hoped for a romantic reunion, for him to be overpowered with emotion at her bravery, for him to declare himself in love with her and ask her to be his wife. Well, he *had* apologised. He had even said he wanted her, but there had been no talk of love, no tenderness, simply that she was ruined now, so they would be married. He was simply doing the decent thing.

She ought not to have come here. *Yet another mistake, Narcissa*, she thought wretchedly, her empty stomach squirming with misery. Tentatively, she lifted the mug to her lips and took a sip. It was sweet, and tasted of lemon and honey, and something powerfully alcoholic. A little puddle of warmth began in her belly and eased through her veins, and so Narcissa settled back against the pillows as she drank and allowed some of her tension to unravel.

He said they would talk later, so she would reassure him that there was no need for him to marry her. No one knew she was here, after all. If he could help her get to Delia's house, she felt certain Delia's brother, the marquess, would offer her his protection until a solution could be found. At least Mr Anson had not seemed angry. He had even kissed her when he'd said he'd wanted her, but what else could he have said or done in the circumstances? She had forced herself upon him and, as he was an honourable man, she had left him no other choice than to make the best of it.

Her thoughts became less coherent as the drink took effect, the alcohol chasing away her worries as exhaustion overcame her. Narcissa closed her eyes and was about to allow sleep to claim her, when a woman she assumed was the housekeeper bustled in.

"I'm sorry to wake you, my lady. I'm sure you're done in, but I've a nice hot bath waiting for you. Do you think you can manage it if I help you? I'm afraid we've no lady's maid here, but I'm quite able to assist you, if you don't mind it. I've raised two girls of my own. They're older than you now, mind."

Narcissa nodded and, though she would much rather have slept, the idea of washing the filth of the past days from her body was not unappealing.

"I don't if you don't," she managed with a weary smile.

The housekeeper gave her an approving nod. "That's the ticket. We'll get you clean and tucked up back in bed in two shakes of a lamb's tail."

Narcissa smiled at the woman's motherly manner and allowed herself to be hustled into the bathing room. It was all very modern, with gleaming white-and-green tiles and a deep bath from which arose a deal of scented steam.

"I took the liberty of adding a few drops of his sister's favourite bath oil," Mrs Fenchurch told her confidentially. "She left it the last time she stayed here, but she's a dear creature and I know she wouldn't begrudge it. I suppose you've had a difficult few days?"

Narcissa smiled, eyeing the lady who was clearly fishing for information. Well, it would be common knowledge soon, no doubt.

"I ran away from home," she admitted. "My father was forcing me to marry Lord Wishen."

"That fat old goat!" the woman exclaimed in shock, and then clapped a hand over her mouth. Retrieving her composure, she said politely, "I do beg your pardon, my lady."

Narcissa let out a short laugh. "There's no need, for I quite agree, Mrs Fenchurch. Though I must tell you he is a kind man. My father tried to marry my sister to Lord Malmsey, which is far worse, for he is truly a brute. She ran away too," she added with quiet satisfaction as Mrs Fenchurch steadied her while she stepped into the bath.

"Hmph. I have heard Malmsey is not a gentleman, for all his fine title. Lord Wishen is old enough to be your grandfather, though," the woman said, her eyes wide, an expression of revulsion on her plump features. She shook her head, her expression contemplative. "I know girls are supposed to obey their fathers, but I can't help but think you did the right thing. Disgusting it is, marrying young girls to old men like that. I thought we was more civilised these days, but it seems—" Mrs Fenchurch sucked in a sharp breath before she finished the sentence. "I was wrong," she said, her voice hard.

Narcissa turned, wondering what had made her sound so angry.

"Your father do that?" the woman asked, her tone softer now, a pitying expression lingering in her eyes. She gestured to the back of Narcissa's thighs, to the red stripes that crisscrossed the delicate flesh.

Narcissa blushed and gave a taut nod. "Yes. I'm afraid the duke is somewhat archaic in his views and his treatment of his daughters," she admitted wryly. She let out a sigh of pleasure as she sat down, and the hot water eased her aching limbs, relieved that the red welts were healed enough to no longer sting. "Mr Anson seems to be a very honourable man. At least, he has been most kind to me. Have you known him long?" she dared to ask, for she had given Mrs Fenchurch the information she was dying for, so it seemed a fair exchange.

"Since he was a little bit of a thing," the woman said with a smile. "I worked for his parents. He is honourable, a gentleman to his bones. A better man you'll not find, nor a kinder employer. People don't know what to make of him oftentimes. What with his mixed heritage and his love of fancy clothes and all that nasty fighting he does. How a fellow can love to make things beautiful, himself included, and then go and knock the daylights out of another fellow and come home all battered and bloody… well, I gave up trying to understand men a long time ago. I shouldn't bother trying if I were you, it's a hopeless endeavour."

Despite the exhaustion tugging at her mind, Narcissa smiled. "I'll bear it in mind."

Once Narcissa was bathed and wrapped in one of Mr Anson's shirts, which hung down past her knees, Mrs Fenchurch tucked her back into bed, fed her a large bowl of vegetable soup, and instructed her to sleep. Narcissa had no problem obeying the command, her eyes closing before the housekeeper had even left the room.

When she woke, the curtains had been closed and she could tell it was nighttime. Only the light from the fire illuminated the room and it took a moment before she realised she was not alone.

"How do you feel?" Mr Anson asked her.

"Better," she admitted, suddenly shy and awkward with him, and wishing she knew what he thought of her being here. His expression was inscrutable, but the firelight gilded his beautiful profile, lovingly casting his high cheekbones in colours of warm bronze and flickering in his eyes in a manner that made him appear rather satanic. He wore a black silk banyan over his shirt and trousers. Heavily embroidered with colourful silks, it was a work of art all of its own, and yet could not detract from his masculine beauty. He wore no cravat, and Narcissa's gaze fell to the little triangle of golden skin at the base of his throat, heat rising to her cheeks as she wondered if his skin was as silky as the robe.

"You sleep like the dead," he observed. "The doctor came to see you and you didn't bat an eyelid."

"Oh," Narcissa said uneasily, discomforted by the idea she had been examined whilst she slept.

"Don't look so worried," he said softly. "Mrs Fenchurch was with him and he's our family physician, a sensible man even my grandmother approved of, and I can tell you she was not easily impressed. She disliked anyone in the medical profession, especially men, but she liked Dr Randolf. He said he thought there was no harm done, but you are to stay abed for a few days until you recover your strength."

"Why didn't your grandmother like doctors?" she asked, diverted by the information and finding herself eager for any scrap of knowledge about him, about his family. For she wanted to know him, to understand him, everything there was to know.

"My grandmother didn't like a good many people, especially men, and did not hesitate to tell them," he said with a wry smile. "I wish she were here now."

"To see if she liked me?" Narcissa guessed.

He laughed a little at that. "Well, not only for that, but she was an excellent judge of character and had an opinion about most things. And advice, too."

Narcissa swallowed, wondering what he thought his grandmother would have said. Seeing the troubled look on her face, his expression softened.

"I think she would have liked you," he said. "And I think you would have liked her, too, though she would have made your hair stand on end with the shocking things she said."

She returned a tentative smile, wondering if he was just being kind or if he really believed that. "I'm sure I would have liked her, if you thought so highly of her, though perhaps I would not meet with her approval after throwing myself upon your mercy," she said sadly, studying his face. "You miss her."

"Every day," he replied with a nod. He smoothed the silk robe where it lay over his knee, his expression wry. "Naani Maa was a wicked old woman with a talent for mischief. She loved tawdry romance books and wore the brightest colours she could get her hands on. No one else has ever made me laugh, nor blush, like she could. She was wise and kind and she would have known what I ought to do, what I ought to say, so that I didn't make a mess of things. As for what you've done, she would certainly have approved of you taking fate into your own hands."

"And would she have approved of you marrying me?"

There was a brief silence. "I don't know," he admitted.

"You don't have to, you know."

"And what will you do when your father comes for you?" he asked, his tone grave, and Narcissa was riveted by the intensity in his indigo eyes. She could not take her eyes off him. "You belong to him, Narcissa. Your only safety lies in taking my name."

Narcissa gazed at the perfection of his beautiful face, emotion rising in her chest as she stared at the handsome man before her. He made her heart beat faster, made her want to be reckless, to throw caution to the wind and do whatever it took to make him love her.

"I want to," she admitted breathlessly. "I think… I think I could be happy as your wife. B-But I don't know if you want me, if it's truly what you want. I'm afraid it isn't. Not really, and I don't want you to hate me for forcing your hand."

He did not speak for a long moment, only stared at her, as if he thought he might see inside her mind if he looked long and hard enough. Sighing, he got to his feet and moved to the bed, sitting carefully on the mattress beside her. Narcissa's senses leapt as he took her hand, his long fingers tracing patterns over her palm, stirring the blood in her veins as if it too wanted to move closer to his touch.

"There is an attraction between us. I feel a… a pull," he confessed as he raised her hand and laid it flat against his chest. Narcissa swallowed as she felt the hard quilting of muscle beneath the silk of his robe, felt the warmth of his body and the steady thud of his heart. "I feel it here, a connection that keeps tugging me towards you. If I let my instincts alone guide me, they would bring

169

me to you. I felt it from the start, much to my dismay. I tried my hardest to fight it, you know, for I believed you despised me."

"You thought *I* despised *you?*" she exclaimed in surprise. "But I never did, and you were awful to me."

He returned a regretful smile, his eyes lowering. She stared at the thick sweep of dark lashes that hid the intense blue of his eyes, waiting for him to speak. "It hurts when the object of your desire is one who believes you are worthless. It made me angry. I assumed, wrongly, that you would have taken your father's beliefs as your own and so I punished you for it before you could hurt me. I am sorry for that. It was unfair of me to judge you when I knew nothing about you."

Narcissa blinked hard, finding tears stinging her eyes. "I'm so sorry."

He looked up, his dark eyebrows tugging together. "What for?"

"For any insult the duke ever gave you, if he ever made you feel... less than you are. Please believe that it only shows me how small-minded and cruel he is, though I have no need of any further proof. I... I came here to tell you how much I admire you, how much I—"

The press of his lips against hers halted the words and Narcissa sighed, closing her eyes and reaching for him. *This...* this was why she had come, her heart told her. She had come because she could not stay away, no matter how selfish it was to throw herself at him. Though she had not expected him to rescue her when he had no obligation to do so, she had hoped he might feel the same way and wish to do so. Surely no one could ever be certain they had made the right choice, that they would be as happy as they hoped to be, but just as his instincts tugged him towards her, she felt the magnetic power of her desire for him as if he'd reeled her in on a line. Not just passion though, not just desire, she wanted to know him, to discover everything about this charismatic man who made her breathless every time he was near. She believed she did understand him a little now, especially with the words he had just given her. If he had believed she thought him beneath her, she could well understand the way he had acted. How it must gall him when stupid, ignorant people acted as though they were superior to him. The desire to protect him from any such hurt again rose inside her, a possessive sensation that filled her chest and made her feel braver than she might ordinarily be.

Narcissa slid her fingers into the silken warmth of his hair as he pulled her into his arms, his lips moving softly over hers.

"I have thought of this," he whispered against her mouth. "I have thought of this every day and every night since I told you to go."

"So have I," she admitted, gasping as he deepened the kiss, taking her mouth ravenously, as though he was starving for the taste of her.

There was a quiet knock, and the door to the room swung open.

"Are you awake, my lady, I just thought—" The housekeeper stopped just inside the door, holding a tray and glaring at Ash, who had moved smartly away from the bed, but not quite quickly enough.

"I'm sure I didn't mean to interrupt," she said stiffly. "I thought the young lady was resting like the doctor told her to."

Disapproval dripped from every word as she glanced from Mr Anson to Narcissa.

Narcissa felt a blush burning her cheeks and dropped her gaze, but it appeared Mr Anson was made of sterner stuff.

"What do you have there?" he asked, ignoring her censure.

"Some nice hot chicken soup. The lady slept right through dinner, and I didn't like to wake her, but she must eat to keep her strength up."

"Indeed," Ash said, moving to take the tray from her. "An excellent point. I will see that she eats every bite."

For a moment, Mrs Fenchurch hesitated, refusing to relinquish the tray. Narcissa wondered if a tug of war would ensue, but the lady backed down.

"Very good, sir," she said. "And I'm sure you'll be certain the lady gets her rest, like the doctor ordered."

"Indeed, I shall," Ash replied, smiling at his housekeeper.

"Hmph." Mrs Fenchurch said. She looked over at Narcissa, saying pointedly, "Good night, my lady," before making a dignified exit.

The door closed, and Ash carried the tray to the bed. "I believe I am in disgrace," he said with a bland smile.

"Not for long, I suspect." Narcissa smiled at him as he set the tray down. "She thinks a great deal of you."

"Naturally. I'm adorable," he replied, his expression deadpan, though amusement lurked in his eyes. "It's my fatal charm."

"Really?" Narcissa replied, staring at him. "I thought it was your waistcoats."

He snorted at that and took up the bowl and spoon, scooping up some of the thick soup and lifting it towards her. "Don't be impertinent. Eat."

Narcissa accepted the mouthful. "I can feed myself; I'm not an invalid."

"I know, but if I feed you, it stops you talking, and I feel that's safest for now."

He lifted the spoon again and Narcissa accepted it, watching him thoughtfully.

"Is that why you kissed me too, to stop me from talking?"

"Partly," he admitted, his lips quirking. "But not entirely. I kissed you for the same reason I always kiss you, because I want to. I find it hard to stop thinking about kissing you," he admitted, his gaze lowering to her mouth.

"But you're not sure that's a good enough reason to marry," she suggested.

Ash sighed and offered her another spoonful. "This is why I'm not ready to talk yet."

She ate the spoonful, speaking quickly before he could press another on her. "Because you are uncertain you wish to marry me at all," she guessed, not that it was a surprise. "I don't blame you for that. But you need only take me to Lady Cordelia Steyning. I'm sure she would give me sanctuary if I asked for it."

"You misunderstand," he said, his expression becoming grave. "We *shall* marry. There is no choice."

"Of course there is a choice!" she exclaimed, clasping his wrist to stop him from pushing the spoon at her again. "There is always a choice. I ran away from home because I did not wish to be forced into a marriage that was not of my choosing. Do you really think I would have you forced into the same situation?"

Ash sighed and shook his head. "It's not the same."

"It is the same."

He set the spoon down with a clatter. "I told you to meet me in that room, Narcissa, I promised there would be no repercussions, but there were. That's on me. I asked you to meet me, and told myself it was for your sake, because I wished to help you, when in truth I wished to help myself. I wanted to have you alone, I wanted to seduce you. I've wanted you to be mine from the first moment I saw you. I've been sick with it, that's why I was so appallingly rude."

The admission did not have the effect he perhaps intended, for a smile tugged at Narcissa's lips, her heart lightening at the idea. "Truly?"

"Well, you needn't look so damned pleased about it," he grumbled.

"But I am pleased, for I wanted you too." She reached out, daring to touch his face. "I wish there were time, I wish everything did not have to be decided at once, so you could get to know me and decide if I was the one for you."

"But there is no time, and no choice, either. We shall be married," he said, turning into her caress, pressing a kiss against her palm. "And whilst that is an unnerving thought, I am glad for it, for I must have you before I go mad with wanting."

Narcissa's breath hitched at the contact, at his words, at the warmth of his mouth and tongue against her skin. Tiny shivers of delight seemed to chase from the place his lips touched, all along her arm, erupting deep inside where a sudden pool of liquid warmth spilled through her.

"You asked me if I wanted you," he said, his voice low. "I told you the truth. I do. I want you badly, Narcissa, but lust is one thing and marriage quite another. We must marry, but I do not wish to find myself tied forever to a woman who comes to resent me for things I cannot change. Women have always sought me out, finding me different from other men because of my heritage. They think I am some exotic creature they can crow about having bedded, but I am not different at heart, love. Once the honeymoon is over and the day-to-day existence of a marriage begins, you will discover I catch colds the same as any other man. I make mistakes, I lose my temper, and I forget things I ought to remember. And those same women who wished to bed me will think less of you for having married me. They may be cruel to you. When that happens, will you still look at me the way you are doing now? Will you still think *I am glad I married him*, or will you wish you'd chosen differently? That is what I think about, the answer I wish I had."

Narcissa hesitated, considering her answer, for she knew it mattered, to him, to them both if they were to have a future together. "I cannot pretend to know what I am facing, not in the way you do," she said, her words careful. "But I am prepared to fight for what I want. I will never regret being yours, Ash. I know that much, but I worry you will feel the same about me, that you will discover 'the diamond' is nothing but a pretty bit of glass in reality, that you were tempted only by a façade, but I fear the only thing that will prove us right or wrong is time."

"Time we do not have," he agreed. "So we must take a chance, and be kind to each other, and hope we can make it work."

"How much time do we have?" she asked.

"I went to Doctor's Commons whilst you were sleeping. We can be married in the morning, providing you are well enough."

"Tomorrow morning," she said faintly.

He nodded. "Finish the soup."

Narcissa ate obediently, her head whirling with the idea she might be married by morning. Once the soup was done, Ash set the tray aside and moved back to the bed. Giving her a considering look, he sat beside her again, but this time stretched his long legs out before him, lounging beside her like an indolent panther. He looked as dangerous too, a glint in his eyes that gave her pause.

"Is this all right?"

Narcissa nodded, though her heart skipped. She smiled as he lifted his arm, inviting her to move closer. With a contented sigh, she snuggled against his chest, delighted with the feel of the silk banyan beneath her cheek, the weight of his arm settling around her. This was perfection, the only place she wanted to be.

Closing her eyes, she basked in the warmth of his hard body so close to hers for a long moment before she spoke again. "Will you tell your parents before we marry?"

"No." His reply was unequivocal, and her heart sank.

"Because you think they'll try to talk you out of it?"

Ash shrugged. "They might, but either way, they will wish to discuss the matter and I will not feel easy until you have my name. No doubt they will be displeased, my sister will certainly murder me, but I do not wish to be arrested for attacking a duke. If he ever lays a hand on you again, however, I'm uncertain I could stop myself."

"How do you know about that?"

"Miss Pinkerton told me." He looked down at her, his hand caressing her cheek as his gaze softened, his voice becoming tender. "She told me what you said to your father, that I was a better man than he could ever hope to be, and he hit you for it."

"I did say that," she said, smiling, relieved that he knew that much. "I was braver then, for I didn't understand the danger I was courting. I never thought he would hit me, fool that I was. I could have borne the slap, however, for it was done in the heat of anger, but the next time—" Narcissa trailed off, her stomach roiling as she remembered.

"The next time," Ash repeated, his hand stilling, his voice expressionless. "What happened the next time?"

Narcissa swallowed, staring at the embroidery on his banyan, tracing a thick swirl of yellow silk stitches with her fingertip. "He was quite calm the next time. It was my fault, he said, my fault he had to do it, to beat the wickedness out of me. He did it the morning before you came to the house. That's why I said nothing in your defence. I'm so very sorry I d-didn't, I wanted to so badly, but I was too afraid. I did not think I could stand for him to do it again. It... It was very bad."

"Christ," Ash said, running a hand through his hair in agitation.

Narcissa glanced up, startled to see such depth of pain and regret in his eyes.

"I'm so sorry, Narcissa," he said, avoiding her gaze and sounding choked. "I'm so terribly sorry you had to endure that. Bloody hell, if only I had realised. If I had known—"

He broke off in frustration, for they both knew that even then he would have been powerless to help her when she was, in the eyes of the law, her father's property to do with as he saw fit. Moreover, he was a duke, and no one would dare gainsay him.

Narcissa gave a crooked smile. "Not your fault," she said, stroking the warm silk over his chest, aware of his growing tension, the anger burning inside him.

"It was entirely my fault," he said furiously. "And I was fool enough to believe you meant the words you said to me." He shifted onto his knees, regarding her with a soft look in his eyes, such regret behind the words they touched her heart, easing any lingering pain. "Can you forgive me, love?"

"There's nothing to forgive," she said. "And the marks are fading, though riding for so long in such dreadful weather was not terribly comfortable, I admit."

There was a taut silence.

"May I see?"

Narcissa gasped, tilting her head back to regard him in shock. "See the marks?"

Ash nodded. "I want to see what that bastard did to you. I want… to make amends. We're to be married in the morning," he reminded her gently. "I'll be seeing a good deal more of you then, I promise. It's only a few hours away."

"I suppose," she replied, nerves exploding inside her. "W-Well, if you wish to."

Awkwardly, Narcissa got to her knees and turned her back to him. With shaking hands, she lifted the back of the shirt she wore to expose her thighs, still striped with the evidence of her father's beating.

She heard his swift intake of breath, followed by a litany of barely audible curses.

"Are they very ugly?" she asked anxiously. "Mrs Fenchurch thought they wouldn't leave any scars."

"Lay down," he said, not answering her for the moment and she could not judge his mood from the cool command.

Uncertainly, Narcissa lay on her front as Ash shifted to kneel beside her. His warm fingers coasted over the backs of her thighs, making her breath catch and a strange tingling sensation begin inside her.

"Does it hurt still?" he asked, his voice somewhat hoarse as he trailed one finger over a long red mark just above her knee.

"Oh, no. Not now," she assured him, though her mind was reeling from the touch of his hand upon her thigh. Before she could gather her thoughts, however, he had bent and pressed his mouth to the same place, bestowing a soft kiss.

"Poor darling," he murmured against her skin. "No one shall ever hurt you again, do you hear me? I would murder anyone who tried with my bare hands."

Narcissa held her breath, too tantalised by the featherlike brush of his lips to speak.

"I'm sorry," he murmured, pressing one kiss after another along the length of the first faded red stripe. "I am so sorry he hurt you, but I shall make it up to you if you will let me. I shall replace the memory of that vile act of cruelty with one of my own making, one where you feel only pleasure."

His lips crossed from her right thigh to her left, his mouth a delicate touch like the brush of silk, his tongue a diverting swipe of wet warmth that made her shiver, more so as his breath fluttered over it, sending chills of delight climbing up her spine.

"Should you like that?"

Narcissa was so dazed it took her a moment to realise she was being addressed. Only the fact that the delicious touch had paused brought her to her senses.

"Yes. Please don't stop," she told him, sighing and burying her face in the counterpane as he worked his way higher, his hands and mouth making her shiver and gasp. When he got to the top of her thighs and nuzzled the curve of her bottom, Narcissa made a muffled sound, torn between wonder at how lovely it felt, and sheer mortification. Before she could utter a sound of protest, however, he had flipped up the long tail of the shirt to expose her backside.

"He's lucky there is not a mark here," he growled, his voice dark. "Or I should have murdered him, regardless of the consequences. To mar something of such exquisite beauty would be unbearable."

Narcissa gasped as his warm hands caressed her, gently moulding the plump mounds of her backside as her bones seemed to lose their structure, turning molten and languid under the warm slide of his hands.

Ash bent, pressing a kiss to first one cheek, then the other. "So beautiful," he said, the words a soft fluttering of warmth over her skin.

"Are you tired, love? Do you wish to sleep?"

"Sleep?" Narcissa exclaimed, looking over her shoulder at him in outrage. "You expect me to sleep *now?"*

There was a wicked glint in his eyes as his mouth quirked. "No, I expect you to demand I make love to you, but one does not like to act like a conscienceless devil. You have been through an ordeal, and I ought to allow you to rest, as Mrs Fenchurch pointed out. The fact that I have no desire to let you is another matter. I shall accede to your wishes, however."

"Then don't stop!" she replied tartly.

Ash grinned at her. "As my lady commands."

With a huff, Narcissa resumed her position on the bed, her face hidden under her tumbled gold curls. Ash's hands pushed the shirt she wore up and up until it bunched around her shoulders.

"Lift up," he told her.

Narcissa did as he asked, allowing him to strip the shirt from her and cast it aside, shivering as the cool air caressed her naked body. Burrowing back into the counterpane, she did not look at him, not ready to face him yet. His palm slid under her unbound hair, resting on the back of her neck. Slowly, he stroked it down her spine.

"So tense," he murmured. "Something must be done. You will never rest properly when you are in such a knot."

Narcissa squeaked in surprise as he moved, straddling her thighs, the cool material of the banyan pooling over her. Ash reached up, settling his hands on her shoulders and squeezing gently but firmly.

"Tsk, every muscle is taut as a bowstring," he murmured, and though Narcissa wondered what else he could expect when she was naked in his bed, she decided it was safest to keep her mouth shut. She didn't want to risk him stopping what he was doing when she was all agog to see what came next. She felt him lean towards the bedside table, heard the drawer slide open and the soft pop of a stopper. The next time his hands touched her, they were slick with oil, the rich, voluptuous scent of it filling her nose. It was an exotic perfume, heady with incense and warm spices.

"That smells divine," she said with a sigh.

"You can thank Nani Maa," he said, amusement lingering in his voice. "It's one of her special recipes, thankfully she passed the secrets onto my mother. You can also thank her for my talent at *maalish*."

"Maalish?" she asked in confusion.

"Massage," he clarified, adding with a chuckle. "I'd say she had more medicinal uses of the skill in mind but, knowing my grandmother, I think that is doubtful."

Once more, his hands settled on her shoulders, caressing and kneading, seeking all the tight muscles and working them with his fingers until they gave in, surrendering to pleasure under his deft touch and leaving her utterly boneless.

Ash worked his way down her back until Narcissa was sighing and so malleable beneath his clever hands that she would have done anything he asked of her.

Dazed and mindless, she was only dimly aware of him laying the banyan aside, of the tug of his shirt as he pulled it over his head. The feel of his warm chest pressed against her back, however, *that* had her wide awake.

"Are you ready to sleep now?" he asked innocently, nipping at her ear.

She snorted before she could think perhaps that was not a very seductive sound and was relieved the counterpane had muffled it. Daring to turn her head, she opened one eye a little.

"No," she said boldly.

"Dear me, you are making me work tonight," he replied with a sigh that tickled her skin, setting her shivering all over. "Whatever could I do next to help you to relax? Hmmm? Any ideas?"

Narcissa shook her head and was rewarded with a low laugh.

"Poor darling, can you not bring yourself to look at me now?" he teased her.

"No," she admitted, not moving.

"I shall cure you of that," he promised. "But you may hide for now if it makes you feel better. Tomorrow night, once we are married, there will be no more hiding, that much I promise you. For now, I shall love you by stealth."

Moving to lie beside her, he eased her onto her side, amused when she protested and covered herself with her hands. Reaching for the banyan, he spread it over her, the cool silk pouring over her skin in a sensuous slide of rich fabric.

"There, modesty is preserved for now, and you will not see the wicked things I'm doing to you beneath," he said, a teasing note to his voice.

Narcissa gasped as his warm hands slid up to cup her breasts, caressing and kneading the soft flesh. His fingers moved to her nipples, gently tugging and pinching until they were hard little buds that sent jolts of lightning bursting through her with every languid pull of his fingers. His breath shivered over her neck as he pressed a kiss to the sensitive place beneath her ear.

"I have longed to touch you this way, sweetheart, wanted so badly to make you mine I could think of nothing else. I was wretched, believing I had lost you."

"S-So was I," she managed, but anything else she might have said fled from her mind as one hand coasted down her stomach until his fingers found the soft nest of curls between her thighs.

"Now, I shall bring you pleasure so sweet you will forget everything else and drift into sleep, leaving me mindless with unfulfilled desire, but you can make it up to me once we are wed," he added, nipping at her ear.

"You will? I c-can?" she said, uncertain what part of that sentence she wanted the most explanation about.

"Mm-hm. Now hush, love. You are in the hands of a master, if I do say so myself. Just lie back and let me work."

The smug words made her huff with combined amusement and anticipation and, if she'd had the wit, she might have teased him for his arrogance. As it was, she swiftly realised he was telling her nothing but the truth. His elegant fingers slid through the curls, easing into her most private flesh and caressing, circling, wringing gasps and sighs from her as he sought the precise place to touch, the exact amount of pressure to exert. Within moments, she was writhing in his arms, her head thrown back against his shoulder.

Ash let out a soft groan as she pushed back against him, discovering the hardness of his arousal pressed against her backside. "Oh, you will repay me for this, sweet," he whispered, pressing his hips harder against her softness as his fingers played inexorably, tormenting the tiny nub of flesh hidden between her thighs.

Narcissa closed her eyes, giddy with the sensations coursing through her, too lost in the pleasure of his touch to even try to make sense of it. Her blood fizzed in her veins like fine champagne, her skin electrified as that secret place throbbed and pulsed and gathered every sensation, drawing it towards that tiny part of her until nothing else in the world existed. His fingers dipped lower and if she had not been out of her senses, the realisation she was slick with moisture might have been mortifying. As it was, she luxuriated in the slide of his fingers over her pulsing flesh and held her breath as some new pleasure beckoned her, drawing her on.

"That's it love, give yourself over to me, I'll take care of you." His caressing words unravelled the last vestige of self-control she had clung to and Narcissa succumbed to whatever powerful force was urging her on. A cry left her mouth, torn from her without her volition as her body grew taut and then shattered.

Ash held her close to him, anchoring her when she felt she might fly away, pieces of herself sent far into the darkness never to be found again. But he held her securely, his wicked fingers wringing every last pulse of delight from her body until she was sated and boneless, utterly spent in his arms.

"You are quite spectacularly lovely," he whispered, nuzzling at her neck. "Whatever happens in the future, sweet, I know I am a lucky fellow. Never think I don't know that. Now, sleep, love. You have an eventful day ahead of you tomorrow."

"Mm," was the most profound remark Narcissa could muster. She sighed as Ash drew the covers up around her, settling himself behind her as she drifted into sleep.

He chuckled as he made himself comfortable, his arm settling over her waist and then sliding up to cup her breast.

"That's it, my love, don't you worry about me. I'll just endure a night of exquisite torture," he murmured, his darkly amused voice following her into her dreams.

Chapter 13

Pip,

Sorry I left without saying goodbye. I was told you'd not return until late and I needed to leave. Something came up.

Thanks for putting up with me. I've said goodbye to Tilly, who promised to give this to you when you got back.

Cheers for everything.

—Excerpt of a letter from Mr Leo Hunt (son of Mr Nathaniel and Mrs Alice Hunt) to The Right Hon'ble Philip Barrington, The Earl of Ashburton (son of the Most Hon'ble Lucian and Matilda Barrington, The Marquess and Marchioness of Montagu).

15th March 1850, Trevick Castle, Trevick, Warwickshire.

"Afternoon, old thing."

Miss Violetta Spencer had been gazing out of the window with a feeling of quiet despair, but the soft, lazy voice caused her to look away with a jolt of shock.

"Leo!" she exclaimed, blinking to be certain she wasn't imagining things. Though she felt she was far too long in the tooth to act like such a ninny, Violetta was mortified to discover a blush tingeing her cheeks. "What the…? How…? Why are…?" she stammered, thrown into confusion by his sudden appearance.

It really wasn't fair, she reflected bitterly, that such a frivolous, pleasure-seeking creature like Leo had been so generously blessed by nature. His dark gold hair shone even in the indifferent light of an overcast day, his broad-shouldered physique and handsome features so familiar to Violetta she ought to be inured to the shock of them by now. She was not.

Though he maddened her and made her wild with frustration, her heart lifted at the sight of him. His travel-worn appearance somehow only highlighted his golden good looks. He moved towards her, all easy grace and magnetic charm. Everyone loved Leo, even when he drove them distracted, they adored him for it. Simply *everyone*.

Violetta sighed and pushed the unwelcome feelings he always provoked down into the dark, secret corner of her heart where she always kept them and did her best to breathe normally.

"Well, this is a surprise. Did we know we had the honour of a visit from you, and from the Honourable Mau, I see. Good afternoon, Mau," she said, smiling at the huge cat, who was draped across Leo's shoulders as usual.

"No, you didn't," Leo admitted with a smile. "We thought we ought to surprise you. Mau was rather concerned after receiving your last letter."

Violetta glanced away, feeling somewhat ridiculous, even though Leo was the one who had started the silly game, writing letters to her on Mau's behalf. But then Leo could be entirely ridiculous and get away with it; everyone else just looked like a fool. Before she could put some distance between them, Leo shocked her by taking her hands in his. He wore no gloves, and his warm callused fingers curled around hers, making her heart beat like she was the veriest schoolgirl and not a woman deemed practically on the shelf. The connection was so shocking she could only stare at their entwined fingers, almost missing the words he spoke in her befuddled state.

"What's the trouble, Vi? Did you miss me?" he asked softly, his blue gaze searching hers.

Violetta snatched her hands from his grasp, a swift intake of breath stealing the indignant retort she wished to speak. Damn him. Why had he to come here and stir everything up? Just to make sport of her, no doubt, for Leo was serious about nothing and no one outside of that wretched club that took so much of his time... or risking his life in stupid sporting events.

"Oh, every second of every day. I am utterly bereft, dying a slow and wretched death, longing for your presence," she said, her voice dripping sarcasm.

"That's what I thought," he replied, his eyes gleaming with mischief.

"Go to the devil, Leo. What are you doing here?" she demanded crossly. "Trevick and the family are away from home. Everyone is in town, so you've had a wasted trip."

"Why aren't you in town, then?" Leo asked, narrowing his eyes at her.

Violetta shrugged. "I didn't feel like it. I find I am in no mood for polite conversation."

Leo made a sound of amusement, his gaze sharpening. "That, I believe. But why are you not out searching for a husband, making every fellow you meet fall madly in love with you, only to step on his heart when you decline to accept his proposal? Why do you keep refusing them, Vi?"

"Step on—" Violetta repeated in outrage. "How dare you imply that I... I torment men only to—"

"Settle your feathers," Leo said, a flicker of irritation in his voice now. "I wasn't implying you were toying with their affections. Lord knows any man with eyes in head falls in love with you at the drop of a hat, it's not like you must try, is it?"

Violetta opened and closed her mouth, too incensed to decide what part of his ridiculous statement she should attack first. Had he come here intending to make her lose her temper? If so, he was doing a wonderful job, as usual.

Mau, sensing the dangerous undercurrent, leapt down from Leo's shoulders and began weaving in and out of their legs, purring sonorously.

"Now look, you've upset Mau," Leo muttered, folding his arms.

"I've upset him! I-I—" she stammered, so overwrought she could not speak. "Oh! Why did you come here? Why do it, Leo? Why must you stir everything up and cause a row and—Good Lord, you make me furious."

"Well, the feeling is mutual," he shot back at her. "Why are you here, all alone, feeling blue devilled and writing to me to tell me so? What do you want me to do about it, Vi?"

"I wasn't writing to you!" she snapped, even though she knew it was ridiculous. "I was writing to Mau."

Leo threw up his hands and stalked to the window.

There was a taut silence.

"You ought not be here, all by yourself," Leo said, his voice quieter now, though some potent emotion she could not decipher still vibrated through the words. "Why are you so determined to end up an old maid?"

"I'm not determined to, that's just the way life is turning out," Vi said coolly. "If I were to meet a good man, one I could esteem, then… then I should marry him. I would be glad to," she added, somewhat defiantly.

"You've met plenty of good men."

"Not one that suited me, clearly."

"I don't think you want a good man at all," Leo muttered, still glaring out of the window.

"I beg your pardon?" Leo turned to look at her and though Vi thought it most peculiar, the air seemed to crackle between them, as if the wrong word, the wrong move, might send them both up in flames. Nervously, Vi took several surreptitious steps away from Leo. It didn't help.

"I said, I don't think you want a good man at all," he repeated, a dark note in his voice that made her heart skip.

Vi fought to hold his gaze, which was far harder than she could have imagined as something blazed there, something hot and unwieldy that scared her half to death.

"I can't think what you mean by that," she said, disconcerted to hear her voice sounding so faint and tremulous.

"I think you can," he said, taking a step towards her.

Vi took another step back and shook her head.

"I think you want something you dare not say out loud," he continued inexorably. "I think you are only pretending to want a good man. A well-behaved, *nice* fellow, one who was scrupulously polite at all times and never upset your world, would drive you mad in less than a sennight. You'd murder him, Vi. Christ, you'd likely break the coffee pot over his head one morning when he failed to rise to whatever bait you'd set to make him furious. Oh, no, love. I think at heart we both know what you want, *who* you want."

"You're m-mad," Vi said, her breath coming too fast, her cheeks blazing, blood seething through her veins like it boiled beneath her skin.

"No. On the contrary, I've finally come to my senses," he said, backing her up until she was flat against the bookshelf on the far wall. He loomed over her, bracing an arm on each side of her head as he stared at her, his expression inscrutable. "I'm not going to let you chase me away this time. I'm not going to let you pretend anymore. Do you hear me?"

"I don't have the—"

"Quiet," he said sharply, making her suck in a breath of shock at the anger she heard there. "I've warned you, Vi. I'll have the truth from you if it kills me."

Vi reached behind her, clinging to the bookshelf as she trembled, terrified by what he might discover if he kept on, by what might happen if she did as he asked.

His gaze softened as he looked down at her and he reached out, touching her cheek lightly with the back of one finger. "I know you don't trust me," he said softly. "I don't blame you for that. I know I've been a frivolous jackass and I've taken nothing seriously my whole life. I know it and I understand I have a deal of work to do to change that, and I will do it, but you must meet me halfway, Vi. I can't do it all by myself."

"D-Do what?" she asked in alarm, too bewildered by this sudden turn of events to fully comprehend what was happening, too terrified to want to try.

"Give me a chance," he said, gazing down at her. "I won't let you down."

Vi stared up at him, refusing to let all the things she had never allowed herself to hope for to escape from the tightly locked place where she kept them. "I don't believe you," she whispered, and ducked under his arm, running from the room before he could stop her.

♡♣◇♤

"Hell and damnation."

Leo watched Vi run away from him and took an unsteady breath. His heart was hammering so hard he felt slightly sick, his palms clammy from such undue agitation.

Mau made a loud, and to Leo's ear, somewhat derisive sound of complaint. Leo looked at the cat, who was sitting at his feet, glaring up at him with a look of pitying contempt.

"I know," Leo muttered. "Not my finest hour, was it? You don't need to tell me. I messed up. Big surprise."

Leo crouched down and Mau leapt nimbly back onto his shoulders. The great cat made a rumbling sound and pushed his head against Leo's.

"Of course I'm not giving up," Leo said crossly. "I'm not that hopeless. I knew it would be hard."

Mau licked his cheek with a sandpaper tongue and Leo snorted.

"All right, I hoped she'd fall into my arms, and we'd live happily ever after. I admit it. Are you happy now? Instead, I've made a great pillock of myself and scared her half to death. Well done me. Lord, I need a drink."

Mau made another sound of protest and Leo sighed. "Fine. Dinner for you first, but then I need a drink. Yes, just one. I know, *I know,* getting foxed is hardly going to help my case, there's no need to tell me."

Leo turned and then halted as he discovered a slightly bewildered footman staring at him in alarm.

"Is there anything amiss, Mr Hunt?" he asked Leo, looking nervously around the room to discover who Leo had been talking to.

"No, nothing at all. I'm going to my room. The usual one, is it?"

"Yes, Mr Hunt. Your bags have been taken up already."

"Excellent, sent me up something to eat, would you? Nothing fancy, bread and cheese will suffice, oh, and a plate of sardines if you would."

The footman glanced at Mau somewhat dubiously. "Er… yes, Mr Hunt. Will there be anything else?"

"Yes, a glass of brandy."

"Shall I send the bottle up, sir?"

Leo hesitated and sent Mau a pained look before letting out a sigh. "No, just the glass."

"Very good, sir," the footman said, and hurried away.

"Happy now?" Leo asked Mau irritably and made his way up the stairs.

Narcissa stretched languidly as she woke from a profoundly dreamless sleep. Her body felt oddly heavy, so thoroughly relaxed she did not wish to open her eyes. Instead, she burrowed deeper into the warmth of the bed, allowing her mind to drift as it would. Slowly, she remembered the events of the previous days, the exhaustion of the endless ride from Hardacre, not daring to sleep other than for an hour snatched here or there whilst she rested the horse. The entire journey had been fraught with anxiety as she feared someone would discover she was a girl out in the world alone. It had been a reckless thing to do, and yet her bravery had been rewarded, for she was here, in Ash's bed, and—

"Oh!"

She blinked awake, suddenly not in the least sleepy as she remembered the events of last night, the way Ash had touched her and made her body sing like she was some exotic instrument only he knew how to play.

Turning, she admitted herself disappointed to discover he was no longer in bed with her, though the delicious aroma of the massage oil blended with the faint citrusy scent of him that lingered on the sheets. Burying her nose in the pillow, she breathed it in, and wondered how she could look him in the eye today, after what he had done to her, after how she had reacted to it. How terribly shocking. And then to fall asleep!

The door to the bedroom swung open, and Mrs Fenchurch bustled in, hefting a tray.

"Good morning, my lady. I've brought you a nice breakfast. There's coddled eggs and hot buttered toast, and I brought you some of my bramble jelly. Mr Anson's favourite, that is. Plus a pot of tea. I wasn't sure if you'd prefer chocolate or not, but I'm happy to bring you a cup if you fancy it. Is that to your liking?"

"Oh, it sounds splendid," Narcissa said gleefully, only now realising how famished she was. She sat up in bed, smoothing the covers as Mrs Fenchurch settled the tray across her lap. "Where is Mr Anson?" she asked, avoiding the housekeeper's too knowing gaze.

"He's readying himself for your nuptials, my lady."

Narcissa nodded, smiling to herself until a thought occurred to her. "Good heavens!" she exclaimed. "Whatever am I to wear?"

Mrs Fenchurch returned a smug smile. "That's all in hand. Don't you fret. His lordship sent word to a friend of his, Lady Latimer. A happily married lady she is too, so don't go fretting over that," she added hastily, as Narcissa's face fell. "He reckoned you were not so different in size, though she's a fair bit taller. Anyway, he asked if she might lend you a gown. Well, she's a dear creature, so naturally she did just as he asked at once. It arrived first thing this morning and I've been shaking out any creases for you. Pretty it is, too, a lovely bright blue with a matching pardessus all trimmed with swansdown. I'll bring it up in a moment. I don't doubt he'll take you shopping for new things as soon as he can. His sister always relies upon his advice, you know. He's got a keen eye for what suits a lady, so she says."

"He thinks of everything," Narcissa said ruefully.

Mrs Fenchurch snorted at that. "No, he don't, for he's a man, but he's not as hopeless as many when it comes to arranging things how a lady might like them. Mind, he's had a deal of practice," she added, *sotto voce.*

Narcissa said nothing, remembering all the things she had heard about Mr Anson. Everyone knew he was popular with the ladies, his affairs being as numerous as they were varied. It was said he was sought after not only for his prowess but for the tact and discretion he was capable of, an indispensable skill when many of the ladies had husbands to manage. The memory made Narcissa suddenly feel anxious and profoundly sad. She had never expected to marry for love and the chance she had now to marry a man she not only desired, but esteemed—one she knew she was close to falling hard for already—had seemed like a dream. But what if those feelings were never reciprocated? What if she fell desperately in love with him, and he carried on having affairs? Her heart lurched at the idea.

"Come now, eat up," Mrs Fenchurch scolded her, upon discovering Narcissa sitting with a spoonful of egg suspended between the dish and her mouth. "Mr Anson told me you must be ready to leave by eight, so that doesn't give us much time."

"Eight!" Narcissa exclaimed, setting the spoon down with a clatter and moving to set the tray aside.

"Oh, no. You're not leaving this house without a proper breakfast after what you've been through the past days. Not when you've a marriage ceremony to get through and then… well, you're not, that's all. And whilst I think about it, I suppose I ought to give you a bit of advice about what to expect on your wedding night. Seeing as you've no mama to do that for you. So eat up, for we've a lot to do."

The housekeeper's colour heightened, but she folded her arms, looking quite as though she would wrestle Narcissa into submission if she did not comply.

Meekly, Narcissa picked up the spoon and forced herself to finish her eggs and a slice of toast, wondering what on earth Mrs Fenchurch would consider good advice.

"One more slice of toast and a cup of tea, if you please, my lady," Mrs Fenchurch said inexorably.

Sighing, Narcissa did as she was bid, though the toast stuck in her throat as she wondered how long it would be before her father arrived on their doorstep. Hopefully, he did not know where Ash lived, but she doubted it would take long to discover the information. The disappearance of Fidelia and Mr De Beauvoir, *and* Alex, all on the same day, must have confused matters, possibly enough that it had taken him some time to discover what precisely had happened, or even that she had gone at all. When she had left, the house had been in uproar, so she very much doubted anyone would have realised she was missing until the next morning at the earliest.

Once Mrs Fenchurch was satisfied, she proved herself to be a dab hand with arranging hair and, whilst she brushed and pinned Narcissa's long tresses into an elegant chignon, the warm-hearted, if no-nonsense lady explained what she thought Narcissa ought to know about her wedding night. The description was brief and somewhat mechanical, and by the end of the recitation, Narcissa's eyes were wide and her cheeks very pink. Though she was grateful to the lady for her kindness, the explanation had been rather mortifying to listen to.

"Any questions?" Mrs Fenchurch asked, her ruddy face glowing more than usual and looking as though she was praying there would not be.

Narcissa shook her head, for she had not been entirely ignorant—one saw animals in the countryside, after all. Visibly relieved, Mrs Fenchurch then helped Narcissa into the borrowed gown. It was far too long, but some quickly made alterations to the hem fixed the problem without too much difficulty, and a few hasty adjustments did wonders with the waistline. All things considered, the effect was not displeasing, and Narcissa hoped her husband-to-be would find nothing to be ashamed of in her appearance. She made a mental note to call on Lady Latimer as soon as she was able, to thank her for her kindness, for with the gown and the pardessus had come matching gloves, an adorable hat trimmed with swansdown like the coat, and lovely little calfskin half boots which were sadly too big. The redoubtable Mrs Fenchurch stuffed the toes with cotton wool, however, so they might serve for the time being.

A peremptory knock sounded before Ash strode in, staring at his pocket watch.

"Tell me you are ready, for we really ought…" He trailed off as he caught sight of her, his expression changing from one of mild irritation to something she could not read.

Mrs Fenchurch gave Narcissa a quick grin, winking at her before she gathered the remnants of the breakfast tray. "If you'll excuse me, sir. My lady is ready as you asked and the hour only just about to strike too," she said with undisguised satisfaction.

Ash said nothing, his gaze moving over Narcissa in a way that made her feel strangely hot all over, as if she'd been caught adjusting her garters in public.

"Do I look quite as I ought?" Narcissa asked hesitantly, not wishing him to think she was fishing for compliments, but feeling so anxious a little reassurance would not go amiss. Whilst she was used to being considered a beautiful girl, she had never wished so desperately to please a man before, and the knowledge that she was wearing a borrowed gown and boots that did not fit her was not helping her confidence.

There was a charged silence whilst Ash studied her.

"Quite," he said, after what seemed like an eternity. "Certainly you do."

"Oh," she said with relief, though it was hardly a fulsome compliment, but she was relieved he thought nothing was amiss. "Thank you."

He let out a breath of laughter and shook his head. "You are a picture, my lady, as you always are," he said, his voice smoother now as he offered her his arm. "Come."

Smiling happily at his words, Narcissa allowed herself to relax a little. She was to be married this morning, to a man who was uncertain he wished to marry her, and she had no idea what the future held, but she meant to do all in her power to see he never regretted his actions.

For now, though, she was content for fate to lead her where it would. It had brought her here after all, and so far, that was the greatest good fortune she could imagine receiving.

Chapter 14

Dear Ma and Pa,

I'm afraid I'm about to do something you may not approve of. At least you may not approve of the manner in which I am doing it, but I have no choice.

This morning, I will wed the Lady Narcissa Ponsonby. I suspect her father will make an unpleasant scene on your doorstep in his effort to track me down. I am sorry for it, but it can't be helped.

Please forgive me. I know you will like Narcissa very much, for she is a dear creature, and nothing like her vile parent. I beg you will save any recriminations for me alone and make her welcome once I am able to make her known to you.

—Excerpt of a letter from The Hon'ble Ashton Anson to his parents, The Right Hon'ble Silas and Aashini Anson, The Viscount and Viscountess Cavendish.

15th March 1850, Albany Street, Regent's Park, London.

Ash led Narcissa down the stairs to the entrance hall, his guts seething with an uncertain mixture of hope, anticipation, and doubt. The sensation had assailed him the moment he had woken to find Narcissa in his arms. The feeling that had risen in his chest at finding her beside him had been one of such pleasure and possessive pride, it had shocked him. He kept telling himself that he did not know her, that he could not trust her—not yet, at least— but it was getting harder to remember that.

When he had entered the bedroom to discover her dressed all in blue, with the fluttering white swansdown like a delicate halo about her face, his heart had done the most peculiar lurch in his chest. Desire had hit him hard and fast, making him want to undo all of Mrs Fenchurch's hard work and take her straight back to bed. Last night she had been so sweet, so giving and trusting, and the idea she might love him if he gave her the chance to do so was one he wanted to believe in. Yet, he still found it hard not to think that a girl so used to privilege, to being viewed as one of the most eligible women of the *ton*, would find her sudden relegation to the lower ranks hard to stomach. How would she tolerate the oh–so-subtle snubs and barbs? How would she feel to discover she was no longer welcomed by some of the high sticklers? Surely that would hurt her, and perhaps she would blame him for it.

Ash was so lost in his own thoughts that the sudden hammering on his front door took a moment to penetrate his brain. Narcissa, though, gasped and clung to his arm, her face blanched white.

"My father," she whispered, trembling visibly.

Ash hesitated. What he wished to do was to open the door and give Beresford a piece of his mind, but he could not risk having Narcissa taken from him by force. He would have to wait until she was safely married to him.

"Come," he said, grasping her hand.

"Don't answer that," he told his butler. "Delay them for as long as you can. Tell Beresford we were married yesterday and have gone to stay with friends in the country."

"Very good, Mr Anson," his butler said, not betraying by word or expression his opinion of such goings on in a respectable household, though Ash did not doubt he'd discuss it to the full with Mrs Fenchurch later.

Ash strode to the back stairs and hurried down them, towing Narcissa with him. "We'll go out the back way," he told her. "The church is on the corner of Regent's Park Road. It's a short walk, and the vicar is waiting for us."

Narcissa nodded resolutely, rushing after him.

Much to Ash's relief, no one was waiting to accost them as they escaped out the back of the house. Though the faint sound of angry voices could be heard as they sped away, they made good their escape, all but running along Albany Road.

By the time they got to the church, Narcissa was gasping, and he shot her an apologetic glance as he ushered her inside.

"I'm sorry, love. I doubt this is the kind of wedding you'd hoped for," he said grimly as they made their way up the aisle.

"It's far better than any marriage I'd expected," she retorted gamely, making him smile even as guilt twisted in his heart.

She deserved better than this shoddy hole-in-the-wall affair, but there was nothing to be done about it. Having paid the vicar well to provide the necessary witnesses and have the paperwork all in order, the ceremony was performed at a cracking pace, with nothing resembling romance, and Ash felt increasingly like a heartless bastard. He thought perhaps they both stopped breathing when the vicar asked if anyone had any objections to the marriage but, miraculously, the duke's furious presence had not erupted upon them. Narcissa's voice trembled as she'd recited her vows, her eyes too bright. By the time Ash gave his responses, he was so het up, his voice was hard and impatient, and he was only amazed she didn't walk out on him there and then.

She didn't, though, and even smiled at him as the vicar pronounced them man and wife and told him he might kiss his bride.

Ash felt the words fall upon his shoulders like a weight, one he doubted he'd ever live up to, but he was caught now. There was no backing out, so he'd best try to salvage the day before Narcissa despised him for bringing her to such a pass.

Startled to find his hand was not entirely steady, he cupped her cheek and lowered his mouth to hers. She raised her face, her gloved fingers clutching at his lapels and suddenly everything went away. Her father, their ignominious escape from his house, the shamefully hasty marriage, none of it mattered. When she pressed her soft mouth to his, all he knew was the scent of her that swam in his head, jasmine and vanilla clouding his mind, invading his senses as the knowledge she was really his settled in his heart. His hand went to her waist, pulling her closer as desire thrummed beneath his skin. *Mine,* said a new and possessive voice in his head, satisfaction rippling through him as the truth of that settled deep inside. He had never known a woman who was his own in every way that mattered. Usually they were someone else's wife, or perhaps widow. Never had a woman been entirely his, not only legally but truly.

"Ahem."

The vicar's disapproving voice reminded Ash they were not yet in private, and he reluctantly let Narcissa go, relieved to see she was looking far happier now than she had done, a soft flush of pink colouring her cheeks. Once they had signed the register and Ash had handed out the necessary coins to thank the witnesses for their trouble, he led her back down the aisle.

Though it seemed ridiculous, he didn't know quite what to say to her. All his legendary charm and sophistication had gone up in smoke as he found himself quite out of his depth.

"What now?" Narcissa asked quietly, for they could obviously not go back to his home.

Though he had written them a hasty note to explain what he meant to do, he was certainly not ready to face his parents yet, and it was likely the duke would go there next, something Ash did not wish to think about.

"We shall visit a friend of mine," he said, not having any better plan.

He hailed a hackney cab and lost no time in helping Narcissa inside and giving the driver the address on Berwick Street. He sat down beside his bride and reached for her hand, relieved when she still smiled at him, though there was concern in her eyes.

"But what shall we do, Ash?"

"I told you, we shall visit my friend. He'll let us make use of his place," he said, wishing that had not sounded quite so tawdry.

Narcissa blushed scarlet as his meaning sunk in.

"He won't be there," Ash added defensively. "He'll stay at the club until… well, until it's safe for us to show our faces. There's no point in being coy about it, love. We need to consummate the marriage to ensure you're safe. It's the only way, and he won't know to look for us here."

"Of course," Narcissa said, her voice faint but composed. "I understand."

Ash gritted his teeth, part of him wishing she wouldn't be so damned agreeable. He was acting like an utter bastard, and she was letting him get away with it. If only the situation had been different and they'd not needed to act so furtively, as if it were something shameful. If only they had celebrated their union as they ought to have done… but he had mismanaged this entire affair from the start, and it wasn't getting any better. He only hoped it wasn't a taste of things to come.

At least the carriage ride was mercifully short, and barely twenty minutes later he handed Narcissa down and led her towards the smart front door of the smart, red brick house on Berwick Street.

"Good morning, Barnes," Ash said, with no preamble. "Is he up?"

"Yes, sir, as it happens, he is. Mr Weston is in his studio." Barnes eyed Narcissa with obvious agitation as he lowered his voice. "But I'm afraid he's a little...er... worse for wear. Not fit company for the lady," he added in an undertone that only Ash could hear.

"Is he now?" Ash replied, frowning. "Well, there's no help for it."

"Perhaps I could see the lady to the parlour whilst you speak to Mr Weston, sir?" Barnes offered.

Ash hesitated. If it were any other man that would be sensible, but Larkin was such an easy-going fellow he could not imagine him saying anything out of the way to Narcissa, even if he was half seas over. Besides, Ash acknowledged the strangely urgent desire to introduce *his wife* to Larkin and have someone congratulate them.

"No, it's all right, Barnes. My wife, Lady Narcissa, and I will go through, if you please."

"Very good, Mr Anson, sir, and may I be the first to congratulate you both," Barnes said smoothly, clearly disapproving of Ash's demand, even if he didn't bat an eyelid at the news.

Barnes led them through to the back of the house and into a large, bright room which smelled strongly of oil paint and turpentine, where he announced.

"Mr Anson and the Lady Narcissa Anson."

Larkin spun around, dropped the glass he was holding, which smashed on the flagstone floor beneath him, and glared at Ash in outrage. "For the love of God! Is it a bloody epidemic?"

Ash stared at him, wondering if perhaps Barnes had been right after all, as the harried servant rushed off to find a dustpan and brush.

"Come again?" Ash asked, frowning.

"You've married a Ponsonby," Larkin accused him, gesticulating somewhat erratically at Narcissa. "I've had Hart here with the other one not two days ago, or is it three? Anyway, the other sister, Fiddle... Fideela..."

"Fidelia?" Narcissa offered politely.

"That's the one!" Larkin said with a snap of his fingers. "Fidelia. Hart married her, and now you! Is there one for me too?"

"I'm afraid not," Narcissa said, a thread of amusement in her voice, though Ash did not find the situation remotely amusing. "Are they really married?" she asked, sounding delighted by the revelation.

"Pity," Larkin said morosely, and picked up a large paintbrush and dipped it in a pot of white paint. "And yes. Happily, blissfully wed, they are, even after all the drama, but at least she found her baby. That's good, isn't it? All's well that ends well," he said, with a snort of derision.

Ash blinked in shock as Narcissa let out a gasp.

"B-Baby?" she repeated. "What do you mean? What baby?"

Larkin paused, and Ash felt another jolt as he realised what he was doing with the brush. There were several canvases littered about his studio, all freshly painted white. The one on the easel before him was not yet complete, only a large white splotch in one corner marring the portrait of Miss Elmira Hastings. Turning slowly, Larkin regarded Narcissa with a bleary gaze.

"Oh," he said, swaying a little as the brush dripped white paint on the tiles. "I may have been a trifle indiscreet."

"Yes, you may," Ash said savagely. "For the love of everything holy, what the devil has got into you?"

With a snort, Larkin shook his head. "The truth will set you free, so I'm told. What utter bollocks."

"Right, that's it," Ash muttered furiously. "Barnes, be so good as to take my wife to the parlour and see her comfortably settled. Mr Weston and I need a little chat. Bring coffee when you have a moment, and lots of it."

"Yes, sir, certainly sir," Barnes said, looking relieved. "Lady Narcissa, if you would be so good as to follow me."

"But Ash?" she said, eyes wide as she tried to convey what she was desperate to know whilst saying nothing in front of Barnes.

"I'll see to it, love, and I will let you know," he promised. "Please, go with Barnes."

Though she clearly wanted to do nothing so much as cross examine his drunken halfwit of a friend, Narcissa did as he asked, leaving Ash alone with Larkin.

He strode across the studio, snatched the brush from Larkin and set it down carefully before grasping his friend's arm. Propelling him out of the back door and into a small courtyard, Ash went straight to the water pump. The bucket beneath it was more than half full, so he picked it up and dumped the lot over Larkin's head.

"F—" The obscenity was lost in the spluttering and choking that followed and Ash stood back, watching his handiwork as Larkin stood rigid, shivering and utterly furious—but somewhat more alert than he had been.

"That's better," Ash said grimly.

"You bastard!" Larkin said, and made the mistake of taking a swing at him. Ash dodged with ease and gave his friend a shove that had Larkin windmilling backwards and sitting on his arse, blinking in surprise. "That was unsporting," he grumbled.

"You started it," Ash muttered, hauling him back to his feet and shoving him back indoors again. "Now tell me what the bloody hell has been going on."

Several cups of coffee later, and Larkin had explained all he could about Hart and Fidelia's elopement, and Fidelia's baby. Once Ash had heard the story in full, he understood his friend's current state of inebriation and the whitewashed portraits of Miss Hastings.

"We'd spoken about getting married," Larkin said, his tone devoid of emotion now as he stared down into his coffee cup. "I thought she trusted me. I certainly trusted her, and all this time she was hiding this secret. I mean, I can understand her not telling me at first, but it's been years, Ash. She asked me to be patient after what she'd been through, and so I thought—" He shrugged, apparently unwilling to go on.

Ash hesitated, not knowing quite what to say. "You were very decent to her, Larkin. Honourable."

Larkin nodded morosely. "And look where that got me. She would have let me marry her, believing the child was hers. Surely, she must have realised I'd figure it out in the end. On our wedding night for example. So why? Why would she do that?"

Ash shook his head. "I can't answer that. I suppose she was afraid of losing him."

Larkin's expression darkened. "Yes, to his mother. All this time, and she never considered that maybe Fidelia had not given up the baby willingly. She must have known that was a possibility, but it was easier to think ill of the child's mother rather than try to contact her, to give her a little peace of mind. The poor woman has driven herself half mad over the past years, and Elmira could have reassured her the boy was safe, at least, even if she did it anonymously."

"I'm sorry," Ash said, seeing the disillusionment in Larkin's eyes. "Though in truth she had no valid reason to think the mother hadn't been willing. Perhaps she feared contacting her would cause the child more trouble, that she would lose him, and she did take the boy as her own."

"Yes, she did. She sacrificed everything for him, and I shall never cease admiring her for that, but… but she didn't trust me, Ash, and she never gave the boy's mother a second thought. She's not the person I thought she was. All this time, I waited for her, doing everything I could to ensure she knew she could trust me, and for what?" Larkin ran a hand through his hair, looking so utterly miserable Ash's heart went out to him.

"What now?"

Larkin shrugged, his familiar lopsided smile not meeting his eyes this time. "It's over. We both said too many things that cannot be undone. She says her brother's behaviour made her wary, but to compare me to that damned scoundrel? Bloody hell, Ash. Now I see she has always held me at arm's length, and I cannot marry a woman who refuses to trust me, and that I can no longer trust in return. That is no basis for a future together."

Ash considered Larkin's words, hearing the ring of truth in them, and knowing he had been doing the same to Narcissa. He had been holding back, not ready to trust her with his heart when she had trusted him enough to put her entire future in his hands. Not only was she far braver than he'd given her credit for, she *was* his wife now. If he wanted them to have a future together, he must put his trust in her, no matter how daunting the prospect.

"So, what will you do?"

"I'll go to the club and give you some privacy, for starters, though I still can't believe you're married," Larkin replied ruefully. "And then I shall get drunk enough that no amount of coffee will sober me. After that... who knows? Perhaps I'll stay with Muir and Hamilton and see what mischief they're up to these days. I've missed out on a good deal, it seems, as you and Leo have not ceased to rail at me for. You were right, weren't you? I ought to have stayed away from Gillmont."

"If you think either of us would take any pleasure in saying 'I told you so,'" Ash said grimly.

Larkin waved a hand. "No, no, I know that. Don't mind me, I'm just blue devilled. But I shall come about, just see if I don't."

Ash smiled. "Of course you will."

"Congratulations, by the way. She's certainly a beauty. The season's diamond, too. Well done you, Ash."

Ash grinned, feeling pleased with himself despite the circumstances.

"You must let me paint her portrait," Larkin added thoughtfully.

"Don't push your luck," Ash replied, getting to his feet and stretching. "She'll probably have decided to divorce me for leaving her by herself for so long, in any case."

"Good lord! You rotten scoundrel. What are you thinking? And on your wedding day, too," Larkin said in alarm. "Tell you what, I'll do a portrait of the two of you. My wedding gift to you. How's that?"

"That's a charming idea, and I'm sure she'll be delighted. Thank you," Ash said, meaning it, for Larkin was exceptionally talented, but cautious about exhibiting his work. He rarely took commissions. "And, once we're settled, you're always welcome, you know that."

"Oh, yes, I'll come and play gooseberry," Larkin said with a snort. "Don't you worry about me, old man. I'll be fine."

Chapter 15

Dearest Fidelia,

If the scandal sheets are correct, you are now Lady Fidelia De Beauvoir. I am so happy for you, my dear friend. I wish you every future joy in your marriage and congratulate you for having escaped what I am told was a very unhappy situation.

I wish you had confided in me a little about your circumstances, though I quite understand why you did not. It is hard to tell another what is in one's heart when there are things it is difficult to admit, even to oneself. It sounds so much like ingratitude, does it not, to bemoan the state of one's existence, when so many others have much harder lives?

Do tell me how your romance with Mr De Beauvoir came about. I would love to know about your shocking elopement. It sounds wonderfully exciting, though I can imagine at the time it was fraught with danger and uncertainty. How I admire you for having grasped fate with your own hands and taken such a terrifying chance. I do not know if I could ever be so very brave as you have been.

Please write and tell me the secret, Fidelia. How do you stop feeling so terribly afraid?

—Excerpt of a letter from the Hon'ble Miss Violetta Spencer (cousin and adopted daughter to The Right Hon'ble Kitty and Luke Baxter, Countess and Earl of Trevick) to The Lady Fidelia De Beauvoir.

15ᵗʰMarch 1850, Berwick Street, Soho, London.

Narcissa waited for what seemed an interminable amount of time until Ash reappeared. Barnes had done his best to entertain her, and kept her supplied with tea and biscuits, but by the time her husband came back, she was a bag of nerves.

"I've had the housekeeper prepare your room, sir, my lady," Barnes said, avoiding Narcissa's eye, for which she was grateful, even as heat rose in her cheeks. "If you'd like to follow me."

Narcissa grabbed Ash's arm as he gestured for her to precede him out of the room. "What's happening?" she demanded, having worked herself into a stew of anxiety over Fidelia. "Did you—"

"Yes, love. I know what happened. Hush now and I'll tell you everything once we are private."

Bursting with impatience, Narcissa held her tongue whilst Barnes showed them into a lovely, sunny room, the walls papered with a pretty design of lush yellow roses.

"This is Mr Weston's sister's room," Barnes informed them with a proud smile. "She picked the wallpaper herself, and the furnishings. A lovely eye for colour, has Mrs Oak."

"It's beautiful, Barnes," Narcissa said, for as desperate as she was to hear what Ash could tell her, she was grateful to discover her wedding night was not taking place in some dingy little back room as she had feared.

Barnes looked pleased by the comment but a fierce glance from Ash had him clearing his throat and hurrying out. "Yes, well, if there's anything you need, don't hesitate to ring the—"

"We will, thank you, Barnes," Ash said, closing the door in the fellow's face.

"Oh, Ash, tell me!" Narcissa said, running to him and clutching at his coat.

"You're wrinkling me," he protested, though his lips quirked in a smile as he took her hands in his. "Come and sit down, then I shall tell all."

Narcissa did her best to hold still as Ash removed her bonnet and pardessus, before he sat down in a chair by the newly lit fire. The room was rather chilly still, but the fire was cheerful, giving off a good amount of heat.

"Come, love," he said, holding out a hand to her.

Narcissa blinked, realising he wanted her to sit on his lap. Awkwardly, she turned her back to him, trying to arrange the vast swathes of her skirts before she dared lower herself, but she felt his hands at her waist a bare second before she was tugged backwards.

Letting out a squeak of surprise, she tumbled into his embrace with a flurry of petticoats and was swiftly pulled into a searing kiss. His mouth was hot and urgent, devouring hers as his tongue swept in, his hands moving restlessly over her. By the time he let her up for air, she was entirely befuddled and out of breath.

"That's better," he muttered with a sigh. "So far, this day has not gone as it ought. I thought I should try to remedy things."

Narcissa laughed and rested her head on his shoulder. "It has been rather odd. Oh, but Ash... I'm sorry, I must know. What did Mr Weston mean about Fidelia's baby?"

Sighing, Ash resigned himself to the inevitable and Narcissa listened in stunned silence as Ash told her about the nephew she hadn't known she had.

"All this time," Narcissa said, her voice choked. "My poor sister has been breaking her heart all this time and I never... I never..."

"There now, love, it's all right," Ash said, holding her tight. "Your father kept you apart from her so you would never know, and he threatened her not to tell you. Neither of you are to blame for his wickedness. He's made you both miserable, but you are free of him now. From everything Larkin said, it seems Fidelia and Hart are very much in love. They're happy, Narcissa, and there's nothing for you to be upset about. Even your brother seems settled, you see?"

Narcissa nodded, a tear sliding down her cheek all the same. "And what about us, Ash?" she asked, her voice little more than a whisper as she dared to ask the question that had troubled her heart since the moment he told her they must be married. "Shall we be happy too?"

Ash held her gaze, and she looked into eyes of darkest blue, unlike any she had seen before.

"Yes," he said firmly. "We shall be happy, and I intend to start on that now, this instant."

He drew her close again, kissing her softly this time, tenderly, his large hand cradling her face as if she were something infinitely precious.

"Ash," she whispered, as his mouth brushed over hers, one of a thousand tiny kisses as he built sensations that began as gentle warmth and turned quickly to something fierce and all-encompassing.

"Yes, sweetheart?" he replied, his voice husky as kissed his way down her neck.

"Thank you."

He made a darkly amused sound before lifting his head and gazing at her. "For this wonderfully romantic wedding day?"

"I don't mind about that, for we have plenty of time to celebrate with people who are glad for us in the future," she said, smiling at him. "But I want to thank you for believing in me, for giving me the chance to prove I can be everything you want, that you need. I... I know you don't believe me yet, but I am so very proud to be your wife, and I shall never regret it."

He stilled, and she waited, uncertain what he was thinking until a smile curved his sensuous mouth, his eyes warm as they gazed at her. "You cannot know how glad I am to hear that, Narcissa, and for my part, I shall do my best to always be honest with you, to tell you what is in my heart."

Narcissa let out a breath of relief, daring to hope that meant he might put his other women aside, and really give her the chance to be everything he needed. "And what is in your heart right now, Mr Anson?" she asked, a teasing note to her voice as his eyes flickered with mischief.

"I'm not sure it's what's in my heart you need to worry about just now," he said wickedly, taking her hand and pressing it to the place where his body was aroused and hard, the heat of him blazing through the fabric of his trousers.

Narcissa blushed scarlet and Ash chuckled, raising her hand to his mouth and kissing her fingers. "Forgive me for teasing you. You're not afraid, are you, *mera pyar*?"

Narcissa shook her head. "No, only rather nervous, but I trust you. What does *mera py*—" She frowned, stumbling over the word.

"*Mera pyar*," he repeated, leaning in to nip at her earlobe, making her shiver. "It's Hindi and means 'my love.'"

Narcissa repeated the strange words thoughtfully, wondering if he meant them, even a little, or if such endearments were natural for him and given lightly. She considered asking him, but his next question drove that idea from her mind.

"And do you know what happens between us? Did anyone explain?" he asked, his expression suddenly grave.

Narcissa flashed a sheepish grin, remembering Mrs Fenchurch's explanation that morning. "Your housekeeper was so kind as to explain things to me."

"Good God! Did she really? Well, I never. She never ceases to surprise me. I shall have to give her a raise," he added, his lips quirking.

"I think you ought, I don't know which of us was more mortified, but she was determined that I should not be sent off 'like a lamb to the slaughter,'" Narcissa said, laughing.

"Is that what she said?" Ash asked, clearly amused, though tenderness glinted in his eyes. "You don't feel that way, do you?"

"No," Narcissa reassured him, though privately she thought the look in his eyes was more than a little wolfish.

Ash gazed at her for a long moment. "I think the room is warm enough for us to divest you of some of those clothes, don't you?"

Narcissa nodded, though gooseflesh chased over her skin at his words, and she could not have spoken to save her life. Her heart was beating hard, with mingled nerves and anticipation but she got to her feet, standing passively as Ash worked with deft hands any lady's maid would have admired. Narcissa decided she would not contemplate the reason he was so adept at undressing ladies, for that was his life before now. Surely, if she pleased him, he would not need to return to such decadent ways.

"You've not even taken your coat off," Narcissa protested when he had got her down to her drawers and chemise. Shivering despite the growing warmth in the room, Narcissa clutched her arms about herself.

Ash tsked and shook his head. "Never mind that, I'll catch you up. But I promised I should cure you of your shyness, did I not?"

Narcissa swallowed. "I'm not sure that's possible."

"Let's see." Ash sat down, settling himself back in the chair, his eyes glinting. "Go on, sweetheart."

"Go on?" she asked in confusion.

"Take the rest off," he said, amusement threading through his voice.

"B-But you're watching me," she protested.

Ash grinned at her. "Yes, I am."

Narcissa stared at her toes, suddenly unable to move, though she knew she ought. Part of her wanted to, for she had been determined to please him, and she had been naked in his arms only last night, but...

"Look at me." Her gaze flew to his at the command. "You are the most beautiful woman I have ever seen in my life, Narcissa. I still cannot believe you are mine, that you can truly wish to be my wife, but I am so glad you are, and I am so proud to call you my own. I want to look upon you, my own beautiful girl, not to judge, not to cause you embarrassment, but simply to drink in the sight of you, for looking upon you brings me pleasure. Perhaps you shall wish to look upon me, also, and I shall do as you desire, love. Do you see?"

Narcissa nodded and let out a breath, reassured by his words. Telling herself she would not be a ninny about this, she reached for the hem of her chemise and tugged it up over her head before her shaking hands fell to the tie on her drawers. With a slight shimmy, they fell to the floor, leaving her in her stockings.

"Your hair. Let it down."

Narcissa shivered, hearing the way his voice had become low and husky, her confidence rising as she saw the look in his eyes, the obvious desire and approval shining there. Bolder now, she raised her hands, watching him as she took out the pins one by one, letting her thick hair fall past her shoulders in a spill of silken gold.

"Narcissa," he said, his voice low and urgent as he pushed to his feet.

"Oh, no!" Narcissa ran from him, climbing onto the bed and clutching a pillow to herself as a laugh caught in her throat at his shocked expression. "No, you said I could look upon you, too. So… go on…"

She made a shooing motion with her hand and Ash's expression changed from one of bewilderment to delight, his eyes glinting wickedly.

"Ah, I see my lady catches on quickly. Well, far be it from me to disappoint you, sweetheart. I suppose you had best look upon your husband, just in case you have a last-minute desire to change your mind."

Giving her a provocative wink, he began stripping off his clothes, making her laugh as he performed for her, giving a theatrical bow once he had bared his top half. By then Narcissa was too stunned to do anything but stare, however, for although she had desired him, and had known he was quite the most beautiful man she had ever seen, she had not been prepared for what lay beneath his clothes. Fully clothed, Ashton Anson was a work of art. He dressed with exquisite taste and even when his waistcoats were rather outrageous, he wore them with such style and assurance, in a way no other man of the *ton* possibly could. Naked, however, he was magnificent. Years in the boxing ring had honed his body. Pure muscle moved beneath skin of golden silk, his chest lightly furred with dark hair that arrowed down beneath his waistband. As he pushed his trousers and smallclothes aside, Narcissa could only stare in wonder.

The devil knew just what he looked like, and he sauntered towards the bed with a smug expression that she could not blame him for in the least.

"Well, love. Do I meet with your approval?" he purred, climbing onto the mattress like some big, sleek cat, prowling towards her as her pulse sped up.

"C-Can't breathe," Narcissa said, as he tugged the pillow from her grasp and cast it aside. She lay back as he moved over her, gazing up at him in wonder.

"That seems like the correct reaction to me," he said, giving her swift smile that showed strong white teeth before he lay over her.

The shock of his hot skin was so profound she gasped with pleasure, her hands going to his back, sliding over powerful muscles as she revelled in the touch of his body against hers.

"Ah, beautiful Narcissa, how I have longed for this moment. I have wanted you from the first," he whispered, and stole any reply she might have made in a passionate kiss that made her giddy with longing.

Too lost for any further conversation, Narcissa gave herself over to her husband, trusting in him to care for her, to please her and show her how to please him. He turned onto his side, taking her with him, and Narcissa shivered as his hands moved over her, caressing and inviting her to touch him in return.

Somewhat nervously, Narcissa accepted the challenge and touched her finger to his nipple, smiling a little as the tiny disc puckered beneath her touch. Emboldened by the look in his eyes, she stroked her hand down his broad chest, drawing her fingers through the wiry dark hair that led her lower, until her fingers touched skin more silken and delicate than any she had known before. He sucked in a sharp breath, letting out a muffled groan as she curved her fingers around him. Pleased to have discovered something he liked after the way he had made her cry out in wanton abandon last night, Narcissa firmed her grip a little and stroked. Ash closed his eyes, an expression that seemed close to pain on his handsome face, though Narcissa knew enough to understand that was not what he was feeling. She experimented a little, moving slowly and then quicker, adjusting her grip and exploring the strange, masculine part of him until he let out a muttered curse. Her triumph short-lived, he tumbled her onto her back once more, removing her hand and pressing it against his chest.

"I will let you torture me to your heart's delight the next time, sweetheart, but I am too impatient to allow it tonight. I need you. I need to make you mine. Can you let me?"

The words struck her heart with possessive pleasure as the unguarded truth held in them rang in her ears. He needed her, just as she needed him. Perhaps it had not just been him who had rescued her from a miserable future... just perhaps, she had done a little saving herself.

"Yes. Yes, please," she whispered, pulling her down to him and coiling about him, drawing him close so that he might finally make her his wife. His hand coasted down between her legs, and he stroked her gently, stirring her body to life with slow, tantalising touches that had her arching towards him, seeking more. He watched her as her sanity unravelled by slow degrees, her colour heightening with her temperature as her skin flushed with passion. Though she ought to have felt self-conscious, such considerations had fled her mind, chased away by the awed look in her husband's eyes as he gazed down at her, the satisfaction he took in giving her pleasure more than obvious.

The intimacy of his touch, the murmured love words and tender kisses he bestowed on her combined with his sweetly insistent caresses until she could go no further and shuddered in his arms, clinging to him as her body gave itself over to the pleasure he brought her. He held her for a moment whilst she luxuriated in the receding waves of delight, and then gasped as she felt him settled between her legs, felt the heat and the strength of him surrounding her, invading her as he pushed gently inside.

"I'll try not to hurt you," he promised, his voice as taut as his body as her indolent limbs stiffened with shock.

Narcissa clung to his powerful shoulders, squeezing her eyes shut as a sharp pinching sensation within her made her muffle a cry against his chest.

"I'm sorry," he murmured, stilling at once, seeking her mouth and kissing her. "I'm so sorry, love. Try to relax, try to let me in."

Narcissa gazed up at him, seeing the concern in his eyes, the regret for having caused her a moment's pain, and she let out a sigh as her taut body softened around him, welcoming him as best it could.

"That's the way," he said, his voice a low purr of approval as he moved deeper and more assuredly.

Narcissa could only hold on, at first enduring the strange intimacy of it, until the feelings changed from discomfort to something else, something that made her breath catch as she watched him rising above her, felt the power of his body loving hers.

She stroked her hands down his back, the sleek, damp skin and shifting muscle beneath her palms a delight to her. Like before, the rest of the world went away as the uncoiling of sensation at her core caught her attention, drawing her on, determined to chase it, but this time Ash was there too. Narcissa was aware of his muscles tensing, of his movements becoming increasingly urgent and erratic as his breath became harsh, his eyes closing. Now she watched him as he had watched her, understanding the pleasure he had taken in observing her as she saw the moment he lost control, giving himself over to the intense release shuddering through him. The sight of his powerful frame trembling as a rough cry tore through him was the most erotic sight she could ever imagine, and the next thrust had her following eagerly in his wake.

Narcissa held on tight as everything went dark and hot and pleasure-filled, clinging to her husband as joy suffused her body and her heart and made their hasty, unromantic wedding day into one she would remember with wonder for the rest of her life.

Chapter 16

Dearest Aunt,

I am well, I thank you and yes, happy enough. I find a good deal of pleasure in my work. My charge is an irrepressible little monkey, but I rather adore her for it. She is outspoken and horribly spoiled, and trying to turn her into a well-behaved child whilst keeping her spirit intact is a challenge, I admit, but one I relish.

Her father is another matter. He seems to take great delight in vexing me. Indeed, I feel certain he is becoming more provoking by the day, goading me into retaliating. I won't, naturally, for such displays are beneath my dignity. He's such an arrogant devil, though, I fear it has become a game to him. One I shall not play. Men like him think women are sport, something to be conquered. No doubt he thinks his beautiful face is enough to have me swooning at the slightest scrap of attention he throws my way. You'd think after knowing me for some years now, he'd know better. I cannot fathom why he has suddenly turned his attention to me. Perhaps his latest light o' love is a dull creature, and he has nothing better to do. Either way, I shall not let this latest turn of events trouble me. He is just another man, and he will grow tired when he cannot gain a response.

—Excerpt of a letter from Mrs Harris (governess to Ottilie Barrington) to her aunt.

17thMarch 1850, Berwick Street, Soho, London.

Narcissa stared down at her gorgeous husband, unable to keep the smile from her face. He lay sprawled on his front, his arms bracketing the pillow. Her gaze drifted over his muscular biceps and big shoulders, wondering how on earth his tailor made him appear so refined when the body of a prize fighter lay hidden beneath all that beautifully cut cloth. She let out a breath of laughter as she considered his taste for extravagant waistcoats and lavish embroidery, remembering one that had been covered in delicate pink peonies. Narcissa could think of no other man who would dare wear such a thing, yet Ash went his own way, choosing things that pleased him no matter what anyone else thought.

"Are you laughing at me?" he murmured sleepily as he cracked open an eyelid.

"As if I would," she said, reaching out to stroke his hair.

He made an indistinct sound of content and closed his eye again, drifting back to sleep. A swell of happiness filled Narcissa's heart, such deep contentment that her eyes brimmed with tears at the overpowering emotion. She had never known such peace and joy as he had brought her in the days since they had married, had not known she could feel the way she did. But he had filled the past two nights and days with lovemaking and in sharing himself with her by telling of her about his childhood, of his beloved Nani Maa, and the parents he so obviously adored. His twin sister was clearly a woman he held in the highest regard, and Narcissa knew she must do everything in her power to become friends with the woman or else life might be difficult indeed. That Ash valued

Vivien's opinion above all others was a truth she had become increasingly aware of, and that his twin shared some indefinable bond with him, one she must accept. She only hoped the woman did not dislike her for the way they had married and did not think Narcissa had manoeuvred him into a hasty marriage for her own sake.

Though they both knew they must return to Ash's own home and face the world, every time they had tried to dress and leave the intimacy of this little retreat, they could not make themselves go. Whilst no one knew they were here, they were safe from the opinions and judgements of others and they could simply enjoy this time together, getting to know each other in ways they could not do until now.

The sound of the front door knocker did not trouble Narcissa, for no doubt it was someone looking for Mr Weston, and Barnes would send them onto the club as he had done several times already. Yet this time she heard raised voices, and something of a commotion. Anxious, Narcissa gave Ash a little shake.

He sighed and stretched languorously, turning onto his back and regarding her with a wicked glint in his eyes.

"Again?" he asked mildly. "My lady, you are ins—"

"Ash, listen," she said, increasingly unnerved as she heard footsteps mounting the stairs.

Suddenly awake, Ash sat up. There was a knock at the door before Barnes spoke. "Mr Anson, my lady, beg pardon for disturbing you but Lord and Lady Cavendish are here. They wish to see you, Mr Anson. At once."

"Bugger," Ash said succinctly, running a hand through his black hair and making it stick up all over. "Tell them I shall be down directly and then come back with hot water so I can shave."

"Yes, sir."

"Your parents," Narcissa said, wide-eyed with dismay.

"So it appears," Ash replied, hurrying out of bed.

The next twenty minutes were a frenzy of activity as Ash played lady's maid and shaved himself at record speed. He'd had Mrs Fenchurch send over clean clothes for him, and Mr Weston's housekeeper had freshened up Narcissa's gown so at least they did not look horribly rumbled and dishevelled by the time they made it downstairs.

"I feel sick," Narcissa admitted as Ash led her to the parlour, where his parents waited for them.

"There's no need, it's me they'll be furious with," Ash said, which did not make her feel any better.

"What if they don't like me? What if they think I tricked you into marrying me? What if—"

Ash stopped and pressed a finger to her lips to silence her. "They will love you. Stop fretting," he said calmly, before giving her a swift kiss on the mouth and facing the door. "Here we go, then," he muttered, before guiding her through.

Narcissa was uncertain what she had expected of Ash's parents, but upon seeing them both, her husband made perfect sense. His father was a large, powerfully built man who looked more like a fellow who'd spent his life doing manual labour than being an aristocrat. His hair was a little on the long side and peppered with grey but that did not diminish the sense of restless energy that emanated from him. Eyes of intense blue the exact same shade as Ash's settled on her with interest, and Narcissa held her breath whilst she took in his mother. Here was where Ash had inherited his stunning good looks, then. Though her raven black hair was streaked with white, the strong cheekbones, dark gold skin, and stunning figure were that of a woman half her age. The Countess of Cavendish was simply gorgeous and Narcissa did not doubt men still turned their heads to watch her instead of women young enough to be her daughter.

"Father, Mama, allow me to present to you my wife, The Lady Narcissa."

Gathering her nerves, Narcissa executed a low curtsey and dared to meet his mother's eyes.

"Good morning, child. Why, you are a ravishing creature. I can quite see why my son ran off and married you without a word to anyone," she said, smiling, though there was something in her eyes that told Narcissa she was not entirely pleased.

"It might have been nice if you'd troubled yourself to introduce her to us a little earlier," Lord Cavendish added mildly. "Especially when her father presented himself upon our doorstep with such insistence. His visit to your home was even more eventful, according to what Mrs Fenchurch told us this morning when we visited."

"My lord, I am so terribly sorry," Narcissa said, taking a step towards Lord Cavendish and then checking herself. "I'm afraid my father is n-not a very good man, nor a kind one, and… and he did not wish for me to marry Ashton. Indeed, he did not know I meant to do so."

What his lordship might have said in response to this she would never know, as Ash spoke before he could reply. His voice was hard, the words ringing through the room.

"He beat her, Father."

Lord Cavendish stilled, his eyes growing dark. In that moment Narcissa remembered what Ash had told her, that his grandfather had been a brute and had beaten his father until he ran away from home to escape the violence.

"I see," Lord Cavendish said, before returning his attention to Narcissa. "I cannot tell you how profoundly sorry I am to hear that."

Narcissa smiled at him, touched by the sincerity of his words. "Thank you, but I am quite well, and I feel I ought to assure you that is not the reason I married your son. Though he saved me from very difficult circumstances, and from a marriage I viewed with revulsion that is not—"

"The duke intended her for Lord Wishen," Ash cut in, and his mother gave a little gasp of outrage.

"But I married Ash because… because I care for him very much," Narcissa carried on. She blushed at having to speak so in front of people she had only just met, but she needed them to understand. She glanced back at her husband, her chest swelling with emotion as his eyes met hers. "Very, *very* much indeed," she added, her voice little more than a whisper.

There was a brief silence before his mother spoke.

"Well, of course you do. I'm afraid the dreadful creature is adorable and, what's more, he knows it."

Lord Cavendish snorted at that but held out his hands to her. "Welcome to the family, Narcissa. We are very glad to meet you at last, and more than glad to know our reprobate son has decided to settle down at last, and not before time," he added dryly, giving Ash a look that made him shift awkwardly and clear his throat.

"Oh, congratulations, darling," his mother said, hurrying to him and pulling him into an embrace. "She's delightful. I'm sure we shall get along famously."

Narcissa let out a breath of relief, as that hurdle seemed to have been cleared, but then they heard the front door open and close once more and Barnes's voice carried down the corridor.

"But Mrs Lane-Fox, you must let me announce you and—"

The parlour door swung open and a woman so lovely she could only be Ash's twin exploded into the room.

"Ashton Anson, tell me it isn't true," she demanded furiously, her lovely eyes flashing with temper. "Tell me you did not go and marry that pretty half-wit without ever consulting me!"

"Vivien!" Ash, his father, and his mother all said in unison.

Disregarding the admonitions, Vivien hurried up to Ash, taking hold of him as if she might give him a hard shake, which, considering the disparity in their size, was rather ridiculous. "Tell me you didn't throw yourself away on that foolish child!" she cried, too impassioned to heed even her father's words as he tried to silence her.

"No, I didn't marry a half-wit, nor a foolish child," Ash said evenly, breaking out of his sister's hold with ease. "And if you don't listen to me, I shall put you out on the street until you can find some manners, you appalling girl. Really, Viv, you are the absolute limit!"

"Oh, Ash!" Vivien said, wiping her eyes as she gazed at him. "You didn't marry her? Only August had it from Larkin and I said he must be mistaken, for you would never get married without telling me first and certainly never...." Vivien trailed off as she finally noticed Narcissa. She turned back to Ash, eyes wide. "But you said—"

"I said I didn't marry a half-wit, though I'm beginning to think I'm close kin to one," Ash said, glaring at his twin. "It was an act, Viv. She was being coerced by her father to make a good match and so she acted the simpleton because the men of the *ton* are too bird-witted themselves to appreciate a woman with spirit and a mind of her own. Happily, that does not include me!" he added, giving a look that warned her to think carefully before she spoke again.

Narcissa, steeling her nerve, knew she must calm the situation and convince his sister that she was not the dim-witted girl she clearly believed her to be.

"Good afternoon, Mrs Lane-Fox. I am so sorry to have caused you distress. I'm afraid the news must have been a shock to you. I know how deeply Ash regretted not having his family with him when we married, but I'm afraid there was no time. You see, I ran away from home, from my father, to be with your brother. If the duke had caught us, it would have gone very badly, I'm afraid," she added, her heart still fluttering with fear even though that was all behind them now. "I know you have no reason to welcome me into the family, and I know I must prove myself worthy of your regard, but I must tell you how happy I am to meet you, and I hope you might come to like me when you get over the shock of how things were done."

"Oh," Viven said, staring at her. "Oh."

"Oh, indeed," Ash said dryly. "Viv, you are the worst sister in the entire world."

"No, I'm not," she retorted. "You know very well I'm the best sister anyone ever had. You take that back."

Ash snorted and shook his head as the front door opened and closed once more and hurrying footsteps sounded in the hallway.

"Good lord, what now!" Ash demanded irritably, folding his arms as the new arrival burst in upon them.

"Vivien!" A handsome fellow with an untidy shock of gold hair stared wildly around the room until they settled on the lovely young woman at the centre of the disturbance. "Vivien, you wicked creature. I specifically told you to wait for me and not to come here, accusing people of wrongdoing."

"August, don't scold," Vivien said, looking chastened. "Ash has already told me off."

"And so I should think," August said crossly, taking a moment to adjust a cravat that looked to have been tied with more haste than care. "Silas, Aashini, I am so sorry. I tried to stop her."

Lord Cavendish rolled his eyes and shook his son-in-law's hand. "You may as well try to hold back the tide with either of them. I blame their mother," he said with a shrug.

Lady Cavendish shot her husband a warning look before addressing the growing company. "I think tea is in order. Barnes!"

"Yes, my lady?" Barnes appeared magically in the doorway with such speed it was obvious he'd been listening in the hallway. "We'll have tea and whatever refreshments you can bring us, if you would, please."

"Of course. At once, my lady."

"And now everyone will sit down and shut up, and Ash and Narcissa will tell us everything, won't you, dears?"

"Yes, of course we will," Narcissa said, grateful for the opportunity to explain what had made them act as they had.

"Well, maybe not *everything*, Mama," Ash replied, his lips quirking.

His mother returned a reproving look, but there was a twinkle in her eyes all the same. "Do shut up, Ash, there's a good boy."

"Yes, Mother," he said with a grin, and did as he was told for once.

After an afternoon of explanations and getting to know her new in-laws, Narcissa was tired, if delighted by the way things had turned out.

Viven had apologised and admitted she may have been a trifle hasty, for her brother might be an idiot, but he was not a fool. Ash took this ringing endorsement with remarkably good humour, explaining it was the best he could hope for from his twin, who had always been unkind to him. This prompted the kind of bickering only two siblings who knew and loved each other dearly could engage in until their mother shut them both up.

Lady Cavendish, whom Narcissa was to address as Aashini, was warm and kind and quickly made Narcissa feel at home. She promised she would give them a splendid ball to celebrate their marriage and to show the gossiping *ton* they had nothing to be ashamed of. The party would be on such a grand scale that people would talk about it for years to come, and those who were not invited would be sick with envy.

By the time everyone left Mr Weston's house, Ash decided they ought to return home, too. After all, their marriage had been well and truly consummated now and there was no way of undoing it.

"Not that I'm averse to making extra sure of that fact," he added, giving her a lascivious wink as he walked her down the steps to the carriage.

As good as his word, once they had been greeted by the staff and congratulated as Mrs Fenchurch threw handfuls of rice at them, Ash took her straight up to his room and to bed.

Some hours later, Narcissa lay, utterly content and sleepy in her husband's arms. She was contemplating the fact she was rather hungry when Ash sighed.

"Well, my love. I hope you'll forgive me, but I must leave you for a little while."

Narcissa turned to look at him in surprise as he gently moved her aside and slipped from the bed. "Where are you going?" she asked, covertly admiring her husband's splendid rear view even as she felt a stir of consternation at his words.

"Out," he said, somewhat evasively. "I have an appointment I must keep."

Narcissa's heart pitched as she wondered if he meant to meet with another woman, but she quickly forced the terrible suspicion aside. She did not believe he would do such a thing to her, yet he *was* hiding something.

"What kind of appointment?" she pressed.

He slid on his banyan—this one a deep burnt orange with black embroidery—and avoided her eye.

"Ash, what kind of appointment?"

He sighed and turned to face her. "Don't make a fuss," he warned, a look in his eyes that made her already anxious heart skip.

"What kind of appointment?" she asked again, holding his gaze.

"A fight," he said.

"A—" Narcissa blinked at him, hardly believing the words. "A fight?" she repeated, her voice becoming unnaturally high even to her own ears.

"A prize fight. You know very well I box, sweetheart. The match was arranged weeks ago and there is a good deal of money riding on it. I can't back out now."

"But Ash," Narcissa protested. The idea of him putting himself in harm's way made her feel quite breathless with terror.

Sighing, Ash returned to the bed and sat down, taking her hands. "Listen to me. I am the club's unbeaten champion. No one has come close to knocking me down in years. I do this all the time. It's perfectly safe."

"But it's… it's brutal," she said, remembering too vividly the way it had felt when her father had beaten her. The thought that Ash would willingly put himself through something like that made her feel so anxious she could not breathe. "I mean, I can understand you sparring for sport, I suppose, but to fight someone in earnest—"

"Darling, it's not just about violence and brute force, there is skill to it, and a deal of pride at stake. I don't wish to upset you, but you'll have to take my word for the fact I cannot back out." He kissed her hands and patted them gently before getting up again. "You knew this was what I did, Narcissa. It's important to me."

"But what if you're hurt, Ash?" she said, beside herself with worry now. "I-I couldn't bear it."

Ash smiled and shook his head. "Have a little faith, darling. I've survived this long."

He turned away from her to consider the two waistcoats he had laid out earlier, apparently far more interested in his choice of what to wear than the anxiety he was causing.

Narcissa frowned at his uncompromising answer, wondering what to do about something she felt so strongly about, that made her feel sick with fear in case he might be badly hurt. Yet, as he'd said, he had fought for years; it was a part of his life. What right did she have to sweep in and demand he stop?

"Very well," she said, though the words stuck in her throat, but she must try her best to accept this facet of her new husband, despite hating it so much. "I understand you wish to carry on fighting, no matter how much it frightens me, but I shall come with you."

Ash spun around, the waistcoats forgotten. "The devil you will!"

Narcissa stared at him, determined to get him to agree to this much at least. "If you are going to fight, I shall be there to support you. It's my duty. For better, for worse, in sickness and in health, remember? And perhaps if I see you win and how very talented you are, then I won't worry so much in future. Should you not like me to see your triumph?"

"No! Narcissa, you are being ridiculous," he said, frustration in his voice. "Ladies, do not attend boxing matches."

"No ladies at all?" she enquired, with a mild lift of one eyebrow.

Ash's gaze darkened further. "Not respectable ones."

"Well, then we shall make an exception. I've caused scandal enough already by running away and marrying you, I really don't see it can make the slightest difference," she added with a smile, hoping to placate him.

"Narcissa, please don't make this into a row," he said, holding her gaze, a warning note behind the words. "I am not going drinking and carousing, I shan't be dallying with any other women. I am going to fight my opponent, and then I shall come home."

"But I want to go with you," Narcissa replied, equally firm in her resolve. "I know you think I am being foolish, but I cannot stay here by myself, wondering and worrying over you. If you think it so very improper, I shall stay out of sight. You may stash me away in some backroom if you wish. Please, Ash, it's not so very much to ask, is it?"

"Yes, it is, and I am not discussing this any further," Ash said, his tone one that she would have been a fool not to recognise as something dangerous. "You are not going and piling more scandal atop what we have already achieved. That is an end to it. I won't be back until well after midnight. Now do stop fretting over me, love. There's really no need."

With that, he swept up one of the waistcoats and stalked out, calling for his valet as he went.

"Argh!" Narcissa exclaimed. *"The devil you will,"* she repeated in frustration.

Sliding from the bed, she pulled on the banyan he had lent her, this one gold with embroidered peacock feathers around the shoulders and cuffs. It was heavy and far too long and difficult to stalk up and down in, for she was obliged to pick up great swathes of fabric, so she didn't trip.

Finding that striding up and down didn't help a bit, Narcissa flung herself into a chair by the fireplace, and only then noticed a small pile of correspondence. She remembered then that Mrs Fenchurch had told her there were letters for her, but Ash had distracted her so thoroughly when they'd arrived home it had gone clean out of her head. At once, recognising Delia's handwriting, Narcissa snatched the letter up, hoping her friend could help her recover her temper. As she read, however, her heart clenched with anxiety.

Narcissa ran from the room, calling for Ash, only to be told he'd left a few minutes ago.

Sick with worry, Narcissa returned to her bedroom, a dreadful sense of foreboding tripping down her spine as her gaze fell upon the neatly pressed and folded garments she had stolen from her brother when she had run away from home.

Mrs Fenchurch had returned them in perfect order, bless her, and just in the nick of time.

Chapter 17

Darling Cissy,

I have just this minute heard the news. Emmeline tells me the ton is alight with the scandal of the Ponsonby sisters, both of you eloping at the same time! Congratulations, you brave, clever girl! I am so very proud of you, if a little jealous. How lucky you are to have captured such a handsome and interesting husband! I only pray your good fortune will rub off on me, too. I should so adore an adventure. I am tired of reading stories of wicked pirates and highwaymen when the fellows courting me are all so very dull. My most devoted beau is Mr Enoch Goodfellow. I have known him since we were children and he's very kind, the sort you don't have the heart to rebuke because he's so very tolerant and kind. Too tolerant, truth be told. I am quite out of patience with him, but no matter how vexed I get, he does not take the hint. I feel thoroughly suffocated by him, but I cannot seem to shake the poor man off, no matter how hard I try. I have even wondered if he's ~~quite in his right mind,~~ *But I am rambling now because there are things I do not wish to tell you, but I really must, so here we go…*

Have you heard news of the duke, dearest? I hesitate to tell you, for I do not wish to diminish your happiness, but perhaps it is best you hear it from me. It seems he worked himself into such a rage upon hearing about your marriage to Mr Anson he has made himself gravely ill. Not that I think you ought to spare a moment of pity on the brute after the way he treated you. A man reaps what he sows and I'm afraid, from all we are hearing, he is undeserving of anyone's compassion. I do not know how accurate reports of his condition are, some say he has suffered a stroke and is incapacitated, others merely that he has taken to his bed, but I thought you should know.

I beg you will forgive me for being the bearer of more bad news, but Wrexham believes you ought to warn your husband, too. He tells me your brother, Lord Richmond, was so humiliated by his defeat at Mr De Beauvoir's hands that he is out for blood. According to the gossip, De Beauvoir knocked your brother down twice in a row and in front of a large audience. I'm told the print shops are full of images showing Richmond being felled like a tree, and several stories have been published that he is bound to find embarrassing. If you will forgive me for repeating such an impression of your brother, Wrexham says he is a spiteful creature and not to be trusted, but I feel sure you know far better than any of us what he is capable of. Please tell Mr Anson to take great care, for my brother would not say

*such things to worry you unless he truly
believed there was a need to do so.*

*I hope my news has not spoiled things for you,
dearest Cissy, for I am so very happy for you
both.*

**—Excerpt of a letter from The Lady
Cordelia Steyning (youngest daughter of
Philip Steyning, The Duke of Sefton) to
Lady Narcissa Anson.**

17th March 1850, The Sons of Hades, Portman Square, London.

Ash moved through the throng, accepting the shouts of encouragement and cheers as he headed towards the back of the club. Often, fights were held in the club's basement but, of late, Ash's popularity had been such that on the nights he fought the entire membership of the club came out in force, plus guests. So, weather permitting, they held fights in the large but seldom used private gardens at the back. Happily, though it was bitterly cold, the night was clear and bright, and the gardens were illuminated by torches that flickered in the chill breeze.

Ash shivered, reflecting glumly that he had never felt less like fighting in his life. If he weren't here, freezing his arse off, he could still be in bed with Narcissa. They could have shared supper together and talked, drunk wine, made love….

Gritting his teeth, Ash told himself not to think of it, not to remember the hurt in her eyes when he had told her he would not let her come with him. He had behaved like a brute, laying down the law and giving her no say, yet the idea of her being at such an event made his blood run cold. The men often got rowdy, many of them well on their way to being tap-hackled before the fight even began, and the language used should certainly not sully his innocent wife's ears.

"Evening, *a chuilein*, ye have a fine night for a wee brawl." Ash turned to see Muir grinning at him, a silver flash in his hand. "That'll warm the cockles of your heart," he said with a wink, handing the flask to Ash.

Ash drank deep before handing the flask back.

"Thanks," he said, in no mood for conversation.

"Is there sommat amiss?" Muir asked, frowning at him.

"No," Ash replied curtly. "Where's Babbage? Has he got cold feet?"

"Nah, he's coming. Congratulations, by the way. Is it true ye are leg shackled?"

Despite the heavy sensation in his chest, Ash smiled and accepted Muir's ribbing when he admitted he had married.

"And she let ye out of her sight to brawl?" Muir asked incredulously. "And what's wrong wi' ye, man? Have ye nae better things to do with a beautiful new bride awaiting ye at home?"

"I've been asking myself the same damned question," Ash admitted, sighing as he saw Lord Babbage making his way towards the ring.

Babbage was a large man with a shock of unruly red hair that proclaimed his grandmother's Scottish heritage. Ash liked him a good deal, for he was a decent fellow, but right now all he could think of was dispatching the man with all haste so he could go home.

"Well, go and flatten the fellow, aye? I've a packet riding on ye and I stayed in town just for this event. I am away to Scotland on the morrow."

"Oh, well, in that case," Ash said wryly.

Muir laughed and clapped him on the back, accepting the cloak that Ash had covered his bare torso with. "Away ye go then, Ash. Gie it laldy."

Ash nodded and stepped into the ring, shaking hands with Lord Babbage, who grinned at him.

"A pity to spoil your pretty face and send you back to your bride in pieces," the fellow said, winking at him.

Ash grunted with amusement, almost pitying the poor devil. Though his heart was not in the fight, his desire to return to Narcissa and make amends for speaking to her so harshly was uppermost in his mind. He wanted this over and done, and quickly. So, instead of giving the audience the show they'd come for, Ash circled his opponent warily. It was some time since he had seen Babbage in the ring, but he stripped to advantage, his muscular frame impressive in the flare of the torchlight. Babbage threw two hard jabs with his left, followed by an impressive uppercut, and Ash danced backwards, testing the length of his reach, weighing up the danger.

The audience was deafening, cheering and shouting, offering advice to whichever of the men they had laid their money on. Ash ignored the roaring in his ears, filtering it out until only the man in front of him held his attention.

Ash returned the same sequence of blows, holding back, pulling his punches and just grazing Babbage's chin but inflicting no damage. The man was built like a brick outhouse, far heavier than Ash but, like many big men, he was slow. Babbage came on again and Ash evaded him easily, the jaw-shattering blows missing him by a mile.

"Come on, pretty boy," Babbage called cheerfully. "Don't be shy."

The man swung again, vast power behind his massive arm, but so slow that Ash dodged and stepped close, delivering two fierce body punches to his ribs, followed by a right that had the fellow windmilling backwards. Ash felt the solid connection to the fellow's jaw, knew the impact had been spot on, and watched with cool satisfaction as Babbage fell with a crash that echoed around the enclosed garden.

The crowd continued to shout and scream, demanding Babbage get to his feet and carry on, but Ash knew that would not happen. The fellow was out cold. Returning to his corner, he found Muir grinning and shaking his head.

"Ye have somewhere to be?" he asked, his eyes glinting with mirth. "I reckon ye have a deal more sense than I credited ye with. Gie yer wife my kind regards, aye?"

"Goodnight, Muir," Ash replied dryly and hurried back into the club to get dressed before anyone could stop him.

Using the back stairs, Ash avoided running into any of his friends. He flung on his clothes with less care than he had ever done in his life and hurried out of the club. Scanning the environs of the square for a hackney cab, he muttered a curse, as none were to be found. Thinking he'd have better luck on Oxford Street, Ash opened the wrought-iron gates that led into the garden at the centre of the square and walked quickly, his mind filled with thoughts of Narcissa. She had clearly been worried, frightened even, and had that not been what he wanted, someone to care for him, to love him and worry if he did not come home? He ought to have at least discussed it with her, explained his reasoning more clearly. How was she ever to trust him, confide in him, if she believed everything she asked for would be refused out of hand?

Despite his distraction, Ash was not such a fool as to walk about London at night with his head in the clouds. A prickling sensation on the back of his neck told him he was not alone, and he focused on his surroundings. The night was dark with only a thin sickle moon visible, the streetlamps doing little to illuminate the centre of the gardens, yet Ash became aware of movement around him. Three men? Four?

He was ready for the attack when it came. The first man wrapped his arm about Ash's throat and tried to pull him off balance. Ash stiffened his stance and threw his head back, hearing the crunch of a nose breaking and a muffled cry of pain.

"Get 'im!" bellowed a harsh voice to his left, but the attack came from his right and Ash had only a moment before a man stepped out of the darkness, swinging wildly. He was no match for Ash, who felled him swiftly, but another grabbed him from behind, pinning his arms as the fellow he'd knocked down scrambled back up and delivered several hard punches to his gut. Ash grunted, well used to such abuse and so not unduly alarmed, but he was too impatient to get home to enjoy dealing with some dim-witted ruffians who thought they'd found an easy mark.

Shouts from the direction of the club told him someone had got wind of another mill in progress, and he knew he'd have an audience soon if he didn't deal with this. He stamped hard on the foot of the fellow who held him. The iron grip around his arms loosened and Ash jabbed his elbow backwards, winding the fellow who staggered away. Ash turned to deal with the fellow more comprehensively, but paused, suddenly aware that the odds were a lot worse than he'd realised.

Whilst the fellow whose nose he had broken was sitting on the ground as blood dripped in a steady stream from between his fingers, five more men faced him, four of them clearly hired thugs.

The fifth Ash recognised as Lord Richmond, Narcissa's older brother.

"Did you really think we'd let you get your filthy hands on one of our own and do nothing about it?" the man demanded in disgust.

Ash regarded him critically, noticing the livid bruise at his eye and another staining his jaw.

"Did Hartley do that?" he asked conversationally. "He always did have a brutal right hook."

Richmond coloured so vividly that it was discernible even in the dim light of the garden.

"One sister lost to gutter scum, the other to a half-breed. You've given his grace a stroke, I hope you realise. If he dies, it's as good as murder."

Ash snorted. "And you're praying he kicks off so you can inherit, I don't doubt," he said, regarding Richmond with derision.

Even before he'd met Narcissa, he had hated the man. The Sons had voted unanimously to refuse him membership to the club, all of them holding him in contempt for his cruelty and the disrespect with which he treated anyone he did not consider his equal.

"Better that than watch Narcissa sink herself so low with her marriage to you, the son of an illegitimate Indian whore."

Ash did not think, he simply reacted. If Richmond had believed himself safe with his little army of bully boys, he quickly reassessed the situation, as Ash felled two in as many seconds. The man's puffy, florid face blanched, and he stumbled back, screaming at the remaining men to do what they'd been paid for.

"Kill the bastard!" he yelled, hurrying out of the way as Ash had no choice but to divert his attention to the men who came at him with murder in their eyes.

Narcissa sat shivering in the hired hackney cab as it pulled up just around the corner from the club on Portman Square. She'd had the devil's own job in escaping the house without Mrs Fenchurch noticing and she feared the fight would be long over by now. Yet, she must warn Ash to be on his guard. As a child, she had feared her brother and had been more than glad that he rarely noticed her existence. Her little brother Alex had suffered the brunt of his spite, bullied by both him and their father, though Richmond's attentions were worse, needlessly cruel and humiliating. He had thought it frightfully amusing to lock Alex in a large chest and leave him there for hours, listening to the poor boy crying and begging to be let out.

Narcissa had been too young and afraid of Richmond to stand up to him, though she had run to her father who had put a stop to it. He had thrashed Richmond for being an ignorant brute and coldly instructed Alex to stop being a snivelling baby and stand up to his brother instead of weeping like a girl. Narcissa had not escaped his scorn either, though she got off lightly in contrast, sent to bed with his furious voice ringing in her ears and with no supper for tattling on her brother. It had hardly been an ideal solution, but at least Alex had been free, and she had comforted the poor boy as best she could once he was safely out of Richmond's way. After that, things had been worse for Alex, however, as Richmond was far more dangerous when he'd been humiliated or bested. The boy's life was made a misery as Richmond set traps that ranged from cutting the girth of his pony's saddle, to leaving bone-crushing animal traps in the garden in the places Alex liked to play. Thankfully, Alex had escaped serious injury, but all three siblings understood just how dangerous their older brother was. Happily, Richmond had returned to town soon after and they had all breathed a sigh of relief.

If he was smarting from his confrontation with Mr De Beauvoir, however—a fight which seemed to have been not only over before it began, but humiliatingly public, with many print shop caricatures and stories about the event—she could only imagine the depths of his rage. Richmond would be out for vengeance, and she did not expect him to be a gentleman in how he went about it.

Peering out of the grimy carriage window, Narcissa squinted into the darkness toward the club. Men were hurrying out of it, heading towards the centre of the sizeable garden that covered much of the square. Their excited voices reached her in a low rumble of sound and her skin prickled with apprehension. The sudden conviction that Ash and Richmond were at the heart of whatever it was drawing everyone's attention struck her square in the chest and would not be dislodged.

She jumped awkwardly down from the carriage, paid the driver, and asked him to wait before she ran towards the centre of the garden. She pulled the hat that covered her thick hair on more securely, aware of it shifting and knowing there would be a terrible scandal if she was discovered here, dressed like a boy. As she ran, she prayed, begging God to keep her husband safe, and promising to be a more biddable and well-behaved wife if only he was unharmed.

As the nightmarish scene before her took shape, however, the breath left her lungs in a rush, leaving her cold with terror. Ash was fighting for his life, three men trying their best to pummel him on all sides as he blocked and countered their savage fists. Narcissa ran forward, too frightened to scream, the sound feeling as though it was trapped in her lungs as she tried to reach him. To her relief, she saw the men from the club rush in, intervening and pulling his opponents aside, leaving Ash breathing hard, bent double with his hands on his thighs, spitting blood onto the floor. Someone went to help him, but he waved them away. Then Narcissa saw Richmond standing alone, off to the side. She saw the look in his eyes as he stalked towards Ash, his face a mask of hatred. No one else had seen, no one else had noticed the knife in his hand, too entertained by the men who were continuing to brawl in their efforts to escape. Narcissa screamed, the sound tearing from her as she ran harder than she ever had in her life before, throwing herself towards Ash, desperate to warn him.

Ash's head came up, his eyes widening in shock as he saw her running towards him. His attention was riveted upon her and though Narcissa tried to cry out, to warn him to look, she had no breath, only managing a shriek of fear that had Ash reaching out for her. Narcissa crashed against him, pushing him sideways with all her might. He took a sideways step, more out of surprise than any force she delivered. Her hat fell to the ground, her hair tumbling down her shoulders as he stared at her in alarm.

"What the devil—"

A hard punch to her side stole the breath from her lungs and Narcissa gasped, swaying in his embrace, her eyes wide.

"Holy hell!" Ash said under his breath. "Narcissa, what are you doing here?"

He broke off as he withdrew his hand from her waist and saw the blood staining his palm. Ash pulled aside the too-large coat and Narcissa looked too, feeling as though she was watching through someone else's eyes as she saw the small dark stain spreading upon her waistcoat, the neatly cut slash in the fabric. Narcissa glanced up at him in confusion, seeing the colour drain from his face, leaving him ashen with terror. As bewildered as she was, Ash stared at her, not comprehending what had happened until he glanced up and saw Richmond.

Narcissa followed his gaze to see her brother watching them, his mouth agape, the knife still in his hand.

"Ash, what the hell—"

Narcissa recognised Muir Anderson, saw him realise who she was, and then he registered Richmond standing there, bloody knife in hand.

"I'll kill him," Ash said softly, the words all the more terrifying for the quiet manner in which he spoke them.

"Nae, ye can no leave her, Ash. Ye must care for the lassie. Ye may leave the blackguard to me, though. I'll deal with him," Muir said, his expression dark with fury.

The last glimpse Narcissa had of her brother was the look of terror in his eyes as the intimidating figure of Muir Anderson advanced on him.

"Here," said a calm voice, and Ash shifted, taking something from whoever stood beside him. Narcissa cried out as Ash pressed hard against the burning pain in her side, her mind whirling as she fought to stay conscious.

"Sorry, I'm so sorry," Ash said, sounding wretched. "Hold on to me, darling. There's a good girl."

His voice was gentle as he wrapped her arms around his neck and lifted her into his arms, treating her delicately as if she were made of spun sugar.

Narcissa sobbed and pressed her mouth against his shoulder.

"The club?" a familiar voice asked but Ash gave a curt refusal.

"No. I need to get her to my mother. I don't trust any damned quack doctor. She'll know what to do."

His tone was businesslike, but Narcissa heard something else behind the taut words and knew he was afraid for her.

"There's a hackney there, look."

She closed her eyes, concentrating on breathing as the pain in her side intensified.

"Ash?" she whispered, remembering there was something urgent she needed to tell him.

She needed to warn him, except suddenly everything was a jumble in her head. What had been so important? Was he in danger, or was it her? The horrifying scene, the terror she had experienced had her heart pounding madly, and incoherent thoughts tumbled in her mind; Try as she might, she could not grasp at them. She shivered, burrowing closer against his warmth as the freezing night air seemed to invade her veins, chilling her to the bone.

"Don't try to talk, sweetheart. I'm taking you home. It will be all right, I promise. Just hold on." Warm hands stroked her face tenderly, pushing the tumble of curls that fell down into her eyes out of the way. "Everything will be all right," he said again, keeping his hand pressed firmly against the wound on her side.

Narcissa closed her eyes, drifting for a while. Waking with a start, she noticed the sway of a carriage, her senses registering the burning pain, and beneath that encompassing throb of heat, Ash's warm body close to hers, cradling her carefully in his lap.

"Hurts," she whimpered, feeling like a petulant child, wanting him to make it stop.

His voice cracked as he bent down and pressed a kiss to her forehead. "I know, sweetheart. I'm so sorry. What were you doing there? Why did you come?"

"Richmond!" she said, suddenly galvanised by the idea he was in danger. "My b-brother—"

"It's all right," he soothed her, his voice gentle.

"No, he'll hurt you," she said, sobbing with anxiety. "He's spiteful, he'll—"

"Hush, my love. I'm fine. I'm perfectly fine, and I promise you, I won't ever fight again."

"You won't?" she repeated, a little stunned by the sudden turnabout. "B-But you said—"

"If you get well, I won't ever fight again," he said, a tremor in his voice. "But you must promise me, Narcissa. Promise me to get well—"

"Ash?" she said, feeling suddenly giddy. The events of the day seemed suddenly overwhelming, and exhaustion swept over her. The pain in her side was throbbing like fury, making her feel sick, and she was so terribly cold. "Ash—" she said again, and then closed her eyes as darkness swept over her.

Ash had never been so glad in his life to get to his parents' home. He wished with all his heart that Nani Maa still lived, for his grandmother would have known just what to do to care for Narcissa, but she had passed her knowledge onto his mother, as she had to Vivien, and he knew they would do whatever it took to help Narcissa. Though the wound had not looked so terribly deep, there had been enough blood to scare him to death and he had been too terrified to investigate and risk doing further harm, or cause Narcissa undue pain.

Larkin jumped down ahead of him and hammered on the front door hard enough to wake the dead. A startled footman opened the door and Larkin told him to wake Lord and Lady Cavendish at once as Ash tried to climb out of the carriage without jostling his wife.

She had fainted on the journey, which had terrified him until Larkin had assured him her pulse was strong if rather rapid.

Ash carried her up the stairs, kicking open the door to what had once been his room whilst voices came from his parents' bedchamber. Moments later, his mother appeared, tying the sash of her dressing gown as she hurried in.

"Whatever has happened?" she asked, her face a mask of concern as she looked at his stricken face.

"Help her," Ash begged, his eyes blurring with tears as the fear that he might lose Narcissa before they had even begun tore at his heart. "Please, help her."

"Oh, my boy. Of course, I shall. Move aside now. Let me see... Good heavens, the poor child. Who did this?"

"Her brother. He meant to kill me, but... but Narcissa—"

Ash swallowed hard as a firm hand settled on his shoulder. "Deep breaths, son. Narcissa will need you to be strong for her."

Ash nodded, acknowledging his father's steadying presence and knowing he was right.

"Silas, I need scissors and hot water, and Nani Maa's medicine chest," his mother said, before gesturing for him to come. "Help me, Ash. I need to get these things off her."

Ash nodded, moving automatically, as if he were stuck in some terrible dream, though his mind kept returning to the stupid argument they'd had just hours earlier. Why hadn't he cancelled the fight? Why hadn't he stayed at home with Narcissa? Part of him had wanted to, but he'd been too damned stubborn to admit he'd rather be with her than fighting. Like he'd been afraid she would change him too much if he let her, and now… and now he'd do anything if only he knew she would not be taken from him. Pain and regret filled his heart, making him sick with it.

His father returned with the medicine chest and scissors, and he helped his mother cut away Narcissa's clothes. Her brother's clothes, he realised, his stomach twisting. Somehow, she had got wind of what Richmond had been about tonight and she had come to warn him. His brave, beautiful, reckless girl. A swell of love and longing pushed at his ribs, as if his chest could not contain the sensation as he gazed down at her pale face and he took her hand, his chest contracting as he found the delicate fingers so terribly cold.

"Will she… Will she be all right?" he managed, almost too afraid to ask, his voice unsteady as his mother swabbed the wound, studying it in the glare of the lamps she'd had set around the bed.

She did not answer at first, and Ash held his breath, knowing she would not placate him with pretty lies if the situation were grave.

Aashini looked up, her beautiful eyes grave but calm. "Yes, love. The wound is not terribly deep, though we must thank goodness she decided to wear her corset under her clothes. I think that's what saved her. If we clean it well and use Nani Maa's poultice, that will keep the infection away. I think she'll be just fine."

The rush of relief that hit Ash square in the chest was so powerful he couldn't speak, his throat working as he struggled for composure.

His mother reached out and took his hand, squeezing hard. "She put herself in harm's way for you, my son. She must care for you very deeply."

Ash nodded, knowing he would never doubt her again, would never allow himself to believe she did not know her own mind. Narcissa was far stronger and braver than he had ever given her credit for, a mistake he would never make again.

"You love her," his mother said with a smile.

Ash let out a shaky laugh and raised Narcissa's hand to his lips. "I do," he whispered, watching his beautiful wife sleep, and sending up a prayer of thanks to whoever might be listening, that he would be given the chance to tell her so.

Epilogue

The hitherto irreproachable Ponsonby family seemed destined to remain mired in scandal as the body of the Duke of Beresford's son and heir was found yesterday, floating in the Thames.

Lord Richmond was last seen during an altercation outside the notorious Sons of Hades club in Portman Square, where he attempted to murder Mr Ashton Anson in retribution for eloping with his younger sister. Though this correspondent is unclear not only about why the lady was at the scene, but furthermore – dressed as a boy – it appears Lady Narcissa courageously threw herself between her husband and her brother, incurring a knife wound to her side.

We do not yet know how serious the wound is as no one at Cavendish House has yet deigned to give a statement.

The marriage between Mr Anson and Lady Narcissa took place after the lady ran away from home to be with her lover, despite her father forbidding her to have anything to do with him. Mr Anson - who is of Anglo-Indian descent via his mother, Lady Aashini Cavendish - is notorious for his pugilistic talents, as well as being a fashionable if somewhat scandalous figure among the ranks of the ton.

What happened after Lord Richmond left Portman Square remains a mystery, though he was observed leaving in company with a Mr Muir Anderson, younger son of The Earl of Morven. Attempts to contact the gentleman have so far failed. It is believed he may have returned to Scotland to escape further questioning.

As for his grace, The Duke of Beresford has recovered somewhat from the stroke that afflicted him on hearing of his younger daughter's marriage to Mr Anson, but according to this correspondent's sources, remains bedridden.

—Excerpt of an article in the Morning Post's society column.

18th March 1850, Cavendish House, The Strand, London.

Narcissa opened her bleary eyes, blinking until the blurry figure before her resolved itself into that of a man. A handsome, beloved man, the sight of whom made her heart give an erratic thud. He was sitting close beside the bed, his head braced in his hands, shoulders slumped. The poor darling looked weary and wretched, his clothes rumpled and all in disorder.

"Ash," she whispered, watching as his head came up with a jerk.

He moved from the chair to the floor, kneeling beside her in one fluid movement, taking the hand she stretched out in his warm grasp and pressing it to his mouth. "Narcissa, oh, Christ, love. I've been so bloody afraid."

Narcissa looked at him in surprise, wondering what he was so agitated about. Trying to sit up, a sudden burning pain in her side lanced through her and she gasped, stilling immediately.

"Don't move!" he ordered, his voice stern. "Please love, don't move. You'll be just fine, but you must rest. My mother has cleaned and treated the wound, but you must keep still so you don't dislodge the poultice."

"W-Wound?" Narcissa repeated, bewildered for a moment until the events of last night came back to her in a rush. "Ash! Ash, did Richmond... are you hurt? Did he—"

"Hush," Ash told her, pressing a finger to his lips, his face taut. "You can see I'm fine, apart from going out of my mind worrying about you. Lord, Narcissa, why didn't you just send a message? You could have sent a footman. Why did you come yourself? You nearly died, you—you foolish, idiotic, brave, *brave* girl."

She returned a weary if pleased smile, for she had been brave, if a little reckless, and she had kept him safe, just as she had meant to do.

"Don't look so damned pleased with yourself. I've a good mind to spank you myself once you're well enough," he grumbled, though she could tell he didn't mean a word of it. His eyes were shadowed, but the deep blue was soft with concern, his words born of frustration and fear rather than anger. "I might have lost you," he said, his voice cracking.

"But you didn't, and you won't," she said, smiling up at him.

Ash pressed his mouth to the palm of her hand and kissed the tender skin there as though he could imprint the touch of his lips to her soul. "Don't ever frighten me like that again," he said wretchedly.

"I won't if you won't," she whispered, before narrowing her eyes. "Are you thinking of staying there, or are you going to get into bed with me?"

He looked at her indignantly, his scowl so forbidding she almost laughed. "You're injured. If you think I'm going to take advantage of you in this condition, you're out of your wits."

"It's not taking advantage if I ask you to do it," she pointed out, thinking this quite reasonable.

"No," he repeated firmly.

"A cuddle," she wheedled, pouting now. "Just a cuddle. I deserve that much, don't I?"

"I still haven't decided if you deserve a medal or a birching," he muttered, but she could see the desire in his eyes, and it made her heart lift with joy.

"Please," she whispered, knowing she had him now.

Grumbling the entire time, Ash stripped off and then slid into the bed, lying down carefully beside her so as not to jostle her.

"Closer," she demanded, grinning at him as he rolled his eyes.

"I'm going to get into trouble for this, I hope you realise."

"Then you'd best make it worth it," she teased.

Ash lay on his side, gazing down at her in a way that made her heart swell with happiness.

"I love you," she whispered, not caring if she was the first to say it, or if perhaps he needed more time before he was ready to tell her he loved her too, for she could see it in his eyes.

Silently, Ash lowered his mouth to hers, closing his eyes as his lips lingered against hers for a long moment. He drew back just a little, eyes still closed, as the words fluttered over her upon a warm breath. "I love you too, so don't do anything like that ever again, you reckless girl. Please, *mera pyar*. I don't think my heart can take it."

"Your heart is safe with me, Ash," she told him, gazing up at him.

At last, she knew he believed her, and she believed in herself too. She was brave enough to face anything, as long as he loved her back.

"I know." He kissed her again. "And from now on, I shall be as courageous as my beautiful wife and hold nothing back. I'm yours, Narcissa, heart and soul, so I hope to God you're ready to take me on."

"Must I take your waistcoats too?" she asked, striving for a sceptical tone even as tears of gladness gathered in her eyes.

"Don't mock my waistcoats," he reproved. "They are non-negotiable."

"Oh." She sighed sadly. "I suppose… *if* you insist."

And she pulled his head down for another kiss.

Coming next in the Wicked Sons series…

Kidnapping Cordelia
Wicked Sons Book 7

To be revealed

Please turn the page for a sneak peek of Kidnapping Cordelia.

Prologue

25th March 1850, Cavendish House, The Strand, London.

"Ash, do stop fussing," Narcissa said impatiently as they approached the staircase.

"I'll stop fussing when I'm entirely certain you are well," he grumbled, still unhappy about his mother's decision to allow Narcissa to come downstairs.

"Ash, don't, I'm perfectly capable—"

Narcissa huffed and glared at him as he swept her up into her arms before she could set foot on the first step.

"You are impossible," she said, though she linked her arms about his neck and kissed his cheek all the same.

"Impossibly wonderful," he corrected, giving her a look that dared her to challenge this description.

"Impossibly wonderful," she agreed, laughter in her voice, though her eyes softened as she gazed up at him.

"Keep looking at me like that and you won't make it to the parlour," he warned her. "I'll take you straight back to bed and keep you there."

A warm breath of amusement fluttered over his skin, and he wished he'd thought of doing that anyway instead of letting his mother talk him into letting Narcissa take tea with the family. She had been through too much during the past week, what with hearing of her brother's death in such strange circumstances. Ash could still see Muir's set face as he stared at Richmond. Though he did not much care what had happened, he hoped for Muir's own sake he did not have blood on his hands. That the fellow had disappeared was a concern but, despite his predilection for trouble, like a cat, Muir usually landed on his feet.

"Ash?"

He looked down at his wife, pausing at the bottom of the stairs as she gazed at him with her heart in her eyes. "Have I thanked you for looking after me so splendidly, for being so very kind and patient when I know I've been dreadfully trying?"

He snorted at that. He was the one who'd been nigh on impossible until he was entirely certain the danger of infection had passed.

"Yes, love, but there's no need. I wouldn't have it any other way. You saved my life, remember?"

She blushed a little at that, still uncomfortable with the lavish praise the family had poured over her for being so courageous. "But Ash, I wanted to tell you, if... if you still wish to fight, I wouldn't stop you. It's only that I was afraid you would be hurt, and I wouldn't be there, I wouldn't know what had happened. Do you see?"

He saw all too clearly now what he would put her through if he carried on fighting and knew he would never let her worry that way over him.

"Yes, love, I do understand. Perhaps I'll have a friendly bout now and then to keep my hand in, and I'll keep sparring, but I'll not carry on fighting like I have been. I promised you I wouldn't, and I meant it. The truth is, I've lost the desire to do it anymore," he admitted, gazing at the beautiful woman in his arms in wonder. "I've got more important things to think about now, like the future we have together, and how I can make it as wonderful as possible."

She smiled and cupped his cheek. "There's no secret there, Ash. Just love me."

"I do," he said. "And I will."

He bent his head, kissing her there in the hallway, only breaking the kiss when he heard giggling and turned to see two maids blushing and smothering their faces with their aprons as they rushed towards the backstairs.

Laughing, he carried Narcissa through to the parlour where his parents, his twin sister, Vivien, and her husband August were waiting for them with their four children. Eight-year-old Sabrina and six-year-old Ben came rushing up to Ash, demanding to know why he was carrying Narcissa. Ivan, who was five, was sitting quietly with his grandfather, solemnly watching proceedings, but little Priscilla, who was not yet three, wriggled out of her mother's hold and demanded Ash carry her instead.

There was a good ten minutes of noise and chaos whilst Ash got the children over-excited and was soundly scolded by his sister, and then everyone settled down to tea and cakes.

Ash looked around at his family, watching how easily Narcissa had become a part of it. Sabrina was sitting beside her, showing her a book of beautifully illustrated stories that her father had given her for her birthday, and gazing at Narcissa's lovely face with a look of devoted adoration. Narcissa glanced up, perhaps feeling his eyes upon her, and the smile she gave him made his heart expand in his chest. One day they would have children, perhaps a daughter who would sit with her mother and listen to her read a story. For the first time, he found the idea entirely enchanting, and could not wait to see what life would bring them next.

A knock at the door was followed by a footman who announced the arrival of Lady Wrexham.

Ash stood, hurrying to Emmeline as he saw the lines of strain around her eyes.

"Em, what is it? What's wrong?" he asked, taking her hands.

"I came to see Narcissa," she said, her voice taut with anxiety. "To ask if she knew where Delia was."

Narcissa gasped, alarmed by Emmeline's obvious distress. "No. I received a letter from her two days ago, telling me about the ball she attended on Saturday, but I haven't seen her since Friday."

"And she never mentioned a beau, perhaps someone she was meeting in secret or—"

"No!" Narcissa shook her head. "No, nothing of the sort."

Emmeline's hand went to her mouth, and Silas and Ash guided her to a chair.

"I'm sorry," she said faintly. "Wrexham is out of his mind with worry. She was supposed to stay with his aunt, you see, but she never arrived, and her aunt has only just informed us. She's been gone two whole days without any of us realising, and I just thought perhaps… but I should have known she would not run off without telling us, no matter the circumstances."

"Two days!" Narcissa repeated in alarm, the colour leaving her face. "What do you mean, she's been missing for two days?"

Ash went to her, wishing she had not been here to receive this news, not after all she had been through. He did not wish her to be troubled, but Delia was her dearest friend, and he could not have kept the news from her.

"Just what I say," Emmeline said, her voice trembling. "We… We believe she may have been kidnapped."

Silas went to Emmeline at once, getting her to repeat everything that she knew.

"I'll contact Montagu. He's in town, and he'll know who to contact to conduct a discreet investigation."

She nodded. "Wrexham is speaking to my father now. But if there is anything anyone can do…. Oh, Ash, I'm so worried, my poor darling Delia. She is such a little innocent. If anyone has hurt her—"

"There, there, don't fret. We'll have her back home before you know it," Ash said, his voice soothing, even though he could not deny the circumstances of her disappearance were disturbing.

"Ash, will you come to speak to Montagu with me?" his father asked.

"Of course," he said at once. "I'll return Narcissa to her room first, though."

"Please, don't worry about me," Narcissa said, tears in her eyes as concern for her friend overrode all else.

"Don't be foolish," Ash said gently, taking her in his arms and carrying her out of the room and back up the stairs. "Darling, don't worry. We'll find her, and we'll make sure she's safe."

Narcissa nodded, clinging to him as he carried her back to her room and settled her on the bed.

"She will be all right?" Narcissa asked.

The look in her eyes warmed his heart even as he felt the weight of responsibility upon him. She trusted him implicitly; he could see the belief she had in him shining from her.

Ash sat down beside her and took her hands. "What do you think, love? We'll get everyone out looking for her, we won't rest until she is home again. I shall look for her as if it were you I were seeking, and I'll ensure we bring her home to you, safe and sound."

"Oh, Ash, you are the very best husband in the world," she said, wrapping her arms about him and holding on tight. "I am so glad I married you. I would have been so wretched without you, I cannot bear to think of it."

"Then don't, love."

She nodded, and then her eyes widened. "Ash, I've just remembered the letter Delia sent me. The night I went after you. She mentioned a man, a Mr Enoch Goodfellow. She implied he was bothering her. Being a little overbearing, I think. Too kind and too attentive, if you see what I mean?"

Ash nodded, frowning. "Goodfellow? I don't think I know him. All right, love. I'll look into it at once. Well done for thinking of it, clever girl."

"You'll send word if anything happens?" she asked, catching hold of his hand.

Ash raised it to her lips and kissed her fingers. "I will, and if you think I won't return to you the first moment I can, you really have not understood my feelings."

"I understand," she said softly, smiling a little at his words. "Take care, my love, and hurry home with Delia."

Ash pressed a kiss to her mouth, and with one last look of regret at leaving his beautiful wife alone, he hurried out of the room.

Pre-order your copy here: *Kidnapping Cordelia*

The Peculiar Ladies who started it all…

Girls Who Dare – The exciting series from Emma V Leech, the multi-award-winning, Amazon Top 10 romance writer behind the Rogues & Gentlemen series.

Inside every wallflower is the beating heart of a lioness, a passionate individual willing to risk all for their dream, if only they can find the courage to begin. When these overlooked girls make a pact to change their lives, anything can happen.

Twelve girls – Twelve dares in a hat. Twelve stories of passion. Who will dare to risk it all?

To Dare a Duke

Girls Who Dare Book 1

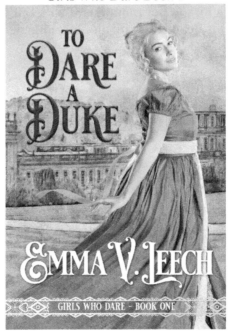

Dreams of true love and happy ever afters

Dreams of love are all well and good, but all Prunella Chuffington-Smythe wants is to publish her novel. Marriage at the price of her independence is something she will not consider. Having tasted success writing under a false name in The Lady's Weekly Review, her alter ego is attaining notoriety and fame and Prue rather likes it.

A Duty that must be endured

Robert Adolphus, The Duke of Bedwin, is in no hurry to marry, he's done it once and repeating that disaster is the last thing he desires. Yet, an heir is a necessary evil for a duke and one he cannot shirk. A dark reputation precedes him though, his first wife may have died young, but the scandals the beautiful, vivacious and spiteful creature supplied the ton have not. A wife must be found. A wife who is neither beautiful or vivacious but sweet and dull, and certain to stay out of trouble.

Dared to do something drastic

The sudden interest of a certain dastardly duke is as bewildering as it is unwelcome. She'll not throw her ambitions aside to marry a scoundrel just as her plans for self-sufficiency and freedom are coming to fruition. Surely showing the man she's not actually the meek little wallflower he is looking for should be enough to put paid to his intentions? When Prue is dared by her friends to do something drastic, it seems the perfect opportunity to kill two birds.

However, Prue cannot help being intrigued by the rogue who has inspired so many of her romances. Ordinarily, he plays the part of handsome rake, set on destroying her plucky heroine. But is he really the villain of the piece this time, or could he be the hero?

Finding out will be dangerous, but it just might inspire her greatest story yet.

To Dare a Duke

From the author of the bestselling Girls Who Dare Series – An exciting new series featuring the children of the Girls Who Dare…

The stories of the **Peculiar Ladies Book Club** and their hatful of dares has become legend among their children. When the hat is rediscovered, dusty and forlorn, the remaining dares spark a series of events that will echo through all the families… and their **Daring Daughters**

Dare to be Wicked

Daring Daughters Book One

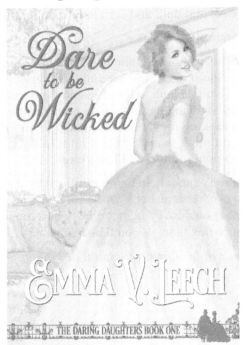

Two daring daughters …

Lady Elizabeth and Lady Charlotte are the daughters of the Duke and Duchess of Bedwin. Raised by an unconventional mother and an indulgent, if overprotective father, they both strain against the rigid morality of the era.

The fashionable image of a meek, weak young lady, prone to swooning at the least provocation, is one that makes them seethe with frustration.

Their handsome childhood friend ...

Cassius Cadogen, Viscount Oakley, is the only child of the Earl and Countess St Clair. Beloved and indulged, he is popular, gloriously handsome, and a talented artist.

Returning from two years of study in France, his friendship with both sisters becomes strained as jealousy raises its head. A situation not helped by the two mysterious Frenchmen who have accompanied him home.

And simmering sibling rivalry ...

Passion, art, and secrets prove to be a combustible combination, and someone will undoubtedly get burned.

Dare to be Wicked

Also check out Emma's regency romance series, Rogues & Gentlemen. Available now!

The Rogue

Rogues & Gentlemen Book 1

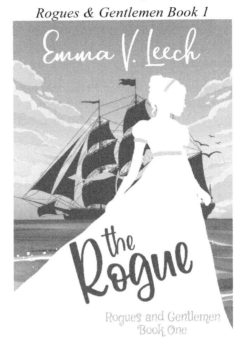

The notorious Rogue that began it all.

Set in Cornwall, 1815. Wild, untamed and isolated.

Lawlessness is the order of the day and smuggling is rife.

Henrietta always felt most at home in the wilds of the outdoors but even she had no idea how the mysterious and untamed would sweep her away in a moment.

Bewitched by his wicked blue eyes

Henrietta Morton knows to look the other way when the free trading 'gentlemen' are at work.
Yet when a notorious pirate bursts into her local village shop, she

can avert her eyes no more. Bewitched by his wicked blue eyes, a moment of insanity follows as Henrietta hides the handsome fugitive from the Militia.

Her reward is a kiss, lingering and unforgettable.

In his haste to flee, the handsome pirate drops a letter, a letter that lays bare a tale of betrayal. When Henrietta's father gives her hand in marriage to a wealthy and villainous nobleman in return for the payment of his debts, she becomes desperate.

Blackmailing a pirate may be her only hope for freedom.

**** **Warning**: This book contains the most notorious rogue of all of Cornwall and, on occasion, is highly likely to include some mild sweating or descriptive sex scenes. ****

Free to read on *Kindle Unlimited*: The Rogue

Interested in a Regency Romance with a twist?

A Dog in a Doublet

The Regency Romance Mysteries Book 2

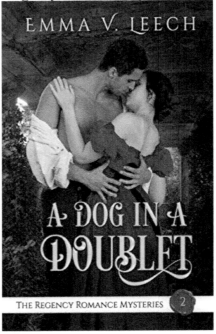

A man with a past

Harry Browning was a motherless guttersnipe, and the morning he came across the elderly Alexander Preston, The Viscount Stamford, clinging to a sheer rock face he didn't believe in fate. But the fates have plans for Harry whether he believes or not, and he's not entirely sure he likes them.

As a reward for his bravery, and in an unusual moment of charity, miserly Lord Stamford takes him on. He is taught to read, to manage the vast and crumbling estate, and to behave like a gentleman, but Harry knows that is something he will never truly be.

Already running from a dark past, his future is becoming increasingly complex as he finds himself caught in a tangled web of jealousy and revenge.

A feisty young maiden

Temptation, in the form of the lovely Miss Clarinda Bow, is a constant threat to his peace of mind, enticing him to be something he isn't. But when the old man dies his will makes a surprising demand, and the fates might just give Harry the chance to have everything he ever desired, including Clara, if only he dares.

And as those close to the Preston family begin to die, Harry may not have any choice.

Order your copy here. A Dog in a Doublet

Lose yourself in Emma's paranormal world with The French Vampire Legend series….

The Key to Erebus

The French Vampire Legend Book 1

The truth can kill you.

Taken away as a small child, from a life where vampires, the Fae, and other mythical creatures are real and treacherous, the beautiful young witch, Jéhenne Corbeaux is totally unprepared when she returns to rural France to live with her eccentric Grandmother.

Thrown headlong into a world she knows nothing about she seeks to learn the truth about herself, uncovering secrets more shocking than anything she could ever have imagined and finding that she is by no means powerless to protect the ones she loves.

Despite her Gran's dire warnings, she is inexorably drawn to the dark and terrifying figure of Corvus, an ancient vampire and master of the vast Albinus family.

Jéhenne is about to find her answers and discover that, not only is Corvus far more dangerous than she could ever imagine, but that he holds much more than the key to her heart ...

Now available at your favourite retailer.

The Key to Erebus

Check out Emma's exciting fantasy series with hailed by Kirkus Reviews as "An enchanting fantasy with a likable heroine, romantic intrigue, and clever narrative flourishes."

The Dark Prince
The French Fae Legend Book 1

Two Fae Princes
One Human Woman
And a world ready to tear them all apart.

Laen Braed is Prince of the Dark fae, with a temper and reputation to match his black eyes, and a heart that despises the human race. When he is sent back through the forbidden gates between realms to retrieve an ancient fae artifact, he returns home with far more than he bargained for.

Corin Albrecht, the most powerful Elven Prince ever born. His golden eyes are rumoured to be a gift from the gods, and destiny is calling him. With a love for the human world that runs deep, his friendship with Laen is being torn apart by his prejudices.

Océane DeBeauvoir is an artist and bookbinder who has always relied on her lively imagination to get her through an unhappy and uneventful life. A jewelled dagger put on display at a nearby museum hits the headlines with speculation of another race, the Fae. But the discovery also inspires Océane to create an extraordinary piece of art that cannot be confined to the pages of a book.

With two powerful men vying for her attention and their friendship stretched to the breaking point, the only question that remains…who is truly The Dark Prince.

The man of your dreams is coming…or is it your nightmares he visits? Find out in Book One of The French Fae Legend.

Available now to read at your favorite retailer.

The Dark Prince

Want more Emma?

If you enjoyed this book, please support this indie author and take a moment to leave a few words in a review. *Thank you!*

To be kept informed of special offers and free deals (which I do regularly) follow me on *https://www.bookbub.com/authors/emma-v-leech*

To find out more and to get news and sneak peeks of the first chapter of upcoming works, go to my website and sign up for the newsletter.
http://www.emmavleech.com/

Or follow me here…

http://viewauthor.at/EmmaVLeechAmazon

Printed in Great Britain
by Amazon

47086533R00162